SUCHEN CHRISTINE LIM

The River's Song

Published in the UK by Aurora Metro Books.
67 Grove Avenue, Twickenham, TW1 4HX
www.aurorametro.com info@aurorametro.com

Editor: Cheryl Robson

Aurora Metro Books would like to thank Sarah Strupinski, Martin Gilbert, Simon Smith, Neil Gregory, Richard Turk, Alison Hill, Anna Festa.

10 9 8 7 6 5 4 3 2 1

Printed by Mainland Press,Singapore
ISBN: 978-1-906582-98-2

SUCHEN CHRISTINE LIM

The River's Song

AURORA METRO BOOKS

On Cavenagh Bridge

Here, years ago
we didn't say a word, though I could tell
you couldn't hold it in. How could I know
there would be stronger feelings yet to quell?

Toh Hsien Min

"My most ambitious plan was to clean up the Singapore River
and Kallang Basin and bring fish back to the rivers."

Lee Kuan Yew, former Prime Minister of Singapore
From Third World to First: The Singapore Story

To the memory of my beloved mother

and

the people evicted from the river

Author's Note

My novel is a work of fiction, based partly on the cleaning of the Singapore River. The characters and events in the novel, however, are fictional. Any resemblance to real persons or events is either a fortunate or unfortunate coincidence, depending on one's perspective.

Acknowledgements

I'd like to thank the Moniack Mohr Writers' Centre, Scotland; Toji Culture Center, South Korea; and the Nanyang Technological University, Singapore, for their writing residencies and generous support during the research and writing of this novel; Dr Samuel Wong Shengmiao for introducing me to the pipa especially the solo piece, Shi Mien Mai Fu, which led me to the heart-pulling music of the Chinese bamboo flute, the dizi.

A very special 'thank you' and big hug for my writing pal Melissa De Villiers for her wonderful support and comments, and friends, Jeffrey Low, Clarinda Choh and Yvonne Kwan who read my early drafts. Thanks too to Jacaranda, my literary agent.

Part One

The Pipa Queen

1

The man had come to play his bamboo flute. No one knew why. The ceremony was over; the workers were already putting away the chairs and tables. They didn't pay him any attention initially, but their chattering stopped as the first long note of his flute floated over the Singapore River. Bleak and desolate in its longing, the music drew their eyes to him.

A bank teller and a secretary trotting on high heels across Cavenagh Bridge stopped to listen. They pointed him out to their colleagues. The man was standing at the spot where the Prime Minister had stood a while ago. In his white shirt and trousers, his bamboo flute held horizontal at his lips, he was still as a crane.

"See the white headband around his head; he's in mourning," the bank teller said.

"What?" her friend laughed. "By playing the flute?"

There was a long pull of breath. And another long note, a sad mewling cry followed by three sharp trills. Two old men, seated under the angsana tree, turned to each other, their hearts stirring. They knew that sound. It was part of a forgotten song. The man's flute played on. The old men heard the clang of boats once again, the shouts of coolies and lightermen, the heaving and hawing, hammering and clattering in the boatyards long gone. The man's music choked their hearts. Their old eyes turned watery. They gazed up at the steel towers of the banks with names they could not read, with offices they had never entered, and remembered their hawker stalls along this river where their food had once fed hordes of hungry office workers every noon. Today the Prime Minister had declared his Clean River campaign a success. Ten thousand tons of flotsam and jetsam, two thousand tons of rubbish and forty-one thousand cubic metres of putrid mud had been removed from this river, along with the squatters and hawkers.

The grey skies started to weep.

A light rain fell on the small crowd of listeners on the bridge, and they ran for shelter in the restaurants and pubs on the other side. A few turned back to look at the man in white. He was still playing as a wind rose and whipped his hair. Raindrops the size of twenty-cent coins splattered onto the red plastic chairs and tables. The cleaners huddled under the tent used for the ceremony earlier.

"Ack! That flute player. He must be crazy to play in the rain. Who can hear him now?" a woman cleaner grumbled.

"The dead can hear him." The man next to her blew a smoke ring and stubbed out his cigarette in the rainwater flowing into the tent. No one spoke after that. The workers squatted on their haunches, their eyes trained on Weng and his flute.

2

"You know what kind of woman your mother is? A whore!" The man spat.

His spit scalded my thigh and burnt through my school uniform.

"Whore's daughter!" He spat at me a second time.

I turned and fled, pushing against the arms and legs of people on the sidewalk.

"I'm *not* her daughter! Not her daughter!" I remember yelling.

*

– *Damn!* Why am I thinking of such things this morning? What is it with mothers and daughters? Even two oceans and a continent can't keep her claws off me. When I close my eyes, I can see the flash of her red fingernails, the white of her thighs, peeping from the slits of her tight-fitting qipao.

Home for us then was a tiny room on the first floor of the coffee shop in a row of three-storey shophouses in Pagoda Street. Our room had no window, unlike Aunty Molek's room whose window looked into the communal kitchen where the women cooked their meals. There were sixteen of us – women and children – living on this floor, not counting the men who came and went as they pleased. Fathers were dispensable in this tenement, except for Old Kim, the owner of the coffee shop and our landlord, who lived downstairs with his wife, Kim Poh, and their brat, Fatt Chye. Old Kim's three married sons by his first wife lived on the floor above us with their families.

I remember waking up with a start. Grunts and moans were coming from the bed above my head. Lying very still on my sleeping mat on the floor at the foot of my mother's bed, I wondered if someone had come back with her while I was asleep. I didn't open my eyes to look. I didn't want to see the moving shadows. I willed myself to go back to sleep, and wished I were dead. I dreaded going to school the next day. The thought of having to face Linda Tan and her friends made me ill. They had seen the man spit on me. They had heard every word he said. The whole class, no, the whole school, would soon know about my mother. I shut my eyes tightly, and used a pillow to cover my ears.

Towards dawn, I crept downstairs and slipped out into the back alley. This was where we children played, and where strange men came to pee into the drain. My back alley was a planet away from Linda's home on Ann Siang Hill where children, watched over by their grandmothers, rode tricycles on the sidewalks, and little girls skipped rope singing Teddy Bear, Teddy Bear, turn around. In my back alley, we played catch, five-stones and police-and-thieves. I hid behind the stacks of firewood piled up against the wall, and waited for the sun to rise before running away.

"Wong Ping Ping! Come out of there!"

Ah Chek who fetched me to school in his trishaw pulled me out from the woodpile. He hauled me back into the coffee shop and up the stairs.

"Mama! Mama! Please don't cane me!" I begged, but her cane sliced my cheek like a red-hot butter knife.

"Don't ever call me Mama again! No man will marry me if he knows I've a daughter. From now on, call me Ah-ku. You understand? Ah-ku, not Mama."

That's a lie, I thought, but she wanted to be known as my paternal aunt: Ah-ku – not mother. Well, I didn't want her to be my mother. She was a …a … Tears fell as I struggled to utter the word, 'whore' inside my heart.

"Ingrate!" she screeched. "Other girls yearn to go to school but cannot go! You! I give you the chance to study and you want to run away? I queued up for hours to get you a place in the convent school! Rat's shit!"

Her cane bit my shoulders, tore my back and struck my eyes. If not for my arm shielding my face, I would've been blinded. Angry red welts sprouted on my arms and legs. I bit my lips to stop from crying out. Crying would make it worse. She was not the sort who melted at a child's cries.

"Why are you running away? Am I not feeding you well? I would've given an arm and a leg to go to school. I begged my foster mother to send me to school. But the witch refused. Now I'm sending you to school, and you run away? Go then!" She pushed me out of the room. "Go! Go!" I was pushed toward the stairs.

"Spit! Spit! He spat on me!" I clung to the banisters.

"Who spat on you?"

*

The next morning, Ah-ku marched downstairs, armed with a bamboo pole. The morning sky was streaked red and orange, and the rooftops of Pagoda Street were aflame. Whiffs of burnt toast and sweet coconut and egg jam rose from the stove in Old Kim's coffee shop. Truck drivers and trishaw riders wolfing down their pork buns and char siew pao were shocked to see her up so early. Ignoring their calls, she hoisted the bamboo pole onto her shoulders. This was the pole she used for hanging up her bras and panties to dry. The very thing to bang on a bully's door.

"Hey, Yoke Lan! Where're you going?" Old Kim called out to her.

Ah-ku stomped past him without answering. If she were to speak, she would explode. At the junction of South Bridge Road, she held up her pole to stop the traffic, and crossed the road amidst a blare of angry horns. Her long hair twirled into a tight knot at the nape of her neck, she marched up Ann Siang Hill. Men on their way to work gawked. They had seen her at places they would never bring their wives to. Three young hoods wolf-whistled at her as she strode past. These sons of sows had nothing better to do, she thought. Two housewives waddled past. "A roadside bloom," one of them with a neck wreathed in gold chains sniffed. The two snooty cows looked her up and down. She returned their bovine gaze till they looked away. She knew how respectable women regarded her – a siren strumming her pipa to entice their menfolk.

She stopped in front of a terrace of two-storey townhouses. The house in the middle was painted a pale green with dark green shutters, and pretty squares of pink and green floral tiles beneath its windows. She checked the house number. Yes, this was it. Her bamboo pole hit the front door. A woman's head popped out of the window on the upper floor.

"What do you want?"

"I want to talk to your mister."

The woman's head disappeared. Minutes later, it popped out again.

"My husband says he doesn't know you."

"Tell him I want to talk to him."

"He doesn't talk to women like you."

"What's wrong with women like me? Aren't you a woman yourself?"

The window slammed shut. She raised her pole and hit its shutters again and again till the window opened and the woman's head reappeared.

"My husband says he does not talk to women like you!"

"Tell him to fall on his knees! Kowtow to Lord Buddha that a woman like me wants to talk to a coward like him!"

A crowd gathered round. She turned to them.

"Aunties! Uncles! You be the judge. This man works in an office. He went to an English school. He speaks English! He's educated.

He'd passed exams. And yet…" She held up her forefinger. "And yet he daren't come out to face me! Do you know why?"

"Tell us why!"

"Aah, I will, Uncle. That I will. This man! This man has a small heart. A small man with a small heart. For only a small-hearted man will spit on a small child."

"Hey! If you blacken my husband's name, he will sue you!"

"Go ahead! Sue me! Let him tell the judge why he spat on a child and called her aunt a whore! Do you know why? You're his wife. Let me tell you. Your husband. He spat on a little girl. Not because the little girl did him wrong. No! Because of me! I didn't want to drink with him in the teahouse. So he beat the dog to spite its owner. You go and tell that husband of yours! The dog's owner is here!"

"He has nothing to do with the likes of you! You're mad!"

"Aunties! Uncles! Here I stand. Am I mad? I'm waiting for her husband to be a man. Let him come out and spit on me, the adult. Not the child. The child has done nothing wrong. Her only crime was to be born the daughter of a pipa songstress! We're not whores! We sing for men. It's true. We entertain men. It's true. We keep them company at night. That's also true. It's not high-class work. Not like office work. But work is work! Do we steal from you? Do we rob? Do we beg? Have we no pride? No skill? Which of you can play the pipa like us? We pipa girls, we sell our music and our songs. Night after night, we sing for pigs like her husband! We mop his brow. We laugh at his jokes. We listen to him complain about his wife when he should be at home. With devoted wives like you, Aunties."

The women nodded, and the men, looking foolish, smiled.

"I ask you. Which man will spit on a child? Not a man, I tell you, but a flea! A flea in the dog's backside. Look! There it goes! Look! Insect!" She stamped her foot on the imaginary bug. She raised her bamboo pole and brought it down hard on the invisible insect. "Damn flea!"

The people laughed. "Crush the insect!" they shouted.

Her bamboo pole hit the earth again. And again. The crowd cheered her on. Oh, she's audacious, this hussy! They applauded her. "Bravo! Bravo!"

"Thank you. Thank you." A low, theatrical bow. "Thank you, Uncles and Aunties."

She hoisted the bamboo pole onto her shoulders once again, and marched back to Pagoda Street with the crowd following her. The housewives fanned out to the market and shops, eager to tell their friends and neighbours what they had witnessed. All morning, stories about the pipa songstress, her bamboo pole and the flea in a dog's backside flew like crows all over the market place. That night, men flocked to the teahouse to hear her play, and the Pipa Queen of Chinatown was born.

*

– Wallet. Checked.

– Credit cards. Checked.

– Pipa. Checked.

– What else now? What else should I pack?

I sit down on my bed, overcome by fatigue. Outside a cold, grey fog hangs over Berkeley's rooftops. The university's trees have turned a dull grey-green. The rain is showing no sign of stopping.

– I insist this time you stay with Kit and me. Plenty of room in the flat now that the bitch and John have moved out with their two boys. Now I've one son less. And no grandsons. No more trouble from that lot.

– You will stay with me, won't you, Ping?

I thought I heard a catch in Ah-ku's voice on the phone, just a tiny quaver locked within her combative tone. Hardly noticeable, but I'd heard it, and the upshot was that I agreed to stay with her and Kit during my two-month sabbatical in Singapore. I am to fly home in time to celebrate her sixtieth birthday.

She's still Ah-ku or Aunt to me after all these years. I can't call her 'Mother'. In fact, I had stopped thinking of her as my mother when she forced me to leave Singapore at seventeen. I try to suppress my apprehension. What if I'm wrong about that catch in her voice? Ah-ku does not cry easily.

My memories are stirring up a storm. The girl is slipping in and out of my head as I pack the old pipa into its worn leather case, its faded red string still tied to the handle. I had never thought of cutting it off.

I see my six year-old self holding Ah-ku's pipa. Sunlight was streaming down from the skylight in the roof. It lit up the pipa in my arms. My fingers stroked the glowing beauty, its body curved like a golden brown pear. I touched its four strings gently, and plucked one of them. A soft 'ping!' uttered my name scattering silvery dust across that room above Old Kim's coffee shop. I plucked it again. An arrow hissed across the sky. An emperor cried, 'Ambush!' His cry pierced my heart. I hugged the pipa tight against my chest. The cry of the betrayed emperor is the start of the most complex piece of pipa music in its ancient repertoire. Starry-eyed, I dreamt of playing it some day.

– *Rat's Shit!* A violent kick sent the pipa flying cross the room.

– *Did I send you to school to play this damn thing?* Ah-ku's cane flamed my arm; her knuckles almost cracked my skull.

Shocked, I blink away my sudden tears. Half a century has passed, yet the memory still hurts. There's something cruel, violent and lyrical in the music of the pipa, I often tell my freshmen class in UC, Berkeley. Originally designed for strumming on horseback, the pipa sings of war and heartbreak. Plucking its strings, Chinese military musicians had led thousands to their death in the snowy plains of the Yellow River. Like flies they fell building the Great Wall in the bitter snow, while the Son of Heaven and his concubines played their pipas to serenade a lonely moon in the Forbidden City. Once, an imperial maid playing the four-string lute caught the Emperor's eye. In a fit of violent jealousy, the Empress ordered the maid's hands chopped off and her eyes gouged out and served to the Emperor on a golden platter at the imperial banquet.

Do you know of any scholar who'd kept count of the number of women killed, abused or sold into slavery in the history of the pipa? Find out and tell me after the summer break. It's the signature assignment for my course on Asian music each year. Sometimes, I play them a song that Ah-ku used to sing:

'O, we scale the stars, and climb the moonshine,
Fight with dragons fierce and wild.
We ride the ocean's waves,
We, the pipa girls, the weavers of a hero's dreams.'

When Ah-ku was living in the big house in Juniper Garden, she was full of songs and stories of these pipa girls, stories that she trotted out whenever the tai-tai, the wives of the rich and famous, visited her. They used to sit by the swimming pool, sipping their iced jasmine tea, and feasting on the piping hot dim sum that Kan Jieh, her amah, had made.

Pipa girls used to sing in the teahouses and music halls along the Singapore River and in Chinatown. Thousands would come each night to gawk at these girls. They floated like butterflies in their silk qipao, gliding up the stairs. Just to see and listen to these girls sing was heaven to me when I was a child. Such sweet joy and sorrow in their songs I tell you! She embroidered and gushed as if she had never been one of these gilded butterflies. A load of rubbish, of course. My research as a musicologist has shown that pipa songstresses were nothing like what she described. Those pubescent girls were often locked up in pleasure houses and forced to learn the pipa and the art of pleasing men from a very young age. Nothing as romantic as Ah-ku likes to paint, now that she's a respectable matron.

My phone rings. It's my ex.

"Honey, two months before the deadline."

"Rajeev, you're a bloody slave driver!"

I always use his Indian name instead of the American version, Jeev, when he annoys me. But this morning Jeev is beyond annoying.

"It's my job, hon," he chuckles, knowing how I hate being called 'hon'. "You voted me in as slave driver."

"Damn."

But I have to admit he's doing a very good job, managing the egos of divas like me in the music department. With him in charge, everyone and everything in the department has worked in sync even in the hell and damnation build-up to our annual concert each spring. In our early years together, Jeev and I had fought like cats on heat. I didn't think then that he could handle ego and temper with the grace and forbearance he shows these days in his grey beard age. Nor did I think he had the acuity to deal with the orchestra's finance and contracts. Still, I'm glad that we're no longer man and wife.

"You'll have no time to yourself in Singapore."

"Don't you worry your sweet head. I've bought an open ticket. I can cut short my stay and take the next flight out if I have to. But I can't just fly in for the old bird's birthday and fly out the next day. A sixtieth birthday is a big thing for us Chinese. She was on to me again last night, talking like a house on fire for more than an hour till I had to lie that the battery in my phone had run out."

"Hmmm, Chinese mothers."

"Indian mothers too."

We crack up like an old couple chortling over remembered jokes about Asian mothers. Such pals we are now, Jeev and I. We no longer harbour great expectations of each other. There's no hidden agenda, no unfulfilled ambition or emotional obligation. Just music, simply the music we enjoy making. And I like it this way. I like the purity. Like a garment washed and beaten clean with a stick by the Indian laundryman, standing waist deep in the river. Durable and torn in places but still wearable, and should the garment wear out in time, it can be discarded without too much pain on either side. If only all relationships could be like this.

"D'you think you'll be able to work in Singapore? You'll be eating ten course meals every day. Swamped by hundreds of relatives and your old lady's pals."

"Jeev, I'll shut the door and lock myself in if I have to. Or come home. I promise."

Home. Home is here. In Berkeley, not Singapore. A decision I made at seventeen when Ah-ku threw me out. What is the sound of anger? The bloody clash of cymbals. With ten thousand trumpet blasts and a hundred drums booming. A whole symphony had threatened to explode in my head when I was writing Prelude to Fury for Orchestra & Pipa Solo. An experimental piece. Discordance and dissonance are the hallmarks of my compositions. Inspired by my intense phone conversations with Ah-ku screeching across the Pacific's choppy grey waves when she found out that Jeev and I were living together.

- Who is he?

- A friend.

- What kind of friend?

- A friend! Boyfriend, okay?

- What's his name?

- Why are you interrogating me?

- Have you something to hide?

- No! He's Peter Rajeev Acharya.

- That doesn't sound American. Is he American?

- Do you think everyone in America is European, white and blond? He's American. And a professor! Happy now? A pro-fes-sor!

- Don't shout! I can stop asking, you know! Stop phoning! Stop caring! America is such a big country. Millions of people. And whom do you choose? A black man!

- You're a racist! He's not black. His family is from India.

- I don't care where they're from. If you fail your exams, don't come back!

- I won't come back even if I pass!

I shut my eyes against the light. The fog outside my window has lifted and the rain has stopped. Berkeley looks fresh in the golden light.

"Hey, knock, knock! Are you still there?"

"Sorry. Just thinking what else to pack for the trip."

"Your work-in-progress. And a reminder to text me when you reach Singapore. I want a daily update."

"Stop being tiresome."

"Honey, you love it when I'm tiresome."

3

A loud cheer rose when Ah-ku came on stage. The cheering was the loudest in the history of the teahouse, people said. That night, after the incident of the bamboo and the flea, the teahouse had standing room only. All the seats and tables were taken by early evening.

"My friends, thank you for your support, thank you. What would you like me to sing tonight?" she asked, looking slim and alluring in a pink qipao with high-cut slits at the side that gave the men at the front tables teasing glimpses of her fair thighs.

"Sing us a song about the flea in a dog's backside!" shouted a man, his gold front teeth glinting in the lamplight.

"Ah, ah," she wagged a finger at him. "Naughty, naughty, Towkay Tan. You know that story already. Shall I sing you a new ballad instead?"

"Yes, yes!" the other patrons shouted.

"Thank you, and so I will. Please drink a cup of wine and sip a cup of tea if my song pleases thee," she began, making up the words as she went along, stringing them together to fit a popular Cantonese folksong. This was her gift. She could make up songs and get her audience to sing along, and the men loved it. " Shall I sing you a song of a young man and a pretty maid?"

"Yes! Go on!"

She struck the pipa's soundboard, and her audience of mostly men listened in rapt attention.

"Listen, my friends, and listen well. One fine morning when the willows were green, and the swallows were young, a handsome lad saw a pretty maid. But alas for him, she was on the opposite bank of the raging waters of the Si Choon River. Struck by her beauty, the young man raised his voice above the rushing waters. Hey, hey, hey! Pretty as a blossom, what's your name? Hey, hey, hey, won't you tell me your name?

Washing clothes on the other side, the girl ignored him. The young man went on singing. Hey, hey, hey! Pray tell me your name. Day after day, the young man came to the river to woo the maid. Come. Sing with me, all of you."

"Hey, hey, hey! Pray tell me your name!" the men roared.

"One more time!"

"Hey, hey, hey! Pray tell me your name!"

"The poor young man sang his heart out louder and louder till he fell into the swirling waters. The girl jumped in and saved him. Her heart was smitten when she pulled him to the bank. Now standing on the same side of the Si Choon River, they sang to each other. And the young man was pleased. The maid could sing better than him. Will you marry me? He asked her. No, she will not! The girl's father roared. Penniless singer! What can you offer my daughter? Before the sun rose the next day, the young maid had fled the Si Choon River. She met the young man, and they boarded a ship and sailed away from the shores of China. Braving the storms and winds, they reached this beautiful island, where the streets are paved with hope and gold. Paved with hope and gold! Sing with me!"

"Where the streets are paved with hope and gold! Hope and gold!"

Her audience sang lustily, not knowing that this was the 'in memoriam ballad' to her mother. She never went beyond this point. Never told her audience how the young man turned bitter and violent, how he drank and beat his pretty wife for singing better than him, how he forced himself on her each night so that burdened with child, she could not go on stage to sing, and how in despair after their tenth child, his wife drank poison and killed herself.

"Encore! Encore!"

Her strumming grew louder and faster. She sang song after song. Boat owners, coolies and lightermen alike, they loved her songs about the river and the folk in their villages back home in China.

Night after night, the story of her bamboo and the flea drew large crowds to the teahouses, gaming houses, and the Majestic Theatre whenever she performed. So popular was she that there were nights when she had several engagements, and her trishaw man, Ah Chek, had to pedal at breakneck speed to take her from one teahouse to the next. The men's clubs clamoured for her. The mahjong clubs on the riverfront were her favourite patrons for they paid well. The boat owners were the most demanding, but they celebrated her songs about the river and the twakows. Where did you learn these songs, they asked. Nowhere. They come into my head like sunlight into a room. They loved her coquettish laughter. When they pressed her for an answer, she brushed them off with a song about her birth on the river, and how the river gods had given her songs. The boatmen lapped this up and cheered. But she didn't tell them that the river was her mother's deathbed, and her father's grave. His body was found under an old bumboat the year the Japanese surrendered.

"One more song! Encore! Encore!"

She shook her head. Towkay Ong and his friends were waiting. The first table in the front row of the Majestic Theatre Teahouse was her patron's table, a sign of his status as the Majestic's premier customer.

"To our queen of the Singapore River! Yum seng!" Towkay Ong and his friends drained their wine cups.

"To our pipa queen of Chinatown! Yum seng!" the men at the next table immediately raised their cups.

"To the queen of the river!" Towkay Ong shouted.

"Born on this river! One of our own!" his friends added.

"But she lives in Chinatown now! Chinatown is where the pipa queen reigns!"

The men at the next table laughed, shaking their heads at the bumboat men.

"It doesn't matter where she was born. It's where she lives now!" they laughed.

"Why, these lily-livered accountants! Who do they think they're shaking their heads at?" Towkay Ong fumed. "Here! To our queen!"

"Born on the river! Queen of the river!" the boatmen bellowed, "Huat-ah! Long may she prosper!"

"Living in Chinatown. The pipa queen of Chinatown! Long may she reign!" the traders countered to great laughter in the teahouse.

With each round of drinks to the queen, their toasting and rivalry escalated. Neither side would stop. Their voices rose higher. Their hands kept drumming the tables, their faces grew red and their voices grew more insistent. The moment the wine cups were filled, they were drained. She had to skip from one table to the next trying to calm down these arrogant airheads. First, she drank with Towkay Ong and the bumboat owners. Next, she drank with the accountants and traders. Cooing and murmuring, she soothed their ego and silly male pride. From table to table, she drank, laughing and flattering her patrons to make sure that the men at the other tables did not feel neglected. At each table, they pressed her to drink two to three cups of sweet rice wine. It was a matter of face and pride to see which table could get the beautiful Pipa Queen to down one cup more than the previous table.

"One more toast, my Beautiful! One more! One more!"

Head reeling, she was floating with her pipa, tottering on her heels. "No more, gentlemen, no more."

But they were merciless, these men. She had to drink if she

wanted them to return night after night. And so it was way past midnight when she tottered out of the teahouse and climbed into Ah Chek's trishaw. The river was heaving before her eyes. Bursts of light and clusters of dancing stars made her giddy. The shouts of coolies unloading the boats were deafening. Three ships had dropped anchor near the river mouth, Ah Chek told her. If she held her head still, she could see the bumboats and twakows swarming around the ships, their lamps bobbing like fireflies on the water. Ah Chek's trishaw sped past the mahjong clubs and restaurants, spitting out their gamblers, hustlers, entertainers and women of the night. She lurched forward and threw up the contents of her stomach.

"Ahhh, so sorry," she groaned.

"You've had too much to drink. Everyone is talking about your bamboo pole and the flea in a dog's backside. People said you played extra well tonight."

"Those swine!" she swore and threw up again, wiping the spit with the back of her hand. "I was serenading fools and buffoons tonight."

"They call you the pipa queen. You're their heroine! That flea is an inspector in the hawkers' department. Did you know? He acts big. Talks big. Makes your life a misery if you need a hawking licence from him. All down the riverfront, the hawkers cheer you. You've rubbed that bugger's nose into the dirt. And serve him right! He took away Ah Teck's licence. How to sell noodles now? Seven children to feed. Last week he waited one whole day for the flea's signature. And what was he doing? Sipping coffee in the canteen! Got to grease his palm under the table. If not, no licence! The insect! He used to work for the gwailo English in City Hall. Speaks their language. That's why he can act big. Fatty Ong who sells pork down by the river had no coffee money. So that louse declared Fatty's pork illegal and unfit for eating. A public danger, he said. Look, Fatty Ong yelled. My family ate the pork. My ma's alive! My pa's alive. My whole family's alive. Every single one of them not gone to hell yet! But the flea ignored him. What could Fatty do? He can't sell pork now. Good that Miss Yoke Lan ripped off his face, Fatty said to me."

"Aiyah! I've no idea that I was doing the hawkers such a great service."

She wiped the drip from her nose.

"Even the women say, tell Miss Yoke Lan, we thank her."

"Are they calling me Miss Yoke Lan?"

"They not only call you Miss, they also call you Queen. And hear this. The aunties at the market even said you deserve a husband."

"Aiyoyoh! Did they really say that? Did they?"

Her pipa trilled like a young girl in a new dress all set to welcome the Gods of Good Fortune and Prosperity. Her fingers skipped and galloped, plucking laughter from her pipa strings. Like birds pecking rice grains on a bronze drum, her notes fell from the rafters of the teahouse. Then they flew upwards like swallows weaving in and out of the audience singing with gusto. Her songs had men tapping their feet and clapping their hands. That New Year, the Majestic Theatre and the teahouses by the river, the men's clubs in Club Street, China Street and Keong Saik Street resounded with her pipa's music and songs. The mahjong clubs and gaming houses fought for her pipa each night, and raised her fee for a night's entertainment.

Towkay Ong, the owner of several bumboats and twakows, was her most ardent fan. The big-boned man with a face that told of hours in the sun trailed her from teahouse to teahouse, bringing with him other loud speaking, hard-drinking boat owners and their men. They waited for her, and took her out to the restaurants near the river where Towkay Ong nibbled her ear, resting his paw on her thigh.

One night a silver-haired trader came to the Majestic Theatre teahouse. He had a soft voice and refined ways. His dressing and manners made the twakow and bumboat owners looked like country bumpkins. People addressed him as 'Millionaire Towkay'.

His friends were the traders who worked in the remittance houses and shops in the city. They fingered their abacuses all day, counting the beads and keeping huge sums in their heads while their brushes inked in hundreds of thousands in a neat script into the accounts books. One of them approached her. The silver-haired gentleman would like to take her under his wing. She understood at once what the old man wanted, for that was how such arrangements were phrased. She asked for time to consider the proposal and how she should thank Millionaire Towkay properly.

Back in the tenement shophouse, she called Molek Ee and Mrs Lee into her windowless bedroom, and the three of them sat on her bed.

"What's there to consider?" Mrs Lee was flabbergasted. "You can't say no. You might never get another proposal like this again."

"I know, Mrs Lee, I know. I did think of that."

"Did you tell him about the girl?" Molek Ee asked.

"I told him that Sum Koo, my foster mother, was the one who adopted Rat's Shit."

"And what did he say?"

"Nothing. Just that she could live with me."

"So there! What're you waiting for?" her two friends screeched.

She looked at them, and sighed, "He's as old as my grandpa if he were alive."

"Aiyah, Yoke Lan. Do you want to hawk the pipa all your life?" Molek Ee was exasperated with her.

"I know, I know. But all my life, I've prayed and dreamed of living in a house with a garden and a mango tree. And a husband who comes home every evening."

"Wa-ah! Such a big dream you have."

"Don't you dream big, Mrs Lee?"

"No, I dream small dreams. Like a small flat tummy."

A fit of giggles seized them. Mrs Lee's belly was big as a barrel. The three women lay on their backs on her bed, gazing at the yellow globe hanging above them.

Mrs Lee sighed. "What for I dream big? I don't want big, I tell the gods. Not big. Not big with child. But the great Goddess of Mercy, does she hear me?"

"Ack! The Goddess of Mercy is deaf. Better depend on myself than the gods," Molek Ee sat up. "I hold my fate in my hand. Our fate is written in the left hand. The life we make is written on the right. My advice to you is this, my girl. Land your big fish now. He might be old as your grandpa, but all the same, marry him."

Yoke Lan closed her eyes and sank deeper into the lumpy mattress.

"What now?" Molek Ee poked her ribs.

"How can you call it marry, Molek?"

"Ack, why not? If he looks after you and accepts the girl, it's marrying you, isn't it?"

"Listen." Mrs Lee sat up. "My man and I were married according to tradition. I served tea to his parents. I kowtowed to his ancestors at the altar. What good did that do? Where's my man now? I'm left with four dustbins to feed. I tell you, Yoke Lan, between money and ceremony, choose money."

4

"I remember the first morning of the great change. . ." I begin to tell Dr Forrest, but I can't go on. Pain and joy collide when I think of those days in Chinatown. How thrilled I was with the light flooding our new room. Ah-ku had moved into the largest bedroom in the three-storey tenement shophouse. It had a window that looked out onto the street below. Our landlady, Kim Poh, Molek Ee, Mrs Lee, the hawker's wife and the butcher's wife, and some of the other tenants had crowded into our room to gawk at her new bed and dressing table with a huge, round mirror. I can see them now preening in front of it, teasing each other and talking about Ah-ku's catch.

"I thought Yoke Lan would go with the bumboat owner, the one with the gold teeth," the butcher's wife said.

"Ah no, this one is richer. This one, people call him Millionaire Towkay. That's how rich he is. Just look at the size of this bed he'd bought for her."

"I can see that. A queen-size bed for a king-size romp," the hawker's wife giggled.

The women's tittering made Ah-ku smile. The butcher's wife opened the new wardrobe and peered inside. "Waah! A three-door wardrobe with three drawers! Cost a bomb, I tell you. Not even our Kim Poh can afford such furniture. Right, Kim Poh?"

"Those pipa girls in Temple Street, their spit is turning into vinegar."

"Envy will choke them," the hawker's wife giggled again. "We poor folks, we're happy to sleep on a plank. Which of us owns a cupboard?"

"Not me," Molek Ee said.

"Nor me," the butcher's wife laughed. "A box under the bed. That's my grand wardrobe."

"Aye, she's grand, our Yoke Lan."

"She's the pipa queen now."

"You can't come in!" Fatt Chye stood arms akimbo, barring the way.

"Kim Poh, tell your fat boy off!"

"Don't mind him. Come and see my sister's new furniture."

"Oooh la la! When did Yoke Lan become your sister, our Kim Poh?" Mrs Lee asked, and the other women chimed in, "Yes, Kim Poh, when? When?"

"You people! What do you mean when? I've always treated her like family. Gave her credit. Let her have a room even before she could pay me. Ping-ping, come over here."

She thrust a lollipop into my hand.

"Waah! The sky will fall today. Our Kim Poh is so-oo generous."

"Stop teasing her, Molek. She's been very good to me. Thank you, Kim Poh."

"No need, no need, Yoke Lan. I knew you'd do well. Why, I was the one who told Old Kim to let you have the room on credit."

"Aiyoh, Kim Poh! Why don't you treat me like your sister too?"

"Molek Ee! Look into the mirror."

"No need to look, lah! I've got a seamstress face. Not a beautiful songstress face. If I were a songstress, our Kim Poh would've called me Sister too. Right or not, Kim Poh?"

"All of you think I'm money-faced. Ask our Yoke Lan. Ask her how much she had when she first came to me. Look at her now. Renting the best room in my house. And she's even caught herself a big fish!"

"A very big fish. What if his wife finds out?"

The laughter stopped.

Molek Ee glared at the butcher's wife. "And how is the wife going to find out if you people shut your big mouths?"

"Molek Ee, this is Pagoda Street. Can people keep a secret, meh?"

My new bed was a mattress instead of a mat on the floor. I sat on it, sunlight streaming in through the open window. I looked down into the street below, marvelling at the stalls selling all kinds of food and desserts, and realised with a start that Ah-ku had not scolded me in the last three days. Thrilled and giddy at this, I felt as if I had stepped onto a rollercoaster, and was scared that I'd fall. Happiness felt strange.

"Are you ready?" a gruff voice asked.

Framed in the doorway, the silver-haired elderly man smiled at Ah-ku, his gold-rimmed glasses glinting in the evening light. His white hair was pomaded and combed back with a side parting.

"Aiyah, Towkay dah-ling, come in. You're early. Ping. What do you say?" Ah-ku hissed at me.

"Pa!" The word burst from my mouth and fell with a thud at the old man's feet.

"Shall we go?" he asked as though I had not spoken.

Heads turned as we walked down Pagoda Street. Ah-ku's flaming red qipao and Millionaire Towkay's gold watch were pointed at and commented on. The eyes of the men in the coffee shop trailed us, the smoke of their evil-smelling cigarettes choking my nostrils. Fatt Chye and his gang nudged each other. Fatt Chye made a funny face to attract my attention, but I ignored him. Behind my back, the urchin girls were giggling like idiots. I held my head high as I walked behind Ah-ku and Millionaire, aware that all eyes were on the three of us. I kept my eyes focused on the street lamps until we stopped in front of a magnificent black Mercedes. Wa-ah! Is this

Pa's car? My Pa? I peered into the red plush interior, and wished, oh how I wished Linda Tan and that man who spat on me were here. Imagine the surprise in their eyes. How foolish and contrite they'd feel.

"Get in! What are you waiting for?"

Ah-ku's bark startled me. I lurched forward and stumbled into the backseat.

"Clumsy oaf, Rat's Shit!" Fatt Chye yelled.

The children hooted. I refused to even glance at them. So what if I fell. I was the one in the car, not them. I looked into the rear view mirror, and a bright-eyed girl with two front teeth missing, grinned back at me.

One week later, following a trip to a photo studio, a black-and-white photograph of the three of us sat on top of Ah-ku's cabinet. It showed a solemn girl with two missing front teeth seated wedged between a smiling young woman with long black hair and a grave old man with sparse white hair.

*

"No more men's clubs for me from now on. So what if I'm a kept woman? I'm a tai-tai now, a rich man's woman, right or not?"

Ah-ku fanned herself slowly, sitting on the floor of the passageway outside our room that served as the tenants' living room. The women sat here in the afternoon to talk, sew or iron while their children were out in the streets. The day was hot and humid. Molek Ee put down the skirt she was hemming as Mrs Lee reached into her bag for cigarettes.

"Ack! Don't you let the busybodies worry you, Yoke Lan," Molek Ee said as she bit off a thread from the skirt.

"Who says I'm worried? I'm just waiting for the day when I can move out of this dump. As soon as Millionaire buys me a house. Somewhere in Katong or Siglap, I tell him. That's my dream. Be rich and respectable."

"Aiyoh, isn't your life good now?"

"Molek Ee, please. Think a little deeper, can or not? An old man comes into your room for an hour or so. He takes what he wants. Then he leaves. He's in a hurry. Always in a hurry. He has to go home. Sometimes he takes you out to a dinner or to a picture show. Sometimes he plays mahjong and you sit for hours behind him, pretending to be interested but always watching and waiting. Then you don't see him for days. You wait. You play mahjong with friends. You shop. And you wait. Then without warning, he shows up at your door and shuts it. He fucks you and then he leaves. Is this a life? Is it good enough? I'm only twenty-one."

"Aye, Yoke Lan, it's lucky you've someone while you're still young. In a few years, other men will see you as an old hen. Finding a good man is like searching for a needle in the rice field."

"Let me have him if you don't want him," Mrs Lee said.

"Here, have a smoke instead."

Molek Ee threw her a pack of cigarettes. Mrs Lee pulled out a stick from the pack and handed it to Ah-ku. She lit up, sucking in the smoke before letting a wisp seep out from between her lips. The other two followed suit and three smoke rings curled and rose in the beam of sunlight coming down from the skylight in the roof on that hot, lazy afternoon when the witches struck.

A shrill voice shrieked in Hokkien, "Where's the whore? Where's the slut?"

Heavy footfalls pounded up the stairs. Three women in sarong kebaya rushed up brandishing their brooms.

"Ping! Run to the back! Go!"

Ah-ku pushed me out of the way. The women elbowed her aside and dashed into our room. A cup flew out. I dived under Mrs Lee's table. Things were smashed against the wall.

"Stop! Stop! You can't do this!"

"Who says I can't? These are bought with my husband's money! Who says I can't? There! And there! And there!"

Cups and saucers flew out of our room. Glasses and plates fell with a resounding crash. A bottle of perfume was hurled against the wall. Lavender and jasmine scented the turbulence as more bottles and cosmetics flew out of the room. The three women were shrieking like wild cats. Their brooms swept the air. Mrs Lee and Molek Ee warded off their brooms with stools and tried to shield Ah-ku.

"Suay-ah! Suay-ah!" the three witches screeched in Hokkien.

"Stop! Stop!" Kim Poh ran into the room. "I'm calling the police!"

"Call them! Let them close down your brothel!"

"This is not a brothel! It's a respectable house!"

"It's a brothel!"

"Stop fighting!" Old Kim, Ah Chek and some men pushed their way through the melee of arms and brooms.

"Don't touch us! We'll sue you gangsters!"

"No, Madam, it is I who will sue you. I am the landlord and the proprietor of the coffee shop below," Old Kim spoke in formal Hokkien. "You, Madam, are trespassing on my property. I request that you and your friends leave at once."

"My husband's whore lives in your brothel!"

"Madam, this is not a brothel."

"But the slut lives here!"

"I repeat, Madam, this is not a brothel."

"I don't care what it is! You tell that slut. If I catch her with my husband again, I will scratch out her eyes. Gold digger!" she spat.

Old Kim and the men escorted the three witches down the stairs. The other women followed, pulling their curious, frightened children along. Kim Poh, Molek Ee and Mrs Lee remained upstairs. An uneasy silence had settled on the passageway. The door of Ah-ku's room was shut.

"Yoke Lan," Kim Poh knocked softly.

No response. She tried again. "Ping, go in."

I opened the door and stepped inside.

Glass shards and fragments of mirror littered the floor. Broken plates and cups were everywhere. Clothes wrenched from the wardrobe were strewn on the bed, crumpled and ripped. Others were cut up. A pair of scissors lay on the bed. The pink lampshade was crushed underfoot. The lamp was smashed. The round mirror of Ah-ku's prized dressing table had a large crack down the middle. The crack cut Ah-ku's face in two, and her dark eyes were staring out of the mirror at me. I backed away, and she sank into the armchair with her back towards me.

I took a step toward the glass cabinet that once held the figurines of animals of the Chinese zodiac. Its glass doors were shattered and the figurines smashed. On the floor lay fragments of the black-and-white photograph of the three of us. The photo had been ripped out of its silver frame and shredded. Bits of dark eyes and grey face lay scattered among the shards. I picked up one half of Pa's face. A jagged bit of Ah-ku's smile. Part of her long hair. Then a fragment of my face and toothless grin. I started to cry.

"Ma…"

"I'm not your Ma. Get out of my sight!"

*

Yoke Lan tried the phone and put it down again. It'd been like this for weeks. The moment the other side heard her voice the line was cut, and the phone in the old man's office was always busy or off the hook.

"The number has been changed," Old Kim muttered, taking back the phone and wiping the mouthpiece with a white towel as though her bad luck might infect the instrument.

In the coffee shop and tenements, they talked incessantly about the three Hokkien women who had wrecked her room and life. At the end of the month, she pawned her gold chain and a gold ring. No, she told Molek Ee firmly, she would not return to the men's clubs and teahouses. She couldn't bear the smirks of the other pipa songstresses. It was a great loss of face. The old man would come back, she declared. He had spent a fortune on her, so why wouldn't he come back? He'd be back, she said; he wouldn't let his money go to waste. She visited his club at night, and left word with his friends. The men standing at the entrance of the club blocked her way. They smiled and asked after her health, and promised to look out for him. Fucking liars, she thought. The old man was inside.

The following month, she pawned another gold chain, and Kim Poh came into her room. "The pawnshop is not the answer, Yoke Lan."

"I don't want to play the pipa again."

Kim Poh looked at her without the usual obsequious smile. "He's not coming back. Your girl's got to eat even if you don't. And there's the rent. I'm sorry but Old Kim . . ."

"Say no more, Kim Poh. The rent will be paid."

Molek Ee took her to the temple to pray to the White Tiger god, the slayer of gossipers, rumour-mongers, wife-cheaters and wife beaters. She offered roast pork and chicken, and took off her shoe to beat the gossipers and Bad Luck spirit. But her luck remained unchanged.

"Nothing more you can do," Molek Ee said. "His wife watches him like a bulldog. That's what I heard. Even if your old man wants to visit you, he can't."

"I must've been a wife-beater in my past life. This is my punishment." She yanked the wretched instrument from under her bed. "Which fool said that the pipa sounds like pearls falling on jade? It's the hiss of tears falling on fire."

That night, she donned her signature red qipao, and sat in Ah Chek's trishaw. At the Teochew Men's Club, the manager arched his brow. "Is this an honour, Miss Yoke Lan? Are you here to play only the pipa? You can offer nothing more?"

"Mr Tan, you know that my pipa songs are entertaining."

"Who doesn't know that? But, Miss Yoke Lan, who comes just to listen to the pipa these days?" He inched closer to her, his voice a leering low. "An old songstress must offer more than songs."

"Don't worry. My songs will bring them in."

"Get down from your high horse, Yoke Lan."

She wanted to slap him. At the Majestic Teahouse, it was the same story.

"Sorry, Miss Yoke Lan, so very sorry. Our patrons want a fresh young face."

The fleas! The parasites! She raged. "Home, Ah Chek! How much is tonight's fare? I'll pay you next week."

"Any time, Miss Yoke Lan. Pay me when you can."

Back in her room, she flung the wretched instrument on to the bed and tore off her qipao. Did they think she belonged to yesterday? She was still young. Didn't they beg her to play not so long ago? No, she would not plead with the dogs. Heaven does not block all roads. Fortune will smile on her yet. "What are you gaping at, you guttersnipe?"

The pipa was hurled across the room. It hit me on the head. I picked it up.

"Put it down! Go and wash up! Now!"

She yanked me up and out of the room. She pulled me into the communal kitchen, and shoved me into the bath hut where she tore off my clothes.

"Burden-on-my-back! You're filthy! Filthy! Stand still!"

She pulled down my knickers. At the first pail of cold water over my head, I shivered like a drowned rat. It was past midnight, and the water was cold. My hair was plastered to the sides of my face. My shivering made her angrier. She swung the pail at me. My head hit against the Shanghai jar. She pulled me up and dunked my head into the water jar. Again and again till I was gasping and struggling.

"Stop crying, you snivelling rat! I'm not dead yet! Not dead!"

"Yoke Lan! What the hell are you doing in the middle of the night?" Molek Ee pulled me away from her. "It's not Ping's fault!"

*

"I remember it as though it just happened," I tell Dr Forrest.

He nods, and waits for me to continue, pen poised above the pad on his knee. I gaze out of the window in his office. Two pots of fern sit on the windowsill wilting in the sun, and the pond glittering at the end of the driveway has attracted the attention of two silky terriers straining at their leash while their owner, a fat man in white shorts, is talking to a woman in blue jeans. When the dogs and their owner move out of my vision, I look down at my hand, amazed that it has twisted off the button on my white blouse.

"We moved back into the windowless cubicle after that night. The bed and the rest of the furniture were sold. The tiny room was packed with boxes of Ah-ku's belongings, but she… she…" I can't go on.

"What else was in the room? What do you see?" Dr Forrest asks.

"The … the pipa." My reply is a whisper.

An image comes to me – I was caressing it when Kim Poh yelled for me.

"Ping! Phone call!" I dropped the pipa like a thief caught in the act, and bounded down the stairs, two steps at a time. The phone crackled with static in my hand.

"Ah-ku!" I shouted. "Ah-ku!" It had been months since she left me in the coffee shop.

"Stop shouting. I'm in Hong Kong… for…" I strained to catch her words, but the sputtering static in the phone and the noise in the coffee shop was making it difficult for me to catch what she was saying.

"Ah-ku! Ah-ku!" I shouted again and again. Only the phone's humming answered me. This experience became part of my childhood nightmares.

"When is she coming back? When?" Kim Poh pressed me for an answer. When I told her I couldn't hear what Ah-ku said, Kim Poh huffed.

"She's dumped you with me. That's what. Three months gone. Where's the money she promised? We don't even know how to get in touch with her. Hong Kong. Hong Kong is so big. Where in Hong Kong? Did she tell you? You're a headache! What if she doesn't come back? What're we to do with you…?"

"Ahem!"

I look up. Dr Forrest is waiting for me. I haven't spoken a word in the past half hour. He's been very patient, but why shouldn't he be? I'm paying for the minutes of silence. It's our last session; tomorrow I leave for Singapore. Dr Forrest removes the writing pad from his knees and recaps his fountain pen. He glances at his watch and smiles.

"You were deep into your memories. I didn't want to interrupt. Why don't you come and see me again when you return?"

"Mm…"

"Enjoy your trip, Ping."

The hell I will!

Part Two

Mongrel Child

5

Three a.m. at the Singapore River.

Weng can't stop the melody that goes round and round in his mind. He hits the railing with his fist.

The dark waters flow in placid indifference to his pain. His insomnia has returned. His nights creep at a snail's pace. Awake at home, he listens to the rumble of memories. Awake at the river, he emits an old man's sigh. Damn. He'd been a fool to love her. He hasn't stopped thinking about Ping ever since Mrs Chang, her aunt, gave him news of her impending arrival. Was that deliberate? Would Ping recognise him? He imagines her grey and ravaged, two bitter lines skirting the corners of her mouth. He'd heard she's divorced and childless. That should be revenge enough. But then he'd found no joy in other women either. The violinist he married had left him and returned to Shanghai. And who could blame her?

"Tien-ah! Heaven!"

His sudden vocal violence shocks the almost deserted quay. Glistening raindrops from a passing shower slide off the tabletops. Inverted chairs cast long shadows across his path. He steps into a puddle and soaks his socks. He strides across Cavenagh Bridge, past the grand post office, now the Fullerton Hotel, and his mind runs off down South Bridge Road, Temple Street, Pagoda Street, with her. How many times had he run with her through these streets and their alleys? Weng Kor-kor! Weng Kor-kor! she'd called, running after him. He was racing ahead, pushing their pram down the lanes of Telok Ayer Street, Pulau Saigon, Boat Quay, Clarke Quay, Robertson Quay, Alkaff Quay, passing the bridges: Elgin, Coleman, Read, Ord, Clemenceau, and pang-sai bridge, the footbridge named after Old Pang, the sai or nightsoil collector. Running across coconut tree trunks flung across the streams and ditches of the Singapore River, they tried to push each other into the water. The memory of those bridges had kept him sane in the detention centre in Whitley Road.

Playing his imaginary flute in his prison cell, he had roamed the riverfront in between the interrogations. Crawling into riverine nooks and recesses with her, wading into ditches and brooks in search of guppies and other fishes, where hadn't he brought her?

By the brook behind the bushes, he had held her in his arms and kissed her, their bodies pressed against the pink honolulus blooming in wild abandon under the angsana trees. Where are those creepers now? Where are the inlets and creeks that led to nowhere and everywhere? He stares past the lights of the condominiums and office towers lining the waterfront. Her hand in his, they are wading into the brown river, eyes intent on the mud banks searching for catfish, catching the sun in each other's eyes. A haze hangs over the river and the humid air is tense and heavy with the fragrance of hot sesame oil, fried ginger and red pepper when she leans over and kisses him on the lips.

Hai! Hai! Hai! Ah-tee, ah! Young brother, you lucky dog!

The coolies hooted and waved from the bumboats. Embarrassed, she sank into the water.

"Ping!" He called and dived in after her, striking out to reach her. Bobbing up, laughing and shaking water from their hair, they were like the statues of naked urchin boys frozen in bronze on the riverbank.

"Weng Kor-kor!" He saw her shouting into the wind, clinging to the pole of the bumboat with one hand while her other hand held on to his tightly as choppy waves heaved their boat in the sea swell.

"Don't let go of me!"

The sun's rays in his eyes, beads of sweat streaming down his face, he was yelling into the wind. "I won't! I won't!"

6

"When the river serpent rears its head, the heavens pour. This is the worst flood in memory, I can tell you," Old Kim said, sweeping the brown water out of his coffee shop.

Fierce winds had swept across the island, felling trees. For two days and nights, the storms had raged, and floodwaters rose waist high in many parts of the city. A footbridge in Clarke Quay was wrenched away in the flood, and a man fell into the river and drowned. Business in Chinatown was at a standstill, but Old Kim kept his coffee shop open, and people came in at all hours to swap stories and complain about the worst flood since their great grandmother's time.

"Just look at what the government is doing," Old Kim complained. "Trees cut down, houses are torn down. Everywhere the land is bulldozed and churned up. You see those twenty-storey blocks? They jut up into the sky like fists, raised against Heaven. Sure to make the Sky God angry. Those blokes in their air-con offices, what do they know? English-educated assholes. They won't let the workers build an altar to the Earth God at the building sites. No praying allowed. Cannot build an altar. Superstition, they say. Good. Now see what happens. Floods everywhere. The construction sites are all flooded. In Toa Payoh, three workers were killed. Now those numbskulls say the workers can set up their altars. Ha!" Old Kim slapped his thigh. "Those fools learn only when someone dies. But," he wagged his finger, "they will never admit they were wrong in the first place."

Two squatters' huts on the riverfront were washed away one night. Stalled cars and buses lined the roads in the pouring rain. In Telok Ayer, Tanjong Pagar and Duxton Plain, the floodwaters rose to knee level. Pagoda Street was a swirling river of brown waters under a grey cloudy sky. Urchin boys clambered up the deserted hawker stalls to launch their paper boats, and the older boys rowed down the flooded streets in soapboxes, taunting the miserable drivers in their stalled cars. One dollar! One dollar! No give dollar, who will push your car?

Weng was swimming in Pagoda Street when he saw a girl in the window above the coffee shop lowering a red pail tied to a rope. One of the urchin boys gave her rope a tug, and the red pail fell into the floodwaters. Whooping and splashing, the boys fished it out and tossed it about. One of them flung the pail into the middle of the flooded street.

"Please! Please give it back!" the girl cried.

"Please! Please give it back!" the boys mimicked her.

Weng dived for the pail. He fought off the others trying to snatch it from him. He was a strong swimmer. With his teeth clamped tightly on the pail's handle, he made for the coffee shop, and raced up the stairs at the side.

"My pail! My pail! Give it back to me!"

The girl's screaming was coming from the front room upstairs. He knocked on her door. Her screaming stopped, and the door swung open. The girl stared at him.

"Here!" He pushed the pail into her hands while his eyes gawked at the beautiful bed and dressing table with the large round mirror. They were just as the aunties in the market had described. What luck, he thought. The bedcover and the pillows were pink and embroidered with red flowers and bright green leaves.

"Waah! So classy." He was drawn to the glass cabinet with its colourful menagerie of porcelain animals of the Chinese zodiac.

"Rat, ox, tiger, goat, pig…"

"Please don't touch the glass."

What's your name?"

The girl was about his younger sister's age.

"I'm Wong Ping-ping."

"Ha! You're a Wong? I'm also a Wong. Wong Fook Weng. Call me Ah Weng."

He shook the rain out of his hair, unaware that he was leaving small puddles on the floor wherever he stepped. "Hey, do you drink from these cups?" He pointed to an English tea set of fine bone china. "They're very easy to break, hor? Do you sleep in this room?"

"Yes."

"And that bloke up there, he lets you?" He jerked his head in the direction of the silver frame with its black-and-white photograph on top of the glass cabinet.

"Of course. He is my Pa."

Her haughty tone surprised him. "He's not your Pa," he grinned.

"He is too," she insisted.

"No lah! He's not."

"He is!" She stamped her foot.

"He's not. Everybody knows he's not your father."

"He is, he is!" tears pooling in her eyes.

"Hey, hey, don't cry. Please don't cry." He started to back out of the room.

"He is; he's my Pa." Her eyes were pleading with him.

He turned and fled down the stairs.

But her face, and those eyes, stayed in his mind.

7

Ping remembered Market Street. Four-thirty a.m. A rat the size of a kitten darted out of the drain. She jumped out of its way. The market was not open yet, but the grannies in black samfoos were already there hovering like black crows waiting for offal, and so were the big boys, who glared at her. She was the only girl, but she refused to be cowed. She had to earn money to buy schoolbooks. A sudden screech of brakes made her leap onto the pavement. Four lorries rounded the corner.

"You fucking beggars! Watch your heads!"

Baskets of vegetables were flung onto the road. Arms shot up around her. Legs kicked and elbows dug into her sides. She tripped and fell when she tried to squeeze past the grannies. They fended her off like ferocious blackbirds, squawking and scolding, as they rammed their bony elbows into her and the boys. More lorries pulled up. Dashing in and out between the vehicles, the boys pounced on lettuces and cabbages that fell out of the baskets. Ping picked up a large box from the rubbish dump and grabbed some greens. She quickly got the hang of things, but just as her box began to fill, it was snatched out of her hands. Two boys threw her box back and forth between them like a basketball as they ran down the road.

"Hey! It's my box!" She gave chase.

"Hey, hey, it's my box!" they teased.

"Bullies!" A third boy leapt out from the shadows and kicked the box out of the bullies' hands.

"My vegetables!" They were scattered all over the road now. Sobbing, she started to pick up the scraps.

"Hey, aren't you the pipa queen's girl? Can't recognise me, is it? I went to your room and gave you back your red pail. Ah Weng. Remember me or not?"

She brushed off her tears with the back of her hand, suddenly ashamed of what she'd become.

"Do you always cry like this? You haven't lost anything, you know."

His eyes were laughing at her. Sun-browned and lanky, he shook away the fringe that kept falling over his eyes and picked up her box.

"Give it back."

"Don't worry lah! I don't want your box. Yikes! I got to deliver newspapers. Want to help? I'll show you later where to sell your veg. You can't set up your stall any old how anywhere or gangsters will bash you.

"Wait! Wait! Slow down. You speak like a machine gun."

"Call me Kor-kor. If you call me Elder Brother, I help you to sell."

She glared at him. There was a twinkle in his eyes and a grin on his face. He had helped her twice, she remembered. "Kor-kor," she said.

"So soft your voice, but okay lah. Come. Follow me. First we deliver my papers."

He worked fast. In no time, all the papers were delivered, and he led her to the backlane.

"You cannot sell in the market. You set up stall in the market, the gangsters will come after you. Look. Do this. Balance the box on your head. Now shout. Cheap veg! Cheap veg! No, no! Louder lah. You're mewing like a kitten."

Impatient with her, he pulled out his bamboo flute from his slingbag and started to play a lively tune. He paused, and bawled loud enough to wake the dead, "Five cents! Five cents! Cheap veg! Cheap veg!" Then he played his flute again and yelled again. "Cheap veg! Cheap veg!"

An old Indian woman poked her head out of her back door.

"Good morning, Aunty! Look, Aunty."

He pushed her forward, and she held out her box.

"Look, Aunty. Very cheap. Very good vegetables, Aunty."

"Berapa ini? How much is this?"

He held up two fingers. "Dua puloh sen saja. Twenty cents only."

"Busok, lah! They're rotten. Are you trying to cheat me, boy?"

"Adoi! Aunty! Don't say that. I'm no cheat."

Speaking a mixture of Hokkien and Malay, cajoling yet respectful in a tone that the old Indian lady seemed to enjoy, he peeled away the blackened cabbage leaves.

"See, still good. Not rotten. I give you special price, Aunty. Fifteen cents only."

"No, ten."

"Adoi, Machik! Fifteen cents, Aunty, and the chillies are yours for free. Okay?"

"Add the spring onions."

"Aiyoh, you drive a hard bargain, Aunty. Want to buy the whole lot?"

"No lah! Buy so much, for what?"

"It'll save you a long walk to the market. These vegetables are dirt cheap."

"You probably stole them."

"Aunty! We didn't steal. Our mother. She's sick. So we sell for her. We just sold some vegetables to the people over there."

Ping held her breath as he pointed in the direction of the houses down the lane.

"Thirty-five cents for everything," the old lady said.

She breathed out a sigh in sweet relief. She'd never met anyone like him before.

"Five cents more, Aunty. Boleh? Can? See I give you cabbage, long beans, lettuce, chillies and spring onions. Make it forty cents?"

"Hmm!" the old lady dropped four ten-cent coins into his palm and pointed a finger at her. "This girl. She's Melayu?"

"Ahh, no, she's not Malay, Aunty. She's Chinese. Aunty says you look Malay."

"Stupid woman," she muttered under her breath.

"Watch it, girl. Indian people in Chinatown understand Cantonese."

"Are you coming back tomorrow, boy?"

"Ya, Aunty. I'll knock on your back door, Aunty. Even if you don't buy anything, never mind. You're my friend. Special service for you, ya?"

"Get off, you!" The old lady laughed and shut her door.

"See? That's how you sell. Thirty cents for you. Ten cents for me!"

"What? Ten cents for you?"

"Hey, I earned the forty cents. I played my flute. I enticed the granny to come out. I sold her your rotten veg and I spoke Malay. What did you do? Eh? What? Better say thank you to your elder brother here. Quick. Call me Kor-kor again. Go on."

"Kor-kor." She couldn't help giggling. She was beginning to like him.

"We're partners now. See? You collect the vegetables and I sell them. Agreed?"

"Agreed."

"Partners forever!"

"And ever and ever and ever!"

It was the happiest day of her life since Ah-ku left.

She didn't mind calling him Weng Kor-kor. He knew the streets of Chinatown like the back of his hand. The backlanes were his terrain where he showed her how to scour for useful things. Here were pebbles, ice cream sticks and bottle caps to be collected and traded with Fatt Chye for a lollipop that they took turns to lick. Here was a wooden crate he could haul home to be chopped into firewood for his stepmother's stove. The tins and bottles he gathered were for selling to the karung guni rag-and-bone man. There's money to be made in garbage. Waste not, want not, his Pa had taught his sisters and him, he told her. And the family ate the fishballs his uncle couldn't sell.

She followed him everywhere.

Like a sunbird, brown and bright-eyed, she flitted beside him, twittering and darting from shophouse to shophouse delivering newspapers, and afterwards she skipped down the back alleys beside him with her box of vegetables yelling: "Cheap veg! Cheap veg!"

She knew every street with its smells, shops, and different kinds of dirt and flies.

Sago Lane smelled of joss sticks, incense and sandalwood from the coffin shops, funeral parlours and death houses where the old, the poor and the sick waited to die, and funeral bands played in the street day and night. The air in Sago Lane was thick with the smoke of incense and the odour of frangipanis and chrysanthemums from the floral wreaths and other offerings to the dead. She avoided Sago Lane, but he didn't mind it. She liked the streets of noodle stalls, Chinese bakeries and clothing shops with heaps of shirts and dresses that spilled on to the pavements, and hawkers yelling, Lelong! Lelong! Cheap! Cheap! Very cheap, sister!

The streets had a vibrancy and a character she could not describe in words. Their sounds and noises rang like music in her ears. During Chinese New Year and the feast days of the gods, opera performances and getai were staged on many street corners. Weng could rattle off the Cantonese names of such streets at the drop of a coin: Hay Yuen Gai, Say Yan Gai, Ngao Cheh Sui Gai. Theatre Street, Dead Man's Street, Water Buffalo Cart Street.

"English, English. Say it in English. Say South Bridge Road," she nagged him.

"But English names are so boring, leh! Let's go and look for Old Fart in the backlane."

The backlanes held secrets few people outside Chinatown knew. Char siew pao, the most delicious sweet pork buns were made on trestles in the backlanes, their minced meat filling drying in the sun on bamboo trays that attracted hosts of houseflies. On hot lazy afternoons, Old Fart could be found in the backlane roasting maize, rice husks and coffee beans in a rusty tin drum over a fire, making the cheap coffee powder that Old Kim passed off as genuine Indonesian coffee.

"He's such a cheat, Uncle Old Kim."

"How else can he feed Fatt Chye his pork every day, eh?" Weng laughed.

They were standing at the back door of Ming Kee Restaurant, drooling at the Peking ducks dripping with honey, houseflies and sesame oil as the birds hung from hooks on a bamboo pole.

"These flies visit the bucket latrines all over Chinatown, Weng Kor-kor."

"So? They add a special flavour to the Peking ducks. Smell them."

They put their noses close to the ducks. Soy sauce, cinnamon, cloves, ginger and sweet plum sauce mingled with wood smoke and roasting meat wafted down their nostrils. Dizzy with the aroma, Weng smacked his lips.

"Oi! You beggars! Clear off or I'll cut off your noses!"

They scampered off, laughing at the fat cook shaking his ladle at them. When they reached the corner of the lane, they turned and waved.

Sometimes, she spent the afternoons alone behind the wood crates and boxes next to the drain at the back of the coffee shop. Hidden from view inside one of the crates, she read the books she had borrowed from the school library, and thought about things she told no one. Not even Weng. Like why did the old Indian woman think she was a Malay? When she found a little mirror someone had thrown away, she held it up and checked her face for flaws. Patches of rust in the mirror hid part of her face. She could only see a small part at a time. Her nose had a bridge higher than Weng's. Her eyes were bigger and rounder; his were shaped like almonds. His hair was black and straight while hers was black and curly. Other than that, she was the same as him. Except that she was a girl and she had dreams. Secret dreams, she looked into the mirror and smiled. Once, she'd dreamt she was Thumbelina, no taller than a man's thumb, and she was flying high up in the sky on the back of a brown sparrow. Last night she'd dreamt she was a pipa player and crowds had come to listen to her. So far she hadn't dreamt of Ah-ku at all and wondered where she was now. Would she come back for her? Yes, she comforted herself; Ah-ku had said she would. But what if she failed to come back? What then? She tried not to think of it. If fear and loneliness overwhelmed her at times, she did not cry. She was ten and half. She was a big girl, and she had Weng Kor-kor.

8

Weng ran out of the hut, pulled off his shorts and jumped into the river. At the crack of dawn the river had stirred to life. Fires were lit in the stoves in his neighbours' huts. Bare-chested boatmen squatted on the decks of their bumboats brushing their teeth with a bit of coconut husk, gargling into their tin mugs like hundreds of tenors and baritones in the choir. This was the music Weng had heard since he was a toddler on his parents' boat, when they still lived on a boat then. He swam out to the middle of the cool brown water. Smoke from the charcoal and wood stoves was starting to tickle his nostrils. Soon the food stalls in the market would open and his stepmother would buy fried dough sticks or fried vermicelli for the family's breakfast.

"Ah Weng!"

He dived at the sound of his stepmother's voice.

"Don't swim too far out! Do you hear me? Weng!"

He bobbed up, shaking the water from his hair.

"Don't stay too long in there. You know what you'll get if you miss school. Have you done your homework?"

Instead of answering his stepmother, he sank back into the murky waters and remained submerged with his eyes closed, unreachable in his subterranean world. Then he swam ashore, pulled himself up on to a crate, and lay on his back, the sun's rays warming his belly.

"Ouch!" A small pebble hit his leg.

"Mister Naked, a very good morning! I heard Aunty Chong Soh yelling at you. In trouble again, are you?" Ah Koon grinned. He was one of the young carpenters, who worked with his father in the boatyard.

"So what if I am? What do you want?"

"This crate. Get off!" Ah Koon made a grab for his leg.

"You missed!"

He jumped down from the box, grabbed his shorts and ran up the road. He slipped behind a hawker stall and pulled on his shorts. Then he nosed his way back to the bumboats further up the river. Here were creeks and streams hidden by tall grasses and weeds where he usually spent quiet afternoons practising his flute or hunting guppies and mud crabs with his friends. By the time he was four, he was already netting crabs at the river mouth at low tide, squelching barefoot through soft grey mud beside his father. They had plenty to eat then, and his father was a happy man and had time to play his pipa, but that was before his mother left them.

He thought about the girl and the Pipa Queen who'd left her in the coffee shop. The girl rarely mentioned her mother or aunt; he wasn't quite sure if the girl was adopted, and didn't like to ask. When he played his dizi, he had noticed the girl's eyes gazing longingly at his bamboo flute. "What?" She looked away.

"Do you want to be a pipa queen too?"

"No!" she yelled. "And stop calling her Pipa Queen." They walked down the backlane in silence. She was carrying the box of unsold vegetables. There had been no buyers for two days.

"Can you play the pipa or not?" He asked her again. It was hard to believe that she couldn't play the instrument. "Listen. If you sell off your pipa, then you don't have to sell veg. You can't make enough to buy books for school anyway. Look, you can't play it. Why keep it? Sell it." She whirled round and boxed his arm.

"I want to play it! I want to play it!"

There! He knew it! He knew it! He knew it! She kicked his shin to stop his prancing, but he was right all along, wasn't he? She wanted to play the pipa.

"Why didn't you say so, Ping?" She would not look at him. Then, in a soft, sad voice, she said: "I don't know how to play it. Ah-ku doesn't want me to learn."

Aiyah, he shook his head at her. "You girls are so dense. Look, where's Ah-ku now? Where? Where? Will she know if you learn to play now? Can she see you? Can she? Can she?" He teased her mercilessly. "My Pa teaches the pipa at the clan association. He'll teach you. I'll ask him."

But instead of thanking him, she ran off.

*

The phone rings. It's Jeev again.

"What now?" I growl.

"Don't bite, honey. Relax. I'll be picking you up at four tomorrow. Best to leave early and avoid that nasty jam on the bridge."

"Thanks." I put down the phone. Grateful and relieved that Jeev is taking me to the airport. My mind's a muddle, wavering between excitement and apprehension. I've been thinking of Weng behind his wall of silence. I'd never breached that wall. I had my pride too. But I did wonder after all these years what had happened to the mountain of mail that I sent him. Did he just burn all my letters? Never replied to a single one… had he erased all traces of our relationship?

*

"This is my village, Kampong Squatters," he told her.

He never thought of her as anything but the girl just as he never thought of Kampong Squatters as anything but his village. It was only much later when the troubles on the river began that he came to see his village as others saw it – a cesspool in the heart of the city.

Children and dogs ran past them. From the thatched huts came the sounds of cooking, the clang of woks and pans, and the hiss of oil and steam. Women washing clothes at the standpipe were shouting at their children and pouring mugs of water over the wriggling bodies squealing, "So cold! So cold, Ma!" Others were queuing to fill their pails at the public taps. A girl pulled down her knickers and squatted beside a drain to pee. Boys shooting marbles stopped their game to look at him and the girl. His friends called out, "Puppy Weng! Who's that with you?"

"Nobody."

"What blew nobody here?"

"The wind, lor!"

"Woo-oo! The wind is blowing his girlfriend home. Woo-oo!"

He was glad she ignored the idiots. Her eyes looked ahead as she walked beside him. She acted as though she were deaf and mute till they reached his family's hut near the creek where the old bumboats lay rotting in the mud.

"Wow, so many tall trees here." She was awed by the raintree near the river. "It looks like a giant umbrella with pink flowers."

He liked that. She was good with words.

"Come on inside. We have two rooms," he announced, pleased that she could see for herself at last how much more space he enjoyed at home compared to her tiny windowless cubicle in the coffee shop. A partition separated the two rooms and a green-checked curtain hid his parents' bed from view. His three half sisters slept in the front room, which was also the family's dining room. Their kitchen was in a smaller hut at the back, and next to it was the family's toilet and bathroom.

"Where do you sleep then?"

"Over there," he pointed to the raintree. "See the camp bed leaning against its trunk? That's my bed. I sleep there. I play my flute there. I'm king out there."

"Ya, king of the alley cats."

His half sisters, Fong, Kum and Leng-leng came out to join them.

"Ping, meet the three troublesomes."

"Hi, Ping."

"Hi, Ping."

"The cats mew when Kor plays his dizi," Fong told the girl.

"And the dogs howl," Leng-leng giggled, hopping from foot to foot.

"Don't listen to them. They've no respect for their elder brother."

"But we have! We have! We respect you as our dreamer, Kor. Ping, he can dream with his eyes open. Like this." Kum pushed up her eyebrows, and the girls giggled.

"Shoo, mosquitoes! Go help Ma."

"What if it rains?" she asked him.

"Then I bring in my bed and sleep inside with these three troublesomes. But I prefer sleeping under the tree by myself."

"You're not scared of… of the river serpent at night?" She was staring at the darkening shimmering waters lapping against the roots of the raintree.

"Better not talk of such things at sunset. I've got dogs anyway. Come. I'll show you something else." And pointed out to her the red chillies, spring onions, Chinese mint, lemon grass, pandan and roses that his sisters and stepmother had planted in rusty tins, earthen pots and discarded plastic pails that he had salvaged from the backlanes. "Come this way. I'll show you Pa's vegetables."

His father's vegetable patch was hidden behind tall bushes. He pointed out the cucumbers to her, the lady's fingers, Chinese spinach and long beans that his father had planted in neat rows of raised earth.

"Weng Kor-kor, you're so lucky to live here."

"Ya, we're lucky. We've water from the river to water the plants, chickens behind our hut so we get fresh eggs every day. Our drinking water is from the public taps you saw. After dinner, my sisters and I will go to the taps to fill our pails and Ma's cooking jar."

"You have no taps in the house?"

"What for we need a tap? We get free water from the public taps. No need to pay. Only got to queue up with our pails. We're used to it. But someday, I'll be a musician. Then I'll be rich. I'll have my own house and my own tap and my own orchestra."

"We heard you, Kor!" his sisters yelled. "Ma said to come in for dinner!"

"Don't listen to him, Ping," Fong sidled up to the girl. "He's dreaming again. Music can't make him rich."

"Why not?" He made a grab for Fong's arm but she slipped out of his grasp and ran into the house.

"Hahaha! Music can't make us rich. Just look at Pa!" she squealed.

His father pushed aside the green-checked curtain and came over to join them at the table. Pale and thin after his recent illness, his father shook his head at Fong.

"What nonsense, Fong. Music makes our spirit rich. When our spirit is rich, it will attract the god of fortune. Not immediately but some day, some day.

"There! Pa agrees with me. When I'm rich, I'll have my own orchestra, and it will play at the funerals of rich folks and earn a lot of money."

"Not just the rich folks, Weng. Everybody deserves good music when they die. People burn paper money and paper houses to the dead. Why not play them music instead? You should sell your idea to everyone. Let them pay your orchestra to play at their funeral instead of a ragtag band that only plays tong-tong-cheng!" his father laughed.

"Your pa is dreaming aloud as usual. Come, children. Let's eat." His stepmother set a large pot of soup on the table and sat down.

Pa laughed. "Ah, then, Ah Weng's mother. Am I a man dreaming I'm a butterfly or a butterfly dreaming I'm a man?" And started to flap his hands like a clumsy moth, which made them laugh including his stepmother.

"Aiyah, Chong, do let these children eat. They're starving while you talk on and on. Come, Ping, help yourself to rice and fishball soup. If you don't, Uncle Chong Suk will talk till my soup grows cold. Come. Eat. Don't be shy."

"Thank you, Aunty Chong Suk. Thank you, Uncle Chong Suk."

The girl ate quietly, too shy to join in the family's banter around the table. Years later, he found out that this was the first time she had eaten with a family who laughed and joked. In the coffee shop, her dinners were eaten in silence except for the grunts and snorts from Fatt Chye and Old Kim.

"Here, Ping, have another fishball."

"Ma, I'm tired of eating fishballs every day." Fong made a face.

"You be grateful. Some people don't even have rice."

"But they have music," Leng leng chirped, and Pa patted her head.

"Pa, Ping wants to learn the pipa," he reminded his father.

"Are you willing to work hard, Ping?"

His stepmother frowned. "Chong, your music is not the kind that pleases men in the teahouse. Not the sort that Ping is used to. Every river comes from a source. Look at her source."

"Hush, Ah Weng's mother. Every river changes course the further it flows from the source." His father turned to the girl. "Are you prepared to work hard?"

She looked apprehensive. His stepmother's words had frightened her.

"Not all who play a musical instrument are talented. Some have desire but no talent. Some have talent but no discipline. Without talent, desire and discipline, there's no music, no art. Do you understand, Ping?" his father asked.

The girl stood up and reached for the teapot. As the family watched, she poured out a cup of tea. Holding the cup in both hands, she knelt before his father.

"Chong Suk Sifu," she addressed him with great reverence as the honoured mentor.

"Whoa! Who taught you to do this, Ping?" his father asked.

"My heart," she replied.

*

The Wong Clan Association was on the first floor of a two-storey shophouse in Sago Lane. Weng followed his father past the dormitory of the coolies on the ground floor. They went up the stairs to the hall where his father's class were already tuning their instruments.

"Good evening, Chong Suk," the men greeted their teacher. There were no women in his father's pipa class.

"Good evening, uncles," Weng greeted the old men reading the evening papers on the other side of the room.

He sat under the gaze of the clan's ancestors looking down from their black-and-white photographs, ashamed of his inability to read the ancient calligraphy, the brush strokes of each word so fluidly and beautifully written. He glanced at the clock on the wall and hoped the girl wouldn't be late. His father was very particular about punctuality. He placed his flute on the chair next to him to keep the seat for her

"It's the Pipa Queen's girl." He heard his father tell his class about his new student. "Never taught a girl in my life, but she served me tea and called me Sifu. Not like you lot."

"Sifu. Chong Suk Sifu!" the men howled.

"Tai chi students in China used to call their teacher, Sifu," his father was shaking his head as he recalled the girl's eagerness to learn. "Let's see how she takes to the learning."

The girl came up the stairs, clutching her pipa case.

"Psst, over here." He waved to her.

She sat down beside him.

His father plucked the strings of his pipa once, and the class fell silent. The men were musicians by night, but labourers, shop assistants, store clerks and salesmen by day. His father sat with the pipa on his lap, still as a crane. He was thin and looked sallow but he shed his tired look as soon as he started to strum.

"What's your pa playing?" Her lips brushed his ear, light as a feather.

"Quiet," he hissed. His ears were burning with a heat that was at once pleasant and startling. "He's playing Shi Mian Mai Fu, Betrayed and Ambushed. You know it?"

She didn't answer him but kept her eyes on his father. He was sorry he'd been so brusque. He hadn't realised that a girl's lips were so soft. He shook off the sensation. The intensity of his father's plucked strings soon mesmerised the both of them, but they were not the only ones. The old men at the table had stopped reading their evening papers. His father's playing tonight had an edginess they hadn't heard before. Perhaps it was the presence of a new student – the girl – that was pushing him to reach for new heights. With a flick of his fingers, a thousand arrows whizzed across the night sky. Stars fell at the emperor's anguished cry. The enemy's armies pounded across the plains as his father's fingers drummed on the pipa's soundboard, and horses' feet, anxious drumbeats, and the soldiers' battle cries filled the room.

The coolies crowded up the stairs, leaning against the banisters in rapt attention. Then just as suddenly as it had begun, the pipa fell silent. Weng held his breath. The girl did not move in the tensed hush that fell on the room. The silenced pipa stood on his father's lap, his father's hand restraining its strings. Then with a sudden twist of the wrist, the strings were released and out sprang the emperor's anguished cry. Soldiers fell and horses neighed and reared in fearful surprise as the pipa plunged down the dark ravines. The emperor's stallion fled from the barbarian hordes. An arrow pierced through his chest, the conqueror had become the conquered, and the pipa moaned his despair. The cries of his imperial stallion grew faint as its betrayed emperor wrenched the arrow from his chest.

For days afterwards, Ping's head was filled with the tumultuous music of Uncle Chong Suk's pipa. Like a fierce white gorge in the mountains, it had rushed through her heart. Listening to him that night, she realised that there were two kinds of music in the world – one that stirred and troubled the heart, and one that soothed the senses and dulled the brain. There was no mistaking which music she most wanted to learn.

She went to the clan association every night but the pipa defeated her each night. At times, she wanted to give up. The pipa was untameable. Like a wild horse, it reared and threw her off each time she tried to pluck its strings. Yield, she commanded, but the pipa would not yield. Her fingers were no match for the stubbornness of its strings.

"Relax your arm. Hold her neck firmly but gently. Like this. Relax your shoulders. Your fingers must not clutch at the strings. Now try again."

The taut strings cut her skin; her fingers bled but Uncle Chong Suk ignored such things. "One more time. The same chords," he said.

She played till her fingers were red and sore, but the pipa would not yield to her touch. She could not sound out its notes the way Weng could with his flute.

"Desire is not enough, Ping. Desire alone can never turn performance into art. Practice, practice and more practice. Each time you fall, get up and walk. Walk. Don't run. Learning demands patience."

"But I've been patient, Uncle Chong Suk. I've practised every day."

"Go home. Go. Come back when you've conquered your impatience. Throwing a tantrum won't help."

Her teacher's harsh words hardened her resolve. She turned up at the clan association every night even on those nights when Uncle Chong Suk had to work in the boatyard, and Weng had to take his father's place to teach her. Night after night, she practised till the skin on her fingers hardened. When Kim Poh found out that she was learning the pipa during the school holidays, she was ordered to help in the coffee shop.

"What's your problem?" Weng needled, "So you work as a kopi girl, but you also earn tips. The blokes in the gambling houses will tip you big when they win. Just for bringing them a cup of coffee. It's better than selling vegetables. You can practise your pipa after the shop closed. Just sleep less, lor. Like me. I practise my flute by the river till very late sometimes."

She wanted to tell him that she didn't mind serving coffee. What she dreaded was bumping into Linda Tan and her classmates when she had to carry trays of cups down Pagoda Street to the gambling houses and mahjong clubs. Pert, haughty Linda haunted her dreams. What? The daughter of a rich merchant is a kopi girl? She learnt to take multiple orders, remembering which uncle ordered kaya toast, and which aunty wanted coffee black, yelling like Kim Poh: One teh si! Two kopi si! One kopi siu tai! She learnt to match orders with faces, and weave in and out of crowded streets with a tray of hot toast, pork buns and cups of coffee and tea, screaming in Hokkien: Sio! Sio! Hot! Hot! The men tipped her generously, and some nights she pocketed one or two dollars that Kim Poh knew nothing about.

After the coffee shop had closed for the night, she emptied the spittoons under the tables and washed them clean for the next day. When the Kims had gone to bed, she slipped out to practise her pipa on the covered walkway. She tried not to think of Ah-ku. She remembered watching a red-lipped songstress peeling a mandarin orange while a man held her on his lap, his hand squeezing her breast as one of the women played her pipa and sang a song that saddened her. She felt a stab of guilt that she was learning the pipa. Ah-ku had made it clear that she didn't want her to become a pipa songstress. But playing the pipa doesn't make you a pipa songstress; Uncle Chong Suk had assured her.

9

"Psst, Ping. Where's Big Tits?" Fatt Chye hissed.

"Why you little pecker! You want to see my tits? Come, I'll show you!"

Miss Rose flung open her door, and the coward fled down the stairs almost crashing into his mother who was coming up.

"Son, what're you doing up here?"

"Your son wanted to see my tits!"

"Choy! What a thing to say, Miss Rose. He's just a boy."

"He was peeping into my room."

Kim Poh laughed and brushed aside the accusation. Ping knew that if it had been any other tenant, Kim Poh would've unleashed her tongue, but it was Miss Rose, the new premier lodger who had taken over the front room, and a hostess in the Southern Cabaret and Nightclub at the Majestic Hotel. Everyone knew that Miss Rose was the magnet that drew Fatt Chye up the stairs each evening to sneak at her sashaying down the corridor to the bathroom at the back, but no one was telling Kim Poh. And why should they? Kim Poh wouldn't have believed that her fat son would do such a thing.

"Ping! Haven't you finished packing yet?"

"She's almost done, Kim Poh," Molek Ee answered as Ping pushed another box of clothes out of her cubicle into the passageway. Kim Poh had ordered her to move out of the windowless room.

"Don't look at me like this, Molek Ee. I lose two dollars every day that Ping stays in this room. I can rent it out for sixty a month, you know. And it's your good friend, Ah Chek who wants to rent a room here. Ping has stayed in it long enough. How long does Yoke Lan expect me to feed and house her girl?"

"Didn't she send you some money lately, Kim Poh?" Mrs Lee stuck her head out of her room down the corridor.

"Oi, you people! Are you keeping count on her behalf? She sent me fifty here, fifty there. Enough to feed, what? Chickens? It doesn't even cover the rent of this room."

"Yoke Lan can't be doing well in Hong Kong. I worry about her."

"You go ahead and worry, Mrs Lee. I can't afford to worry. We lose sixty dollars on this room each month. Sixty dollars on this girl. Ping, you sleep out here from tonight. Have you moved out everything? Move out your mattress now."

"Come, we'll help you to move it," Miss Rose said.

Molek Ee and Miss Rose heaved and shoved her mattress into the wire cage above the stairwell. Her new bedroom was a cage with a wooden platform, just high enough for her to sit up inside it. Used for storing bags of coffee, tea and sugar sold in the coffee shop, the cage was made of thick strong wire, and the door had a latch and padlock. At least she could lock up her things, she consoled herself, and tried not to think of it as a dog's kennel. The main drawback was the lack of privacy. Everyone could see her when she was asleep.

As if reading her mind, Miss Rose handed her a piece of cloth. "Here. Hang this tablecloth up when you sleep."

Su and Noi, Molek Ee's daughters, pushed the box containing her clothes into their already crowded room, which was also their tailoring workroom.

"Don't worry, Ping. You can come in here to get your clothes and change in our room. We'll put the rest of your things under our bed and keep them there until your Ah-ku comes back."

"Look, you people. I'm not throwing her out. This wire cage – I can get ten dollars a month for it. It's a room with a rental worth one hundred and twenty a year. And don't forget; we're also paying for her school and food. For how long? We don't know when Yoke Lan is coming back for her."

"Aye, Kim Poh, no one is saying you're heartless. It's just that this poor girl has no mother now. You're like her foster mother."

Molek Ee placed a hand on her shoulders, but the sudden touch, so warm and caring, almost made Ping burst into tears. She bit her lips and kept telling herself that her bedroom was not a cage. "Don't worry, Molek Ee. I don't mind sleeping out here. I'm not scared of falling down the stairs."

"Right then. You sleep here from now on," Kim Poh said. "I've got to go. Make sure you move out all your things."

"Don't worry, Kim Poh," Molek Ee said, and waited till their landlady had left before whispering to her, "Ah Chek said you could leave some of your boxes in his room."

"And you can hang your school uniform and bath towel on our door," Su added.

"And do your homework in our room," Noi said. "But if I strike the lottery tomorrow, I'll buy a house, then you can live with us and be our little sister."

That made her smile and everyone laughed. How she envied Noi and her sister. At sixteen and fourteen, they had left school, and Molek Ee was teaching them to sew. They hoped some day to sew for one of the foreign clothing manufacturers setting up factories in Singapore, they said. That night as she slept in her wire cage, she made a wish. It wasn't for Noi to win the lottery, but for a bed under the raintree at the river next to Weng.

"Shhh! Come and see the mongrel child in her cage." Fatt Chye pulled off the tablecloth. Three boys stood grinning at her. "Woof! So airy in the cage, hor?"

"You boys leave her alone!" Molek Ee came out of her room

and the boys ran off.

My new bedroom is a loft of light and rainbows. Although it is the smallest room in the house, it is the happiest because of all the secret dreams it holds.

Mrs Singam liked her description so much that she was asked to read it out aloud to the class. She was in Primary Six that year when she started to count and amass A's as though they were pieces of gold. Uncle Chong Suk was pleased with her rapid progress at the pipa too. But no amount of praise or distinctions were enough. She felt grand for a while, but the novelty soon wore off as the year progressed. There was something more pressing on her mind. Old Kim wanted her to stop school after Primary Six, and work full-time in his coffee shop. At twelve, she was old enough to earn her keep, he declared. And Fatt Chye echoed him whenever he had the chance. "No use your A's. Pa is not going to let you go to school anymore. What for you study so hard? Come to a show with me, want or not?"

"No."

"You go to a show with me, I'll persuade Pa to change his mind."

"No."

Molek Ee pulled her into the room.

"Now, listen to me, girl. Be careful with that boy. You're not a little girl anymore. Unbutton your blouse."

She was stunned. "Unbutton?"

"That's what I said. Your Ah-ku is not here so I've got to teach you certain things."

She blushed; her cheeks were burning. She suspected that Molek Ee knew what she had been trying to hide all week. The two little bumps, hard and tender, had appeared on her chest. They had popped up overnight, and now a tender fullness filled her chest that was flat as a washing board before the bumps appeared.

"Look at yourself. Your body is no longer that of a child's. Now you understand why Fatt Chye is eyeing you? You'll be bleeding soon. Down here."

"Down there?"

Noi and Su giggled. Their mother glared at them. "What's there to laugh about? It happens to every girl. You're twelve going on thirteen this year. Soon you'll be a woman. Don't let the boys touch you. Understand?"

*

Music was her refuge besides school. She went to the clan association to practise as often as she could. Uncle Chong Suk was like the father she never had, a stern parent who wanted only the best from her. She was gaining mastery over her pipa, and loved nothing better than to practise with Weng accompanying her on his flute.

"Pa can't come tonight. He's ill, but let's practise anyway," he said one night. "Can you play this chord?" His dizi trilled like a bird, and she plucked the same notes on her pipa strings. "Not bad. Play it again. Watch your fingering. Pa said your playing has improved."

"Don't bluff."

"I'm not bluffing. Pa never praises his students."

"I have an hour to practise. Then I've to run back to the coffee shop. If Kim Poh finds out I'm here again, she'll hit the roof."

"Okay, let's do this piece."

There were no music scores or notes. Everything was from memory. Uncle Chong Suk taught by example. He'd shown her how to tune the pipa's pitch, tugging at the strings a little to lower it, or pressing the head to raise it. Sometimes, the men in the class showed her how to pluck the strings and make them sing at a particular pitch and tone. Sometimes they ignored her, especially when she showed impatience or played badly. Weng had told her that he had to learn from a very young age how to sit still and listen to these lao qian pei, the elderly musicians in the clan association. Through observation and imitation, he had picked up many techniques from the older dizi players, and his father had made him practise a piece over and over until he could hear every pause, every nuance or misstep in his own playing. This could take months. Even years, he said.

"Can we play something else tonight? Just this once for fun?" She struck the chords of a familiar folksong she had learnt on her own.

The old men who were regulars at the association looked up from their newspapers. "Go on, girl," they said.

Surprised, she played the Cantonese folksong to the end, a song that was popular in the teahouses, and one she had heard Ah-ku played many times before. The song sounded even better the second time round. Encouraged by Weng and the old men's applause, she played another folk tune, pleased that her fingers were striking the right chords so effortlessly. Weng joined her with his flute, and their lively melodies soon attracted the coolies living on the ground floor. The young men came up the stairs and crowded into the room.

"Encore! Again! Please play us another song!" they begged.

"Go on. Play another song," Weng urged her.

She played a third song, and then a fourth, to great applause from the coolies, the old men and the elderly musicians. Her fingers strummed the pipa with an ease and fluency that surprised her. Pleased with herself and engrossed in her playing, she didn't realise until too late that Weng was taking a bowl round the room, and the men were tossing coins into it. She stopped playing at once.

"Look, Ping." Weng held up the bowl, laughing like the rest of the men.

She kicked the bowl out of his hand and ran down the stairs, tears streaming down her cheeks. He had betrayed her.

"Ping! Wait! I collected the money for you to buy books! Wait!"

He caught up with her in the back alley.

"What's wrong with you?"

"I'm not a pipa girl!" she sobbed.

She stayed away from the market the next day, and the next and the next, stewing in anger and misery until she couldn't stand it any more. He was her best friend. Her stupid, stupid, best friend. She found him waiting as usual at the market. His face broke into a grin when he saw her.

"Look Ping I found this pram in the dump I've fixed the wheels you don't have to carry a box any more you can…"

"Slow down. Don't talk so fast," she stopped him, laughing at his eagerness to show off his prized find.

That morning after they had delivered his newspapers as usual, and sold off her vegetables, he told her he had a surprise for her, and took her for the first time to his hideout. A secret place, he said. A fishing spot that not even his sisters and friends knew of. She knew it was his way of saying sorry, but she'd already forgiven him. Neither of them brought up the past. They were children then, and the future was more important than the past.

The creek was up the river beyond the warehouses, boatyards and bumboats, along a stretch where there were few huts. Here, the water was cool and clear. Scrub, creepers, lallang and bushes grew in wild profusion, and here and there, clusters of purple morning glory and bright pink honolulus curling green tendrils out of old car tyres and rusty bicycle parts dotted the riverbank.

"There're guppies in the creek," he whispered.

"Are there snakes?"

"Nah." He scoffed at her timidity and took her hand. He led her into the river till the water came up to their knees. "Watch your step here. There're bits of glass at the bottom."

Feeling the shift and roll of soft mud under their feet, slimy weeds, dead leaves and bits of wood, their feet pushed aside the soft mass of water weeds and rubbish at the bottom. Shimmers of rainbows darted out like streaks of sunlight.

"Guppies!" she squealed. "Look, look, tiny wrigglers."

"They're tadpoles."

"Bigger guppies over there. There!"

"Shhh, take this." He handed her a large coffee strainer of fine wire mesh. "Hold it in the water and don't move. When the fish swim in, scoop them up and cover them with your hand."

Yellow, green and orange rainbows darted in and out of the weeds in the sunlit waters. Tiny fishes nipped her toes. She let out another squeal of squeamish delight; his elbow jabbed her ribs. "Quiet. We've got work to do." His tongue licked off the perspiration on his upper lip. A warm humid breeze caught his hair and his fringe covered his eyes as he bent down to peer into the watery shadows. She felt the midday sun's sharp bite on her back, the sweat trickling down her neck, and the heat of his body so close to hers. He was standing still as a crane waiting for its prey.

"Quick! The jar!" He'd scooped up something thrashing in his net.

She held out the jar and three strips of blue and orange fell into it. His next attempt netted two grey females, their bellies swollen with eggs, and he let them go. He searched among the weeds, his look concentrated and his eyes focused on the shadowy depths at their feet. He netted more guppies, and her coffee strainer caught several tiny orange and green males. By the time they had guppies swimming round and round in two jam jars, the sky had turned grey.

"I'll take the jars to the pet shop tonight. They pay five cents per fish. Then they sell them for twenty cents each to people who keep aquariums. You get half the money, okay?"

"How come you didn't bring me here earlier?"

He shrugged, staring into the waters for a long while before he answered. "Today is the anniversary of Ma's death. My own Ma. She drowned in this river when I was five."

She couldn't see his face, hidden by his fringe, and watched instead a bead of sweat rolling down from his temple to his neck before it was soaked up by his tee shirt. A large raindrop fell on her arm. She looked up at the sky.

"It's going to rain," she said.

Grey clouds had massed on the horizon like a huge army and

the air had suddenly turned cool. He packed their jars of fish into a plastic carrier just as large drops splattered down on them.

"Take the pram and head for the backlane. It's a shortcut. Quickly now."

Rain was pelting their arms and faces. The sudden squall was strong. Gusts ripped through the trees. Within minutes they were drenched, their tee shirts clung to their backs, and their hair plastered their heads. Racing down the backlane between the shophouses, she tripped and fell. He pulled her up. The strap of one of her slippers had come off. She took off her other slipper and ran barefoot, splashing in the puddles.

"Here!" he kicked an empty tin to her.

"Ouch!"

"Now what?" He knelt down and examined her foot. "Wah-pia-ah! You've stepped on something. You're bleeding." He pulled out a piece of glass. "Feel anything here? Here? Any more glass?"

"No."

He released her foot. "The bleeding will stop in a while. Put on your slippers."

"Can't. The strap's broken."

"Wait here."

He ran back down the alley and stopped several houses away. Through the pouring rain, she saw him bend down, grab something and came running back, waving something red. Panting and looking triumphant, he held up a pair of red clogs.

"Just there. They were just sitting there. On the steps. Of that back door. No… nobody's," he panted.

"It's somebody's. You stole them," she said.

"I found them."

"You stole them."

"You put them on."

"No."

"Put them on!"

"No! You stole them!"

Their voices rose in the torrential downpour. She was crying, and he was shouting at her for being such a ninny.

"Those people can afford it, stupid! Can you? Can you? You want to walk barefoot? Step on another piece of glass or what? You want to bleed to death, is it? Put them on!" He thrust the clogs into her arms.

"I'll pay back the owner some day!"

"Just wear them! Move! Move!" He slapped her on the shoulders.

"You move!" She gave him a hard shove and ran down the backlane, her red clogs clattering, her tears and the rain streaming down her face. But she was happy. Her body felt light. He had stolen the clogs for her. He who'd never been a thief had stolen the clogs for her. Her heart felt like a leaf in the wind. He was behind her, catching up on her. His pram was rattling and spilling the guppies out of their jars. Suddenly, he let go of the pram and sprinted towards her.

"Think you can get away? Think you can outrun me?" he shouted into the wind. "I'll make you smell my armpits!"

He caught her by the shoulders and locked his arm around her neck. His hand pressed her face against his chest.

"Smell it! Smell it! Smell my armpit!"

He laughed and held her tight against his chest as rain pelted their face and back. The sour-sweetness of his wet body rushed up her nostrils. She could hear the pounding of his heart beating against her breast, felt the ridges of his ribs and the tautness of his arms. Suddenly conscious of his maleness, she pushed him away, and he let go of her, his eyes bright with boyish triumph and mischief.

"Hoi! You two!" His uncle called out. "You two look like you've been rolling in the mud! Look at you. Before we know it, you two be getting married!"

10

– I hate her I hate her I hate her I hate her I hate her I hate her I hate her I hate her I hate her I hate her I hate her I hate her I hate her I hate her…

She tore the pages out of her exercise book and lit a fire in the backlane, watching the sparks fly as she flung another match into the pages.

The news had spread like wildfire down the entire length of Pagoda Street. Ah-ku had married the scion of the wealthy Chang family, and she had a son. A beautiful baby boy, they said. Everyone was thrilled. Molek Ee, Mrs Lee and Ah Chek couldn't wait to tell her the good news the moment she stepped into the coffee shop after delivering drinks to the gaming houses. Not only had Ah-ku married well and given birth to a son, they told her, she had also engaged a Cantonese amah called Kan Jieh to look after the boy. And such Cantonese maidservants do not come cheap, Molek Ee stressed.

I know, I know, Kim Poh had huffed; only the rich can afford their services. Kim Poh was annoyed that Molek Ee was doing all the telling of the news. And it was this Cantonese amah, who had brought the good news and money to pay Kim Poh, Molek Ee told her. The amah had also said that her Madam was living with her new family in Singapore now. Yes, Ah-ku had come back from

Hong Kong, and from now on, Kim Poh would receive a regular sum of money for her board and lodging. Isn't that wonderful, Ping? Molek Ee asked.

She knew she ought to be over the moon, but her heart felt pinched and tight. Even Molek Ee's hand on her shoulders could not ease the tightening in her chest. You're going to be all right, girl. You've money for secondary school now. Your Ah-ku has given Kim Poh two thousand dollars. Molek Ee comforted her. And it's a lot of money too, Mrs Lee added, holding up the fussy dress with pink ruffles and lace. Look at this, Ping. Your Ah-ku bought this for you. The pink frock was like a slap in her face. Why didn't Ah-ku come to see her? The last straw was the bit of paper with Ah-ku's phone number on it and the amah's express instruction not to call Madam unless it is an emergency.

She stood up and dusted the ashes from her sleeves. Her face was smudged. She had no regret writing and burning the hate words. She stamped out the last of the ambers with her foot, and kicked away the smouldering ash.

"Why you worry your head?" She heard Old Kim rasping as she crept upstairs. "Let the kaypohs and busybodies say what they want. Yoke Lan's married now. Do you seriously think she'll come back for the girl? What if she doesn't? What if the two thousand is a hong bao, a little red packet to keep us quiet? Have you thought of that? Remember the time after the war? People abandoned their children. Right here in Pagoda Street. A baby girl wrapped in a pink towel stuffed inside a box. A small hong bao with a few coins inside a red envelope. Not uncommon then, right or not? The only difference now is that the girl is not a baby, and the hong bao is two thousand dollars. But it's clear to me. That woman has abandoned her bastard. The girl's a mongrel. That's why she didn't come for her. She doesn't want the girl."

Each word was like a knife into her heart.

*

The dust slowly settled in Pagoda Street; the coffee shop and its tenants upstairs returned to their routines. The wonderful tale of the rise of 'our Pipa Queen' had spread from the coffee shop to all the teahouses in Chinatown and the riverfront, but nothing had changed for her. The only difference was that Kim Poh had added pork to her meals, and there was money for books and school uniforms, and she could attend the Convent of the Holy Infant Jesus secondary school in Victoria Street.

"It's good you're still here. Good that she sends you money for school. Your money problem's solved, right or not?"

She appreciated Weng's practical stance, and stopped feeling sorry for herself. They continued to deliver his newspapers together and sell the vegetables she scrounged in the market on weekends, now that school had started. He pointed out that there was no need for her to sell vegetable scraps anymore now that Ah-ku had sent her money.

"But what if Ah-ku stops sending? A bird in hand is better than two in the bush," she recited the English proverb solemnly and taught it to him. Besides, and she didn't tell him this, she liked being with him. "If the two thousand dollars run out, Kim Poh might throw me out. She and Old Kim don't like me."

"Don't worry, lah. Good enough that I like you," he grinned. "If they throw you out, you can go to the convent. The nuns will take you in. What's the worry?"

But she was worried. There was something else on her mind, something she couldn't tell him because he was a boy. Lately, Molek Ee had made her wear a bra because her breasts were beginning to show. Twice she had caught Fatt Chye eyeing her breasts. He had grown taller, and had taken to dressing fancy, with his fat hips stuffed into a pair of tight jeans and his shirt collar turned up like Elvis Presley in the movies. He had been coming upstairs too under the pretext of switching off the lights each night. 'Lights out at nine' was the house rule set by Old Kim, and two nights ago, she had woken up with the distinct feeling that someone had thrust a hand through the wire cage to touch her breasts.

"Ouch!" Molek Ee sucked the blood on her finger. "Damn!" She'd pricked herself again. This was the third time in a row that lights had been switched off without warning.

"Fatt Chye! It's not yet nine!" she yelled into the passage way.

"It's nine by my watch!"

Molek Ee switched on her torch. "There's five more minutes to go by my clock."

"Your clock doesn't count. Who's the landlord here?"

"But we pay our rent! We should've light in our rooms."

"Do you want to complain? Complain to my old man downstairs. I'm just doing my job. Lights out at nine except the stairs and the landing."

Fatt Chye moseyed down the stairs, leaving Molek Ee fuming. She knew she could not complain. Cheap rooms were hard to come by. This city was changing. The government was tearing down old buildings to make room for new blocks of Housing Board flats. But even if she could get a one-room flat from the Housing Board, it would still cost more than a room in Chinatown.

The following evening, Molek Ee was still unhappy. "I want to wring his fat neck. He's doing this deliberately," she grumbled to Mrs Lee.

"You better not. Old Kim is pleased his fat boy switches off the lights before nine. That can save him several dollars a month, you know or not? That miser calculates to the last cent. Did you hear Kim Poh crowing this morning? My son is helping his father to keep the electricity bill down! My-yy son!" Mrs Lee screeched like their landlady, sending the rest of the women in the passageway chortling into their food.

It was the dinner hour, Ping's favourite time of the day when the passageway, which doubled as a dining area for the tenants, was crowded with mothers and their children. She sat beside Molek Ee, listening to the women's gossip while they were having dinner, and relaxed after the day's chores.

Mrs Lee scooped up the last bit of rice from the pot and gave it to her youngest boy, ignoring the clamour of her three older girls. The five-year-old was always hungry; his stomach was a bottomless pit. Mrs Lee cursed the boy's father under her breath. The man had gone off again, and she would have to ask her tontine group for another loan to tie her over till he chose to return.

"Molek Ee, good thing you didn't complain," said the butcher's wife. "Old Kim is very pleased with the fat slob. He's the favourite son now."

"Well, the boy did bring Old Kim a huge windfall when he was born."

"What windfall? Stop it!" Mrs Lee hit her son's hand. The five-year-old had tried to grab his sister's fishcake. "Stop snatching your sister's food or I'll show you my cane. What windfall, Molek Ee?"

"When Fatt Chye was born, Old Kim won second prize in the lottery. That's how he came to open this coffee shop."

"Lucky Kim Poh." Miss Rose came out to the passageway to join them. "That boy has failed his exam again."

"You think he cares? He wants to leave school and run the coffee shop. Kim Poh says her boy should inherit the business."

"What about the other sons? Their mother was Old Kim's first wife."

"Aiyoh, Mrs Lee. A dead first wife can't do pillow talk. Kim Poh will get her way. Mark my words. Pass or fail, her boy will inherit the shop."

"Fatt Chye is too smooth for my liking. I saw him ogling your girls, Molek Ee."

"I'll dig out his eyes if I catch him."

"The other night at the Majestic, he was salivating after my friends," Miss Rose laughed. "I told Kim Poh about it, but she wouldn't hear a word against the bugger."

"Don't waste your breath, Rose."

By the time dinner was over, it was past nine when Ping went into the kitchen for her shower. She was usually the last in the queue for the bathroom. Every evening the tenants rushed for the bathroom while there was still light and electricity. Often she had to shower after nine when the kitchen and bathroom were dark, but she didn't mind it. She loved having the place to herself. Besides the kitchen wasn't completely dark. The single yellow bulb hanging in the passageway provided some light, and she usually took a candle into the bathroom with her. She loved to move the flickering flame up and down, and from side to side, making the shadows dance on the walls of the tiny bathroom at the far end of the kitchen. Its zinc partitions did not meet the floor and ceiling so that a large gap exposed the feet, and the top of the bather's head was visible to anyone in the kitchen. Rust had also eaten into the metal, and where the nails had come off, pinholes of candlelight shone through them.

Ping placed her candle on the ledge and proceeded to undress. The air inside was cool and damp. Using a mug, she scooped some water out of the Shanghai jar and poured it over her head, shivering as the cool water streamed down her warm body. She soaped herself and bent down to scoop more water from the jar, pouring mug after mug of the refreshing water over her body. Her eyes closed. When she opened them, another pair of eyes met hers above the partition. Like an animal caught in the glare of an oncoming truck, she froze before a blood-curdling scream shocked her into action. She rushed out of the bathroom, screams ringing in her ears.

"What happened? What happened? Hoi! You!"

The screaming went on and on. People were rushing out of their rooms. There was hollering in the passageway. Molek Ee threw a towel around her. Someone put some clothes on her.

"Hush, Ping, hush. Quiet now. Quiet. You're safe. Safe now. We've caught him. It's all right. It's all right. We've caught him," Molek Ee hugged her. "Come, girl. We've got to go downstairs."

In a daze, she followed the women down the stairs. The coffee shop was thronged with curious onlookers. Even Old Kim's three sons and their families had come down from the top floor of the building.

"What did Fatt Chye do?" one of the sons asked Molek Ee.

"Peeping, that's what he did. He peeped at Ping in the bathroom!"

"Ah! That's why he goes upstairs every night. Ha!"

"I had the feeling that I was watched when I took a late shower," Noi said.

"Why, that buaya, that crocodile!"

"Noi did complain to me, but I said, no, lah. People upstairs, we're respectable. Who would have thought it was Fatt Chye! Shameful!"

"Poor Kim Poh."

"Watch your mouth! Don't you pity me! You're all against my son! But he's the only son, let me tell you, the only son who helps his father! Who bothers to keep our bills in check? You people have a grudge against him. Are you sure it's my son? Did you see him do it with your own eyes? If you haven't, don't anyhow accuse people!"

"We caught him in the kitchen, Kim Poh."

"Are you saying the landlord's son can't go into the kitchen because some slut is taking her shower at night?"

"No, just don't peep at our daughters!"

"Is Ping your daughter? Is she?"

"She's not but Fatt Chye was peeping at her!"

"Her word against his! You!"

Kim Poh's palm slammed into her face. Ping's head reeled. If Noi hadn't braced her body against hers, she would have fallen.

"Is this how you repay me?" Kim Poh raised her arm again.

"Stop that!" a male voice ordered. "Father! Are you going to stand by and do nothing?"

Old Kim stared at his eldest son. The two of them had rarely spoken to each other. His son did not avert his eyes, and Old Kim was taken aback. The challenge to his authority was uncharacteristic. A hot flush rose from the pit of his belly to his cheeks as though his veins were engorged. The crowd in the coffee shop was silent, a silence that grew more menacing as the seconds ticked by. Old

Kim's belly heaved. His breathing grew heavy under the strain. His eldest son refused to look away; he wanted an answer from his father. Sweat poured down the sides of Old Kim's face. His other two sons and their families were watching. His tenants and neighbours were watching. His customers in the coffee shop were waiting to see what he would do next. Under normal circumstances, his three sons would've flinched under their father's stare. He could stare them down. Stare down every bloody son of that cow whose untimely death had left him with these three buffaloes who were now up in arms against him as if they'd been waiting for this day.

Old Kim's breathing was laboured. He inhaled and exhaled rapidly, his face hot and red. His eyes came to rest on the culprit, cowering behind his mother. Old Kim grabbed the nearest object and swung it high above his head. The broomstick hit the scoundrel on the head and broke into two.

"Fatt Chye!" Kim Poh flung her arms around her boy. "Say you didn't do it! Say it! Tell these people you didn't do it!"

Old Kim yanked the cowering teenager from his mother and shoved him hard against the wall. He grabbed his son's hair and banged his head against the wall again and again. "You can't say it, can you?" he bellowed. Kim Poh tried to wedge herself between father and son. "Out of my way, you bitch! Your son has shamed this family!"

He pushed his wife away. A raging bull now that the yoke of restraint had broken, an unholy strength surged through his arms. He yanked the ashen-faced coward from his mother's arms. He ripped off the boy's shirt and pulled down his pants. He whacked him with the broomstick again and again when he resisted.

"Take off your bloody pants! You want shame? You'll have shame! You're a disgrace to this family!"

"Don't! Please don't do this! Please Kim, don't. He's your son."

Kim Poh fell on her knees.

"Out of my way! Or I'll throw you out too! He's not my son! Out! Out!"

The jagged end of the broomstick sliced Fatt Chye's back. Ping covered her mouth to stifle her cry. Horror and pity overwhelmed her. Fatt Chye's pale belly shimmied before him as he staggered out of the coffee shop, the small pale slug between his legs was flaccid and shrunken. He was desperately trying to cover himself with his hands but the broomstick kept hitting him.

"Move!"

Old Kim stabbed his son's back with the jagged end of the broomstick. Blood oozed from deep scratches crisscrossing Fatt Chye's back. Kim Poh tried to wrest the broomstick away but Old Kim rammed the stick into her abdomen, and she crumpled in a heap wailing for her poor boy. Mrs Lee and Molek Ee helped her up.

"Don't come near! I'm warning all of you!" Old Kim bellowed.

The crowd backed off. Prodded like a hog by his father, the stark naked teenager limped out of the coffee shop and down the street. Past the hawker stalls, the shops, the gaming houses, mahjong clubs and tenements, every doorway and window was jammed with onlookers. Diners at the foodstalls were staring open-mouthed at the pitiful appendage swinging between the thighs of the pale fat boy, his arms raised to protect his head from his father's blows.

Ping turned and ran back to the coffee shop.

"Ping! Ping!" Weng caught up with her. "I heard what happened."

"Wait here for me." Tears streaming down her cheeks, she tore up the stairs.

*

She was still sobbing as they stood before the convent's gate and grey walls. Clutching the small bag of clothes she had hastily packed, she kept shaking her head. Weng put down her pipa case and rubbed his arms. He looked up at the glass shards lining the top of the convent's walls. They were glinting ominously in the light from the street lamps. Ping had cried all the way down the streets, past the shops shuttered for the night. He pulled out his handkerchief and thrust it under her nose. She blew into it. The bastard, he thought. How long did he gaze at her nakedness? He wanted to bash Fatt Chye's brain into a mash of bean curd. He reached for the bell, but she stopped him.

"You don't want to go in?"

Her shoulders drooped; she shook her head, and blew into his soiled handkerchief again. He felt a drop, and glanced up at the sky.

"Let's cross to the cathedral. It's going to rain."

He picked up her pipa case, took her hand, and they crossed the road. The grounds of the Good Shepherd Cathedral were in shadows. Tall angsana trees stood along the fence like sentinels, their leafy arms swaying and swishing in the rising wind and drizzle. The church doors were locked. They sat on the stone steps to wait out the rain. The drizzle grew steadily heavier. Cars and buses whizzed past on the road beyond the iron fence. He glanced at her, sniffling beside him, his handkerchief balled in her hand. A bus grounded to a halt at the bus stop. A couple got off and ran up the road in the rain, the man holding a newspaper over his head. A few more buses came and went, and then there were no more buses. It must be past midnight, he thought. The road was shimmering wet, awash with colours as cars whizzed past trying to beat the red light. The heavy rain was showing no sign of easing. The wind blew a shower of raindrops into the porch. He took Ping's pipa case and pulled her up. They retreated further into the shadows and sat on the floor with their backs against the wall of the church. She stopped crying and was clutching her bag of clothes, staring into space.

The road, emptied of cars now, was a glistening black ribbon, and the rain, the steadily falling rain and the wind in the trees were the only sounds in the night. He looked across to the left of the church, to the vast darkness of the football field in front of St Joseph's Institution, the premier boys' school he had hoped to attend some day. Its darkness seemed impenetrable, and the weight of her head on his shoulders was pressing on him. She was asleep, tired out by what had happened. He forced himself to stay awake for her sake, and dared not move lest he woke her. His back began to ache, but it was a sweet fatigue he had never felt before as he studied her sleeping face.

A sudden cry like a bird being strangled came from the back of her throat. He reached for her hand and held it, feeling her warmth creeping up his aching arm and shoulders. Then a sudden breeze brought down a hail of raindrops. She sneezed, and instinctively, he wrapped his arms around her. She woke up with a start and pushed him away. She stood up, trembling like a frightened bird. His head was spinning; he was confused.

"I didn't, I didn't do anything," he whispered.

"Don't touch me. I'm dirty."

"No, don't say that. He just looked at you." His voice was as shaky as hers. "Let's… let's go across. Ring the bell. You've got your Ah-ku's phone number? Tell her this is an emergency."

11

Caught in a ray of the morning sun, the chandelier was a dazzling fountain of splintered lights. Ping gazed at it, marvelling at the decorative cut glass and numerous light bulbs. She had never seen a chandelier before. Had never been inside a house like this before. Cream-coloured curtains hung from ceiling to floor at the french windows that looked out on to the back garden with its swimming pool. The air in the dining room was cool. An air conditioner was giving out gusts of cool air. On the round dining table, that could easily sit ten, was breakfast laid for two. Her eyes travelled from the slices of brown toast on a white plate, the two gleaming knives on the table-mat, the dish of golden butter and two jars of marmalade and strawberry jam with a royal crest and a label that said, 'Made for the House of Windsor' to the two white bowls with an egg in each, two white teacups and saucers, and two teaspoons. Everything was so beautifully laid out. She must be dreaming, she thought. She'd soon wake up in her cage over the stairwell, but across the table, Ah-ku was staring hard at her.

"Sit down, Ping. What do you say?"

"Good morning, Ah-ku." She sat down stiffly on the edge of her chair.

"Did you sleep well? What a ruckus you caused last night. Kim Poh phoned. She doesn't want you back. Not after what you've done. You have to stay here for the time being, and we'll see what to do with you. If you behave, you can continue to stay, but I want to make one thing very clear. I won't have you running with riffraff in Chinatown again. Do you understand? What were you thinking? Running off with that hooligan last night."

Ping stared hard at the egg in the bowl, her eyes beginning to swim. "Weng's not a hooligan, and I… I wasn't running…"

"If you didn't run away, how did you end up in the convent? Do you realise how much trouble you caused last night? Kim Poh was bawling on the phone about what you did to her son. Look at me when I'm talking to you."

The stranger across the table looked years younger than the sultry songstress she remembered. The hair once long and straight was now stylishly cut short in a perm. A string of white pearls adorned her neck, and on her left hand, she wore a diamond ring. Last night, Ah-ku had arrived at the convent in a beautiful lime green dress, accompanied by a tall, handsome man.

"Look up. Were you able to sleep last night?"

Ping shook her head. She had hardly slept a wink although the bed was incredibly comfortable. The sheets were so clean and fresh, and so fragrant that she'd wanted to cry. It was the bed she had dreamt of in her wire cage, and the bedroom was even more spacious and grander than the room in her dreams. Until last night, she hadn't known that such space and luxury existed in this city. Her Singapore was the Singapore of dingy shophouses and cramped, dimly lit rooms.

Her eyes wandered to the rosewood altar with the statue of a smiling Goddess of Mercy in white porcelain, two red candles, a bronze joss urn and an oil lamp. A sideboard held six ivory figurines of Chinese musicians playing various musical instruments including the pipa, and two photographs of Ah-ku in silver frames. One showed her with her husband holding their baby son, and the other was of her playing the pipa in a Chinese ensemble.

"Look at me when I'm talking to you. I want you to remember

this. Juniper Garden is not Pagoda Street. The girls here don't roam the streets. They come straight home after school. They have tuition, music or ballet lessons. Now Uncle Chang is very kind. He says you can live with us. From tomorrow, the driver will take you to school and pick you up after school. Behave yourself and don't disgrace me. You understand?"

She nodded, relieved yet she felt as if a part of her life would be cut off. She knew she should be grateful that Uncle Chang allowed her to live in this beautiful house. She ought to be happy. Wasn't this what she had longed for? In her imagined reunion, she'd seen herself running to Ah-ku, hugging her wildly, and telling her how much she had missed her.

"Tell me the truth now. What exactly did you do to cause all this trouble?"

"I didn't do anything."

"Why did you run away with that boy? Kim Poh said people saw the two of you sneaking off. A good thing that the sister phoned me, but she spoke English. I had to wake up Uncle Chang to talk to her. It was past one in the morning. Heavens! You've given me a headache."

The bowl was pushed towards her, but she couldn't eat. Her stomach had contracted and her insides felt squeezed. Kan Jieh came in with a pot of tea, and the amah's presence had a calming effect on Ah-ku. Her voice softened.

"Wish Kan Jieh good morning."

"Good morning, Kan Jieh."

"She's the housekeeper and Boy-boy's nanny. She's in charge here. If you want anything, you must ask Kan Jieh."

"I hope you slept well, Miss Ping."

"From today onwards, greet everyone in the house when you wake up, and at all meals. Always greet your elders before you sit down for meals. Don't just sit at the table like a lump of clay. And don't rush to eat. Wait for others to start first before you eat your rice. We've got to teach her some manners, Kan Jieh. I don't know what she's picked up at the coffee shop. Please give her an egg each morning before she goes to school. Look at her. All brown and bony like a twig, and her hair is a mess. We'll have to clean her up. The neighbours will think I've brought in a wild urchin."

Kan Jieh laughed. "Madam, I'll see what I can do. I'll see that she gets an egg. How would you like it, Miss Ping?"

"Eh?"

"That's not the way to answer. Kan Jieh asked how you would like your egg done."

"Half-boiled."

"Half-boiled, please…"

"Half-boiled, please."

"…and say thank you, Kan Jieh."

"Thank you, Kan Jieh."

"Now what's the matter? Why are you crying? Did Fatt Chye hurt you? Look at me when I'm talking to you. Eat your egg."

A strand of hair had fallen into the bowl. A thin black line across the yellow yolk. She tried to pick it out with a finger, but the yolk broke and oozed.

"Use a spoon for goodness sake." Ah-ku pushed a napkin into her hand. "Here. Wipe your mouth and fingers. Kwan Yin, ever merciful, grant me patience! Didn't Kim Poh teach you to be clean? Eat up. You haven't touched your breakfast at all. Aren't you hungry? Now let me go over the facts again. You said Fatt Chye peeped at you. Did you see his face? It could be anybody's eyes, you know. Are you very sure it was Fatt Chye, and not some other boy? Not the one you ran off with."

"It's not Weng!"

"There's no need to shout. Did you do anything? Any gesture that might've encouraged Fatt Chye? Are you sure you didn't encourage him? What are you doing? Sit down, Ping! Don't give me any drama. We had enough of that last night. I've got to get to the bottom of this before I phone Kim Poh today. She's Fatt Chye's mother. After what you did to her son, she's got nothing good to say about you. Who knows? I might even have to pay her off to shut up her big mouth. I don't want any trouble. I don't want Uncle Chang's relatives to hear about this. Do you understand? Oh the gods! You were trouble the moment you were born. I must have murdered you in my past life so now in this life, I've got to pay for it. My karma."

"But I didn't do anything!"

"Don't raise your voice in my house. This is not a coffee shop. And look at me when I'm talking to you. Kim Poh said you were a flirt. Always out late. She made you work in the coffee shop to force you to stay home. But you were always gallivanting with that boy. Is that true? Don't lie to me and eat your breakfast."

Ping forced herself to bite into the toast. It was hard and tasted likc cardboard. Last night while Ah-ku and Uncle Chang were cloistered in Reverend Mother's office to decide her fate, she had waited in the corridor of the convent, staring at the glacial hands of the clock on the wall, helpless as a spider dangling on its thread blown by the wind, fearful that the thread might break, and Ah-ku would leave her in the convent's orphanage.

"Eat up. You're lucky that Uncle Chang lets you stay. Call him Uncle and call me Auntie from now on, not Ah-ku. Do you understand?"

What was there to understand? Her mother was distancing herself again, retreating into the distance, changing colour like a chameleon until she was a neutral beige in this crowded city where every middle-aged woman was addressed as Auntie. A polite English term of address, nothing more. Ah-ku in Cantonese meant something more. At the very least, Ah-ku expressed a familial bond even though the maternal bond was denied. Auntie! She detested Auntie, and sobbed into Weng's handkerchief.

"Throw that filthy rag away. What are you crying for? You're going to have a good life here. You'll go to school and learn to play the piano on Saturdays when you've no school."

"I have school." Ping blew her nose into the handkerchief and kept it stubbornly balled in her hand. Something was hardening in her like the kernel of a sour mango.

"The girls around here take piano lessons. Don't you want to be like them?"

"I've school on Saturday."

"The gods give me patience! If you don't want to learn piano, that's fine. I can't change a worm into a butterfly. I was just trying to give you the opportunities I never had. If you can't learn on Saturday, you can learn on other days"

"I have lessons after school on other days," she lied. She was determined to continue the pipa with Uncle Chong Suk.

"It's so difficult to be kind to you. Don't say I didn't try, Ping. I warn you. Behave yourself if you want to live here. Don't slurp your tea."

"Mama! Mama!" The toddler ran from Kan Jieh's arms into his mother's.

"My little dah-ling. How's my duckling? Kan Jieh, how should Boy-boy address Ping?"

"Madam, let him call her Cheh-cheh."

"Cheh-cheh! Cheh-cheh!"

"Listen to him. Aren't you Mama's clever boy? But who's Mama's fussy darling? Who won't sleep without air-con, eh? Won't eat without his Papa? Who? Who? Who?" She tickled the boy and rubbed her nose against his belly. The toddler laughed, waving his arms wildly. "I'm going to tell Ping Cheh-cheh all about you."

"Would you like more toast, Miss Ping?"

"Don't just shake your head. Say, no, thank you, Kan Jieh."

"No, thank you, Kan Jieh."

"Remember, you're not a kopi girl and this house is not a coffee shop. You must learn to speak properly. Uncle Chang's family is very particular. All his brothers and sisters speak English very well. Uncle Chang's sisters – one is a lawyer, another a doctor and another a director of education. I don't want you to disgrace me in front of them. Do you understand? I don't want people to say that I've brought rubbish into their family. When you sit, sit with your legs together. Not wide apart. When you eat, eat with your mouth closed. Not half open. And don't go chup-chup like a pig when you eat. Hold your chopsticks straight. Don't cross them. And listen to Kan Jieh. Obey her. Do you understand? We have to get her some new clothes, Kan Jieh. I don't know why she's in rags. We sent money to Kim Poh. But it looks like it all went into her pocket."

12

The wife of a successful man must have a big heart, Yoke Lan reminded herself. Chang was a regular of the restaurant where she played her pipa for a paltry sum, a member of a group of well-heeled young men who were friends of the manager. You're invited to their table, Miss Yoke Lan, the manager said to her one night. She walked over to the group at once. It was always a good sign when dinner patrons wanted to meet her. It pleased the management and made her job a little more secure when she was seen to be in demand. Chang had pulled up a chair for her and offered her a cup of tea. "Pu-erh-cha is very good for the throat," he muttered as though to himself.

She gave him a smile, surprised at his shyness. "On whose authority, sir?" she asked.

"Ho-ho! On his own authority, Miss Yoke Lan. He'd like you to drink from his cup too. Isn't that so, you dumb mutt? You've been coming here night after night because of her. Speak up now. She's here beside you. Ask if she likes your tea. Maybe she doesn't like pu-erh-cha."

His friends ribbed him mercilessly that first night.

"But I do like pu-erh-cha, mister…?"

"Chang. Just call me Chang."

He was quiet and didn't have much to say, which was a refreshing change from the usual boisterous talk of the men who often called her to their table. He opened up when he found out that she was from Singapore too, and invited her to have supper with him and his friends.

"And don't worry about your pipa. I'll lock it in the boot of my car."

"I'm not bringing it with me. It belongs to the restaurant."

"Oh? I thought all musicians play their own instruments."

"I used to own a pipa in Singapore. But I left it behind and I can't afford to buy one in Hong Kong. Far too expensive here."

The next evening, he came to the restaurant alone and asked the headwaiter for a private room. When she went in, he had a surprise on the table waiting for her.

"Oh my, oh my heart. You shouldn't have, Mr Chang. It's… it's so beautiful!" She cradled the pipa in her arms.

"Will you play it for me, Miss Yoke Lan?"

"Yes."

"Always?"

Carefully, she placed the pipa back into its silk-lined case before turning to him with a smile. "Always, Mr Chang?"

"Always." He drew her into his arms and kissed her.

Since then no one had addressed her as Miss Yoke Lan except Chang when he was in one of his playful moods. To her neighbours in Juniper Garden, she was Chang Tai or Mrs Chang, wife of Chang Soo Beng, the youngest son of a wealthy trading family, and the half-brother of Dr Mary Chang, a gynaecologist, Helen Chang, a lawyer, and Mrs Irene Ting, a deputy director in the Ministry of Education, whose qualifications she listed this morning in a voice tinged with awe to Miss Kok, the retired principal of a girls' school, who was her neighbour and mahjong partner.

"It's a good thing that Chang has little regard for certificates."

"Is it because of your sisters-in-law that you're so keen to learn English, Mrs Chang?"

She poured out the pu-erh tea and handed a cup to Miss Kok before answering. "What to do? Chang's sisters speak English all the time. I can't thank you enough for agreeing to teach me. But I must insist you accept a small fee from now on."

"Don't be silly. We're friends. Besides I'm retired. I've time."

"Being a friend is one thing, Miss Kok. Being my tutor is another. I can't be getting free English lessons from you all the time."

"Why not?" Miss Kok's plump hand reached for one of the rice cakes that Kan Jieh had brought in for their morning tea. "Thank you, Kan Jieh. This rice cake is delicious. I'll have another piece. Now Mrs Chang, tell me. Why do I sense such anxiety all of a sudden? Why the hurry to learn English?"

Yoke Lan sighed and poured herself a second cup. "It's the opening of the family's new cinema and the invitation to the National Day dinner at the Istana. The cinema's official opening is already a very big event. The Minister will be the guest-of-honour. Chang has invited so many MPs and VIPs. With this P and that P coming, everyone speaking fa-lee, fa-leh, I'll be lost on opening night. His brothers and sisters, all can speak English. Aiyah, Miss Kok, I must learn fast. Once a week is not enough."

"But you know some English already, Mrs Chang."

"Good morning. Yes. No. Thank you. They're chicken droppings. Singapore today is not like the Singapore I grew up in. All the important people speak English these days. And now that the girl is living with us, Chang speaks English even at home. Glee-goo-glee-goo, the two of them, I can't understand a word they say."

"Teenage girls are a lot of trouble, let me tell you. Keep an eye on her."

"I intend to. Ever since my mother-in-law passed away, Chang's siblings have switched to speaking English. So you know how I feel when I'm with them."

"Language is a habit. The more you speak, the more you learn."

"Aye, you make it sound so simple. English is full of potholes. One misstep and you fall in. Like ordering coffee. Last night, the waiter at the Shang-gar-lila Hotel asked me white or black. I stared at him. To cover up my gaffe, I said I hadn't heard. Then Helen had to tell me loudly in Cantonese, the waiter asked if you want milk or not. She scolded the young man for not speaking louder. I felt so bad."

"You lack confidence, that's all."

"Aiyah, Miss Kok, you don't understand. When I speak Cantonese, I'm an intelligent woman. When I speak English, I feel stupid, wobbling like a peasant woman tottering on high heels. My stupid tongue just can't roll the arr-ror, arr-ror. I don't know how you people can roll your tongue like the gwai-lo English. I marvel at how Chang can switch from Cantonese to English, to Hokkien, to Malay. With Kan Jieh, he speaks Cantonese like a Cantonese. When we were in Hong Kong, people thought he was native born. And now back here, he's so fluent in English. When we have dinner with his sisters and their families, everyone speaks English because of the nieces and nephews. It was so much better when my mother-in-law was alive. Everyone had to speak Hokkien then. Nowadays, half the time, I don't know what they're talking about. I can't be asking Chang to translate all the time. He'll get impatient."

"Mr Chang must be very busy. It's been a while since we last played mahjong."

"I'll tell him what you said. My husband has little free time these days. Not like when we were in Hong Kong when he had more time and he talked a lot more then," her face brightening at the memory. "Do you know? Chang told me that ai or love was a concept new to the Chinese. The ancients didn't write or talk about love, he said. It was the Westerners who introduced the concept of romantic love into China. Chang said this is why Chinese husbands do not say I love you to their wives. Love. History. Politics. Those were the sort of things we talked about in Hong Kong."

"How romantic."

"Oh no, he wasn't romantic at all, Miss Kok. He believes love and passion have nothing to do with marriage. He didn't even want to register our marriage at first. It's just a piece of paper, he said. Nothing can bind a man to a woman, not even his children, if he has no feelings for her. He said a marriage cert... wait. Let me think. He used some very learned words. Ah yes, yes, he said a marriage cert only ensures the fair redistribution of accumulated goods when we divorce. A marriage certificate is not a declaration of love."

"My goodness! Where did he get such outrageous, such terrible ideas of marriage?"

"Don't worry, Miss Kok, he no longer holds such notions now that we have a son."

But she sounded more assured than she felt. Her past experiences with men had taught her that they were incapable of marital fidelity, and a wife must always be vigilant. The husband of one woman could end up the catch of another, but she kept such misgivings to herself. "Chang's very conservative now."

"He should be. He's in the national committee for family and community development, isn't he? He has to be careful of what he says."

"I know, Miss Kok." She quickly changed the subject. "Did I tell you that he's a director in his family's main trading company now? At last he's on par with his older brothers."

"This is good news, Mrs Chang. Congratulations."

"Thank you. Now you see why I must learn English. I've got to attend official functions with him more often. I don't want to feel useless."

"I'll coach you. Every day if necessary."

"I can't tell you how much I appreciate this, Miss Kok. I don't mind being frank with you. The day I married Chang, I promised myself two things. One is not to give him any reason to be ashamed of me. Two. To always speak properly in front of his family."

"What a strange thing to promise on your wedding day! You're hilarious, Mrs Chang."

But it was no laughing matter to her then. The Changs were

an established family with substantial properties on the riverfront. Their maternal grandfather had been a well-known public figure before his death, and their father, Chang Ah Kow was a wealthy trader. It was common knowledge that he had an affair with a songstress, and Chang was their son, brought up by his domineering stepmother.

"Good of you to come. Sit down. I've been waiting to see your wife," the dragon lady said at their first meeting.

"So you married my stepson in Hong Kong? Well, he's always been impulsive. When he was young, he didn't want to study. I tried my best but he ran wild. He's the only one who didn't go to university. All my own children have degrees. All professionals."

She paused, watching the pair of them intently. Chang sat there, silent and expressionless. "He wouldn't listen. Got involved with unsavoury women in Geylang. Then he met a girl from a good family. But the girl broke off with him and married someone else. Who could blame her?"

Her hand was shaking as she poured tea for the old woman, a ritual that was required before she could be formally accepted into the family.

Cup in hand, the old lady looked at her and said pointedly: "Pipa girls, and hostesses are Cantonese. Are they not? We Hokkien women don't do such work. I daresay no Hokkien woman was a prostitute. And no Teochew women either. Only the Cantonese women do such things."

As she spoke, the old lady's eyes watched her like a cat's but she didn't flinch. She met the old woman's hard gaze, and replied levelly: "Your stepson knows what I did in Hong Kong. I won't bring him shame, I promise."

Then, and only then, did her mother-in-law take a sip of the tea.

"It's Iron Buddha tea, is it not?" The old lady smiled.

13

Some days, Ping had to pinch herself. Juniper Garden was another universe. A secluded, tree-lined Eden of sun-drenched, two-storey bungalows with large gardens and green lawns hedged and fenced in, protected by burglar alarms and gates with signs that warned, "Beware of Dog".

Majestic raintrees shaded the lanes which had few passers-by except the maids walking their dogs in the evening. The estate had attracted those riding the crest of Singapore's newfound prosperity. Businessmen, lawyers and doctors had bought houses here, stocking them with the emblems of their new wealth. Every other house had two cars under the porch, a rock pool stocked with Japanese carp, or a swimming pool in the back yard.

In the afternoon, when she returned from school, a sunlit silence descended upon the road. By then, Ah-ku had retired to her bedroom for a nap with Boy-boy, and the air-conditioner in her room was switched on, which was an unheard of luxury in Pagoda Street. On most afternoons, Kan Jieh dozed in her easy chair in the kitchen while the daily help did the laundry and ironing in the utility room.

She enjoyed eating her lunch alone in the dining room, not having to worry about how she ate. She would read the papers or look at the photographs on the sideboard especially the one of Ah-ku with members of a Chinese ensemble. The photograph intrigued her. It showed Ah-ku had re-invented herself in Hong Kong as a professional musician dressed conservatively in a white top with a high mandarin collar and a long black skirt. It wasn't the sulky woman from Pagoda Street in a slinky qipao with high slits showing her thighs. This was a stranger. There was something posed and fraudulent about her, and yet, this judgement seemed harsh. The more she looked at the photograph the more she felt that a woman had every right to change herself. So why was she begrudging Ah-ku?

In the afternoon, the sun's heat silenced the birds and insects. Juniper Garden was gripped in a leafy torpor. Pagoda Street was alive all day and night with the cries of street vendors, the shouts of children, the ringing of bicycle bells and trishaw bells, and the drums from the Indian and Chinese temples amidst the constant roar of traffic.

She was an outsider here. The housing estate was quiet and dull. There were few children on the road, and those who came out of their houses did not shout or run, and the maids held the children's hands. In the evening, no mothers came out to the road to yell for their children to come home from the playground. There were no street performers at night, no itinerant medicine men to entertain the crowd with snakes and tricks. No squabbles among the neighbours, and no fistfights excited the boys. Indeed, there were hardly any boys, and no backlanes where children could hold betting games with cards, marbles, bottle caps or fighting spiders. There was no trapping of rats, no stray cats or dogs, no aroma of roasting coffee beans or Peking duck dripping with houseflies and honey. The only inhabitants who made any noise in the neighbourhood were the three or four teenage boys who raced their bicycles down the road on weekends, and their closest to a derring-do was to twist the handles of their bicycles and jump over a traffic hump. Weng could do it a hundred times better. She missed him like she was missing an arm or a leg.

*

"Ping! Over here!" Weng was waving and jumping up and down in front of the Good Shepherd Cathedral as buses trundled past.

"Weng!" A loud blast of car horns as she ran across the road.

"You idiot! You could've been killed!"

"I was praying that you'd be here today."

"I waited for you every Friday! Every blooming Friday afternoon."

"I couldn't come earlier. Their car picked me up every day. Uncle and Auntie…"

"Auntie? Who? You're calling your Ah-ku, Auntie? Why in English?"

"Don't know. Don't ask. I hate it."

"Wah-lau! She's become English, or what? Do you have to say, Auntie, good morning. Auntie, good afternoon."

"Stop it, Weng. If you tease me, I won't tell you anything!"

"Hey, you've cut your hair."

"Don't touch my hair. Ah-ku took me to this posh shop. The girl washed and cut and dried my hair with a hairdryer."

"Waah-lau! You're rich. Look at you. School uniform, new. White shoes, new. Schoolbag, new. It's leather some more! Wah-pia-ah! Impressive." He held the school bag to his nose. "Wah-lau! It even smells expensive."

"Stop saying Wah-lau! Wah-lau! You sound so crude like Fatt Chye."

Her tone was sharper than he thought he deserved. It made him suddenly conscious of his once white uniform, now worn and grey, the fabric having grown thin from too many washes. Why does she think his Hokkien slang is crude? His street talk had never bothered her before. Did a few months of rich living change her hearing or what?

"Cannot say Wah-lau! Is it?

"Sorry, I didn't mean to shout. Hey, the ice cream man is here.

I'll buy us an ice cream. Okay?"

"No, I'll buy." He ran off and returned with an ice cream cone for both of them to share. They had always shared an ice cream on hot days after selling their vegetables, usually going to the river to eat it. "Let's sit on the steps. Here, have the first lick." He watched her lean over to take a small bite. "I always pay for our ice cream. Remember? This is not going to change even though you're rich now. Agreed?"

"Nothing has changed. Except that I don't live in the coffee shop any more. How's Fatt Chye?" she asked and hoped he wouldn't talk about her.

"Like that, lor! Daren't show his face. Hides in his room all day. Pa said Old Kim lost his head that night because he didn't want to lose face."

"Poor Fatt Chye."

"Why pity him? Quick! It's melting. Lick it. Lick it. Finish it."

He thrust the ice cream cone into her hands. He didn't know what he was feeling. He couldn't put his finger on it. Something besides the ice cream was melting. Something between them was dripping.

"It's dripped on my uniform. You finish it."

She handed the ice cream back to him, and he stuffed the sodden mess into his mouth and wiped his hands on his pants.

"So tell me. What's it like living in the big house?" he asked.

"I have my own room and bed."

"That's grand. Why do you look so glum then?"

"I'm not glum. Just not used to it yet."

"If you don't like it there, you can come and live with us," he offered.

"But where am I going to sleep?"

"With my sisters."

"Ya, and then have no money to go to school, no money to buy books and school uniforms. Big joke."

"You miss the coffee shop."

"No, I don't."

"Yes, you do. You miss selling vegetables and carrying mugs of kopi-o. Kopi girl."

He tried to ruffle her hair but she pushed his hand away. "Don't do that!"

"Do what? I didn't even touch your hair. How can you not miss Pagoda Street? Or our river? Your Ah-ku, what do you call now? Auntie. Wah-lau! Even the cleaning lady in my school, we call her Auntie."

"Stop it, Weng. What is it to you? Auntie! Ah-ku! Who cares? They're just names. Names!" She turned on him, her face dark with a hard brightness in her eyes. "I'm not as lucky as you. Okay? You've got family – father, mother and sisters. What do I have? Auntie. You want me to leave her? Leave her large house to squeeze in with your sisters? Do you want me to be poor all over again? Never knowing if next year I can go to school? If you were me, will you choose to be poor and live with Kim Poh waiting to be thrown out?"

Weng looked down at the shoe on his right foot and noticed for the first time, a tiny hole where his toe showed. Why were they fighting? Why were they hissing at each other like cats when all he wanted was to tell her that he had missed her sorely?

"Look, my bus is here. Got to go." She sprinted down the steps.

"Are you coming for practice this Saturday?" He sprinted after her.

"Yes!" she shouted into the wind as she ran.

"I like your hair!"

She whirled around. "Idiot!" she grinned, and jumped onto the bus.

*

Dinner was served as soon as Uncle Chang returned from his office. It was mahjong night tonight. After dinner, Ping helped Kan Jieh to clear away the plates, and wash up in the kitchen.

"Miss Kok and Mrs Tan will be here soon. I have to take Boy-boy upstairs for his bath and milk, and put him to bed. I shan't be down. Will you see to the tea and coffee?"

"Yes, Kan Jieh." Ping made a face.

On mahjong nights, she had to serve the players coffee brewed in the way she had learnt in Old Kim's coffee shop. She wouldn't have minded it if it weren't for Miss Kok. Although more than four months had passed since she first served coffee, Miss Kok still picked on her whenever she visited.

"Four rounds or eight, Mr Chang? I'm ready to play as long as you want."

Miss Kok bustled into the house, waving her plump wrist ringed with a jade and diamond bracelet.

"Relax, Miss Kok. Some of us have to work, and Ping has school tomorrow. Mustn't keep her up too late making coffee for you."

"It's very charitable of you to take in that girl. I always tell my friends what a kind soul you are. You didn't mind her one bit."

"What's there to mind? One more mouth at dinner. No difference."

"Aye, you and Mrs Chang are young parents. I've said this many times before, but I'll say it again. Taking someone's child into your home is difficult as it is. But taking in a girl of that age, at thirteen or fourteen is much harder than you think. Girls that age give twice the trouble. I know it for a fact. In my forty-two years as a teacher and principal, thousands of teenage girls have passed through my hands. You don't realise what you've undertaken yet. Why, look at her. She could be Mrs Chang's younger sister, you know."

Ping saw Ah-ku's face brighten as if lit by a ray of sunshine.

"Oh my dear Miss Kok, how kind of you to say that. I have to buy you lunch."

"But it's true, Mrs Chang. Here comes Mrs Tan. Ask her. I'm not flattering you."

Laughter rippled through the living room. Miss Kok was yapping like an excited Pomeranian, and the clickitty-clack of the mahjong tiles and Miss Kok's chatter grated on her nerves.

"Pong! My game!" said her uncle.

"Aiyah! Mr Chang! I shouldn't have thrown that piece and let you win."

"Carry on talking. You ladies play mahjong to talk. I play to win."

"Oh, Mr Chang, please don't say that. We play to win too. Fortification!" Miss Kok called out in a loud voice. "Girl! Where are you? Oh, there you are. Hiding behind your book as usual. Come over here. Bring us some coffee, will you?"

She resented the loudness of Miss Kok, the tone of her voice and the fact that she never called her by name. 'Ping' wasn't so very difficult to remember. Yet it was always Girl this! Girl that! But when it came to Mrs Tan's daughters, Miss Kok would say ever so sweetly, Angelica dear, Jessica dearie, or Felicia angel, please come over. Those names were a mouthful, yet the old cow had no trouble saying them.

"Ah! Here's our coffee. Finally! I'm parched. Wait, girl. Don't slip away yet. Empty your uncle's ashtray and mine. Smoking is my one and only indulgence in old age, Mr Chang."

"Besides mahjong, of course."

"Of course. Girl, come back! Where's the coffee for Mrs Tan and your aunt? You mustn't forget your aunt. You're very fortunate, you know, to have such a kind uncle and aunt who offer you such a lovely home. Be grateful. Always be grateful to those who feed you. Now empty these ashtrays. Make yourself useful. I used to tell my students. Don't just eat and do no work. I like to see a girl do some housework. Good for the soul, you know. Housework rests the brain. Wait! Girl, come back, come back. Don't creep away the moment I turn my back. Here. Take the ashtrays like I said. Clean them and bring them back. Make sure they're washed clean. Very clean. You didn't clean them properly the last time. Must do a good job. Don't be lazy. Don't cut corners."

Ping snatched up the ashtrays. Marched into the kitchen and

hurled the damn things into the dustbin. The resounding crash brought a shout from the living room. She rushed out of the kitchen and bolted up the stairs.

"Ping! What did you break?" Ah-ku shouted.

She slammed her bedroom door shut.

"Come down at once!"

Hands trembling, her breathing coming hard and fast, she locked the door as footsteps pounded up the stairs.

"Open up!" Ah-ku was rattling the doorknob.

She stood up on the bed ready to jump out of the window.

"Rat's Shit!"

She jumped!

"Open up! What's going on in there?" Loud knocking on the door.

She jumped again. And again! And again! As though her bed was a trampoline and the momentum of each jump was bouncing her up and down. She couldn't stop. She didn't want to stop. A demon had seized her limbs. Months of pent up anger and frustration shot through her. Deportment! Good manners! Gratitude! Jump! Jump! Jump! Speak Properly! Sit Properly! Eat Properly! Jump! Girl! Girl! Girl! She stomped on each word. A thunderous boom! The door burst open!

"What in heaven's name…?"

Ah-ku stared at the collapsed bed. Ping stood up. The room was suddenly crowded with heads and bodies, and Ah-ku was shouting and gesturing wildly, stabbing a finger at her. A loud wail from Boy-boy's room stopped her shouting.

"There, there, it's all right, my son, there, there."

Uncle Chang walked into the room with the wailing toddler in his arms.

"Chang! What are we to do with this girl?" Ah-ku screeched.

Ping held her breath as she waited for the axe to fall on her.

In a deadpan voice, Uncle Chang replied, "Buy her a new bed."

*

I stuff two more books into the suitcase, lock it, and sit on the bed, still thinking of Uncle Chang and that broken bed. As I watch the shadows lengthen in the room, I see what I'd failed to see at the time. Brokenness had marked my entry into the Chang family. A broken bed is a bad omen for marital or family harmony. No wonder there had been no peace. How ironic that Ah-ku had named me 'Ping', which means 'Peace'. Damn, why am I thinking like a bloody superstitious old Chinese woman all of a sudden? Is it because I am going back to Singapore?

I get up from my bed, and draw the curtains. The air outside has grown chilly now that the sun has set. I walk into the kitchen, switch on the lights, and pour myself a large glass of chilled Californian white from the half bottle left in the fridge. Then I slip The Yellow River Concerto into the CD player, and soon I'm lost in the brown waters of the river I left long ago.

Part Three

River Troubles

14

Chong Suk gazed at the brown river as he did every evening before going inside to take down the rake from its hook and slap on his straw hat. In another hour or so, the sun would set. Just as he was leaving their hut, his wife called out from the kitchen.

"The long beans are ready for harvesting!"

"How much do you need?"

"Harvest the lot. What're you waiting for?"

How he hated and loved this river when he thought of his first wife. She would always be 'Weng's mother' in his memory; he couldn't bear to recall her name, her beautiful name that reminded him of the plum blossoms in their family's village back in Kwongchow, China. She was his distant cousin, and the matchmaker had laughed and said they were a perfect match for each other. He was seventeen and his village's best pipa player, and she was fifteen with the most beautiful singing voice in the village. When the great famine struck, his father had ordered them to follow their uncle to Hong Kong and sail for Singapore.

Chong Suk pulled down his straw hat and shaded his eyes from the sun. He pushed aside the clumps of bush and grass and walked towards where the undergrowth was thicker. The bushes shielded his vegetable patch from prying eyes, his patch of solitude where he could think without Chong Soh nagging him to do this and that.

He glared at the rows of long beans. There'd be no peace tonight if he didn't harvest the lot. He put down his rake and started at once, pulling at the stalks.

Weng would be home soon to help him. The boy had grown and changed. He remembered the silent, mournful small child who had sat on a box, gazing for hours at the river. Little Weng did not run or swim with the other children. Every day, he'd sat alone on his box under the raintree, staring out at the river for hours at a stretch. He couldn't bring himself to talk to the boy about his mother's death but he had to do something to save their son.

"Weng, come inside."

The boy slipped off the box and came into the hut.

"We're going to town."

His son's face remained blank, his eyes dark and opaque as a mud pool.

"Uncle Wong has to deliver rice in town. He'll give us a ride in his lorry."

His neighbour dropped them outside the Shanghai Bookstore in Victoria Street. He held his son's hand firmly in his and they went inside. The famous shop was a vast treasure house stocked with books, and more books, bamboo brushes, ink slabs, rice paper for calligraphy, and Chinese musical instruments. Displayed in a large glass case behind the counter were flutes of different sizes, made from natural bamboo. The boy stood in awe, holding his father's hand tightly, his head barely reaching the counter as he gazed up at the flutes. Chong Suk chose the smallest flute in the glass case, and told the shopkeeper to pack it in a box. Then he handed the box to his silent son.

"Don't drop it."

The boy gripped the box in one hand and his father's hand in the other. After he had paid for the flute, they walked home from Victoria Street, up North Bridge Road and South Bridge Road, past the shops selling shoes displayed in large glass cases, racks of clothes, and trays of gold watches and gold ornaments. He had always wanted to buy his wife a gold chain, and now it was too late. He glanced down at their son holding his box tightly, and knew the boy would treasure the flute inside the folds of pink satin.

When they reached home, he took the boy to the riverbank behind their hut and sat him on a wooden crate. "You may take the flute out of the box now," he said.

For a moment Little Weng hesitated; then as he watched, his son opened the box carefully as if afraid he might break the cover. The boy reached for the flute and held it to his nose. The delicate scent of natural bamboo must have reminded him of his mother's scent when she held him close to her breast, and Chong Suk, too, breathed in its sweet dry fragrance and shut his eyes, afraid he might cry in front of the boy. Reining in his own feelings, he showed his son the six holes for fingering, another for blowing and one to cover with a small piece of bamboo membrane. The boy's eyes lit up when he showed him how to paste a tiny piece of the fragile inner skin over the hole.

"Hold it horizontally like this and blow. When you blow, the skin will vibrate and create the natural sound of a bamboo flute. Listen."

He made several sounds on the instrument. Intrigued, the boy held the flute to his lips and blew. His first note was like a birdcall. Pleased, the boy blew again and again as if it was the most natural thing for him to do, as if the bamboo flute was his voice, and it was speaking for him. Chong Suk smiled.

"Can you feel its smoothness, son?"

The boy nodded, his eyes bright and clear as his hand ran down the flute's length. The feel and texture of the bamboo felt just right in his hand. Chong Suk showed him how to blow again, and played a tune that made the boy think of water rippling and bamboo leaves swishing in the breeze.

"Teach me, Pa."

"You speak!" he laughed. "You can speak. I will teach you, son, I will. But first, you must sing to expand your lungs."

Every evening when he returned from work, he made the boy sing do-rei-mi-fa-soh-la-mi up and down variable octaves. He had him doing deep breathing exercises. In… out. In… out. He made the boy face the river, singing loud enough to project his voice across the expanse of water till the boatmen on the other side could hear him.

At first, the boy's lungs were weak, and his voice was small.

"Expand your lungs to this, son." He spread out his arms wide as if he were holding a huge balloon. "Stand on the riverbank to sing out your scales. Practise every morning. Your mother is in there. Sing to her. Sing loudly so she can hear you, son. Sing so she'll come home to us," he'd almost choked.

15

The fan on the ceiling stirred the sluggish afternoon air. The classroom stank with sweat and grime. Mr Rodrigues slammed his palm on the desk, and forty boys jerked out of their stupor.

"What would Singapore be like without the Singapore River?"

"Uncolonised and free."

"Who's the smart aleck? There's no such word as uncolonised. Every fool knows Sir Stamford Raffles founded Singapore. You! Stand up. What're you muttering, boy? Speak up."

Weng rose from his seat at the back of the class.

"Sir, if no Singapore River, no Raffles. Then he couldn't come. Then British couldn't colonise us 'cos they couldn't dock their sailing ships and land."

"Yeah!" the class roared.

"Quiet! Sit down."

Weng sat down. The history taught by Mr Rodrigues was different from the history taught by Mr Lee at the Water Transport Workers' Union night school. Mr Lee's history class conducted in Mandarin referred to Chinese history books, which mentioned Singapore way before Raffles and the British did. For centuries, Temasek or Singapura had been a port of call for thousands of Chinese junks and Asian vessels, Mr Lee told the class of young working men and teenage boys.

The river was the island's main artery. Tongkangs and square-rigged vessels of all sizes, Indonesian prows and Bugis boats docked at the river mouth. Goods from different parts of Asia and beyond changed hands in the lamp-lit huts and houses crowding the banks of the Singa River, named after the mythical beast that had brought countless blessings to the traders, long before Raffles had even a whiff of the island's fart, Mr Lee had laughed. Mister Raffles tricked the Malay Temenggong into selling the island for a few thousand silver dollars.

"…within the walls of these ancient fortifications, raised not less than six centuries ago… I have planted the British flag…"

Ack! Mister Raffles was lying; he did not plant the flag at all. It was Chow Ah Chey, the Cantonese carpenter, who planted the British flag on Singapore first to signal to Mister Raffles that it was safe to land. Then came divide and rule. What the English did best.

"Sir, ordinary workers like the boat builders, carpenters, twaylow, swaylo, coolies, lightermen, trishawmen, pipa songstresses and prostitutes built Singapore. But capitalist traders exploited them."

"Where did you learn such rubbish?"

"It's not rubbish, sir. At the workers' night school, sir."

"Are you a student there?"

"I go there on Sundays."

"Then you better leave, boy. Get out of my class. You're a Communist. Those schools are Communist fronts. You'll be a bad influence in my class. I'm reporting you to the Headmaster. I don't want you back here unless I have a letter from your parents and the Headmaster."

The bus sputtered and stopped near Cavenagh Bridge. Weng got off. The hot humid day was still clinging to his shirt. He wiped his clammy palms on his pants, and stood on the bridge gazing down at the two dejected bumboats chugging under it. He'd have to break the news to his father, but he wouldn't go back to that school. He was sick of the crap dished out by teachers like Mr Rodrigues.

Mr Lee's history lessons were sharp analyses of social inequalities, not the bland pulp dished out in the government schools. The lessons were in Mandarin, which he understood much better than English, and the fees in the night school were low. He was sixteen now, time he helped out the family. His half sisters had never attended school. There was not enough money to send all four of them, and being the boy, he was the lucky one, but he was sick of the drain on his father, sick of his stepmother's constant harping. My three girls don't even know the smell of school. So much was expected of him because he knew how to read the black squiggles on a page. Nah! He'd had enough.

He picked up his bag, and hurried down the flight of steps to the river, past the warehouse and bare-chested coolies unloading the last few bumboats before the day's end.

"Hoi! Ah Weng! Tell your pa I got to unload boats tonight. Can't come for practice. There's a carpentering job for him in the boat-yard. He can start tomorrow. Tell him. Don't forget."

"I won't, Uncle. Have you seen Noodle Ting?

"No. Bet he's still delivering noodles."

Weng ran all the way home. He was late. Already, the shopkeepers were bringing out wooden shutters to close shop. Hawkers were lighting fires in their stoves at the stalls, and mothers were calling their children home. A river breeze brought the smell of mud and engine oil mixed with the fragrance of fried garlic, noodles, char kway teow, and deep fried lard. He dropped his bag outside the hut, kicked off his shoes and ran to the vegetable patch. Soon it'd be too dark to water the plants.

He spotted his father among the beanstalks, behind the screen of bush and lallang whose sharp green blades fended off the petty government officers, who liked to spring surprise checks on squatters in the area these days. He couldn't understand how growing vegetables on land no one was using could be considered a misuse or violation of property. The owner was not using the land, so how could it be called theft or robbery?

"Kept in again?" His father had stopped digging.

"No. I'm leaving school, Pa. Not going back."

His father threw him a look of disgust and returned to his digging; his back turned against him, stiff and rigid. Weng picked up the bamboo pole and the two pails, fashioned from kerosene tins. Mud squelched between his toes as he waded into the river and filled the two pails. Balancing a tin at each end of the bamboo pole, he slung the pole across his shoulders, and trudged back to the rows of vegetables. He watered the beans, the bok choy and lettuce, moving methodically down each row. The two of them worked in silence till the orange sun dipped behind the clump of trees, and the shadows lengthened, and still his father would not stop. Weng snatched up the bundle of longbeans and headed back to the hut.

He was washing the mud from his feet when his stepmother entered the small hut that served as their kitchen. "Left your books outside again. Your sisters had to lug your bag in."

"They didn't have to."

"What if it rains? Books cost money. People who have the good fortune to go to school should treasure their books. Not dump them like rubbish."

He went out after drying his feet on the rag in the doorway. His stepmother's cooking was inevitably accompanied by the symphonic banging of tin plates, pots and pans, punctuated by the hiss of hot oil. His three sisters were setting the table when his father came in.

"The bok choy are ready for harvesting," he announced.

"So you expect the girls and I to pick them, cart them to the market and sell them for you?" his stepmother shouted from the kitchen.

"Do what you want."

"Of course, I'll do what I want. Can't depend on you, can I? In name, you're the vegetable gardener. But who waters them? Who pulls up the weeds? Sounds very good, doesn't it? Coolie, labourer, vegetable gardener, carpenter…" She banged a dish of beans on to the table.

His stepmother was unstoppable once something had set her off. Dinner was ruined, but he had no appetite tonight. After dinner, his father went off to the clan association, and he retreated to the riverbank with his flute. He sat on his camp bed under the raintree, and looked up at the changing night sky and the lights of the boats in the distance. The plaintive notes of his flute weaved in and out of the whirring motors and winches of ships weighing anchor at the river mouth. The warm night clung to his shirt, but he couldn't take it off because of the mosquitoes. A baby's wail from a neighbour's hut cut in. Disconsolate, he stopped playing, and tucked his flute under his pillow, and tried to sleep. A ship's horn sounded in the distance. In the dark lane behind the trees, two passers-by laughed, and a man yelled, "Tua-hia, ah! Oi! Brother! What's the news? Let's sup!" People around here always managed to eat a meal no matter what, he thought, as the smell of fried onions, chillies and garlic wafted in from the food stalls. He drifted into slumber, his camp bed creaking softly under his weight.

Late in the night, he was awakened by the sound of voices quarrelling inside the hut. He crept up to the window of his father's room, and crouched under it. The heated whisperings of his stepmother hissed in his ears.

"Haven't you shown it to Weng yet?"

"What can he do?"

"He should read it. The girls and I can't read. And you can't read. Why didn't you show him?"

"Even if he can read the English, what can he do?"

"So you're going to wait till we lose this hut, is it? Wait till they kick us out. It's about time Weng shoulders some responsibilities. Look at Ah Lok's son. The boy is just fifteen. Already he's working on the boats."

In the silence, he imagined his stepmother's lips quivering, her eyes on the brink of tears, and his father lying beside her with his eyes closed.

"You refused to let him learn to build boats, become a carpenter, or cart loads. It's the flute, isn't it? You protect his hands. My girls also have hands. They can't play the pipa or flute. But they wash and scrub and iron all day like their mother. Doesn't that count for something? My girls are your flesh and blood too. I'm warning you. Don't say I didn't. The first man to ask for them, I'll let them go. Noodle Ting is eyeing Fong. It's better that she marries him now than end up homeless like us."

His stepmother's impotent sobbing robbed him of sleep. He lay on his camp bed, staring at the bits of night sky between the leaves above his head. He reached for his flute and held it against his chest as though it had the power to ward off pain. He thought of Ping. Why had she stopped coming for pipa lessons? Was she forgetting him and all those who lived by the river?

He wished he were five again. Life was simpler then. There was music and song every night when his mother was alive. The bumboats crowded around their boat each night, dimly lit by oil lamps, and on their decks were the boat coolies, the red glow of their bamboo pipes piercing the darkness like red eyes. His father's pipa and his mother's singing soared above the dark waters. Her songs floated out to the ships anchored at the river's mouth. Encore! Encore! The boatmen yelled as they rained coins onto their deck.

But fine weather never lasts. Flashes of lightning slashed the weeping skies one night. The wind howled louder than usual. It had rained all day the previous day, and the river was threatening to flood its banks. Their boat shivered and rocked as he lay in the dark under a plastic sheet, rainwater dripping from the boat's thatched roof. He was tense. The river was full of inexplicable hisses and sighs. All night, the distant cries of men troubled him. Something was not right. His parents had left him in the boat. He waited for them to come back, and then he must have fallen asleep.

As a grey dawn woke him, he saw his father crouched on the

deck, head between his knees, his back heaving at each emission of strange animal sounds. The look that his father gave him was that of a cornered, wild beast. His father refused to leave their boat. Night after night his pipa keened and mourned till his friends had to drag him off the boat. They found him a place to stay on land, and the hut became their home. Six months later, his father bought him the flute. And he remarried.

16

The men crowded round Noodle Ting's stall when they heard Weng's question.

"Squatters have no claim to the land, Ah Weng," Noodle Ting replied.

"But Pa pays rent," he protested. "We've lived there for years."

"Listen. You pay rent also no use. If the owner wants the land back, you can't fight the owner. He says move, you move. If not, first, a lawyer's letter will come. Then a second letter. After three letters from the lawyer, your Pa will get a court summons. Then how? No help already! He got to go to court. The judge will fine him for sure. Then after you pay the fine, you also got to move out. You don't move out, they send you to jail. Worse still, right or not?"

"The hell it's worse!" one of the men shouted. "We're all in the same soup, Ah Weng! My family have lived here and worked here, fucked here and shat here all our lives. Since my great grandpa came over from Xiamen. Four generations we worked on this river! Now they want to evict us!"

"It's government land. Like it or not, we got to move one of these days. I'm not the one saying it. It's the people from URA who said it."

Weng watched Noodle Ting trying to calm the men. No wonder Fong was proud of her boyfriend. The way Ting had managed to dig the latest information out of the Urban Renewal Department had won the men's admiration. He hoped his sister would marry the guy soon.

"Ah Weng, tell your father to go and ask the government people for help. See what those blokes say. There's talk about developing the river. That's why the landlord wants his land back. You know who the landlord is? It's them Chang brothers. They own lots of land and warehouses around here. Bumboats too, and a water transport company. A shipping company and cinemas. They are a filthy rich family."

Surprised, Weng said nothing. He kept his thoughts to himself as he listened to the others. Ping had never mentioned her new family's wealth.

"Landlord or no landlord, they can't just evict us. No law, meh?" the chicken rice vendor asked.

"What law? The law says the government and landlords can evict us any time they want to develop this shit hole!" the mee pok hawker answered.

The chicken rice vendor swore at the bureaucrats and greedy vipers.

"Cool it, all of you. At the moment, it's only talk. Many years of talking already, nothing has happened yet," Noodle Ting soothed the rising tempers. "The economy is not good this year. Maybe nothing will happen!"

Weng hoped Noodle Ting was right as he headed home with this bit of good news. But his stepmother was unimpressed.

"At most, they'll let us stay one more year, maybe two. Then what? I still say it's better to apply for a rental flat now. There's a long queue for such flats. The rent is a bit high but I'll wash more clothes if you're worried about the money. Ah Weng will be working soon. The girls will help. Best if we move out of here. What do you say?" His stepmother turned to his father.

"Say something, will you! The sooner we move out the better. That's what I say."

"What for we move out? We're comfortable here. All our friends are here. The air is better here. There's more space here. More trees. We grow our own vegetables here. Have you seen those flats? Like boxes on top of other boxes. Can't grow a thing in a two-room box. There'll be no more free vegetables once we move. We'll have to spend more money. On food, on lights, on water, on transport. Everything will cost more. I will have to take a bus every day to come back here to work. Noodle Ting already said business is bad. Nothing will happen. Not for another few years."

It was the longest speech that his father would make on the subject. The next day, he went with his father to seek Mr Lee's advice.

"Don't worry, Chong Suk. The union will write a petition on behalf of Squatters' Village. There must be a law to protect poor people like us."

*

The following week, Weng stood at the gate to Juniper Garden, and regretted coming. He peered through the grille. The familiar white Mercedes that picked Ping up at school was parked under the porch. He had come on impulse hoping that she would be in the garden so he could ask her what she thought of his plan to speak to her uncle. But now he wasn't so sure. He should've phoned her first before coming here. There was no public phone in this posh estate. To get to one, he would have to walk back the way he came to Bukit Timah Road where there was a public phone near the bus stop. The residents of these houses didn't need to use a public phone; they were rich enough to have their own phones in the house. He should have thought of that. He took out his handkerchief and mopped his brow. His shirt was soaked. To save on the bus fare, he had walked part of the way from

Orchard Road. The sudden thought that Ping's uncle might not want to meet him unnerved him. But he had prepared his speech. Hands in his pockets, he waited to see if someone would come out to the gate. If no one came out after another five minutes, he would leave.

His hope rose when the front door opened, and he heard a child's voice call out, "Ping Cheh-cheh!" From somewhere inside the house, a voice answered, and then the door was shut again. He waited a few more minutes to see if she would come out. She had told him that she played badminton with her uncle in the evening sometimes. And he had pictured them playing in the driveway. The secret wish to watch her wielding a racquet was what had motivated him to come in the first place. She hadn't been to the clan association for weeks. Has she grown tired of the pipa? Has she switched to the piano? What has she been doing? These questions plagued him. He looked through the grille again. No one seemed to be coming out to the garden. He should leave. A stranger loitering at the gate would arouse suspicion, and the neighbours might set their dogs on him or worse, call the police.

He walked away, whistling softly under his breath, telling himself that he wasn't that disappointed. All right, maybe just a little.

"Love all!"

Arrested by the familiar voice, he stopped at the corner that turned down a backlane. His eyes followed the trajectory of a shuttlecock as it smashed into the net strung across the lane. From where he was standing, several houses away, he could see Ping's back.

"Ha! There you go!" Her opponent laughed, his badminton racquet held high above his head as he lobbed another shot at her.

From where he stood, Weng saw that the director of Chang Brothers International was a youthful fortyish man smartly attired in a white polo neck tee shirt, white shorts and white sports shoes. So this was the man Ping admired, with a loyalty so fierce that only those deprived of a parent could understand. He moved closer to the hedges and hoped no one would see him. He had just spotted the former pipa queen coming out of the house in a fancy dress that showed too much flesh. She stood leaning on the back gate watching the players.

"Whoa! I say Ping, have you been practising?"

"No time, Uncle."

"Then you'll lose again."

"No way!" She hit the shuttlecock.

The bunch of feathers flew back and forth in rapid succession across the net. She was forced to skip and dash about the court like a wild thing, her hair flying. The sight sent a thrill through his chest. The sudden memory of her thigh pressing against his was intoxicating. There was no telling what that girl might do at times. She was an alley cat. No one was her keeper. But didn't she have a special place for him in her heart?

"Yeah! Papa scores again!" A boy ran out of the house, clapping his hands, and his mother, caught the boy's hand and held him.

"Ping! Uncle needs to rest. Boy-boy wants to go for a drive."

"Finish the game first, Uncle. Oh drats!"

The shuttlecock had landed in the drain.

"Stop playing now! Time to wash up! Chang! Your son is waiting!"

The shrill Cantonese voice followed him as he turned and strode down the lane in the other direction. His resolve to speak to Ping's uncle about his family's eviction had drained out of him. This wasn't the right time. Perhaps there was no right time. How could these people understand what it is to lose one's home? He shouldn't have come, and started to walk faster, finally breaking into a run as dogs barked from behind the houses' gates. He didn't stop running till he reached the bus stop, panting for breath.

17

"Here, let me take that bag, hon."

"I can manage and stop calling me hon. Save that for your Japanese carp."

"Now, now, don't be like that about Suki. And let's not fight just before you fly off."

"I don't fight with cab drivers," I laugh and give Jeev a peck on the cheek. "Thanks for the lift. I appreciate it. I really do."

Jeev had not only driven me to the airport; he had also booked my flight and re-scheduled my classes so I can leave three weeks earlier than planned to reach Singapore in time for Ah-ku's birthday bash. Knowing her, it will be a grand affair in a Chinese restaurant replete with plates of suckling pig roasts and baskets of longevity buns shaped like pink peaches.

"Don't forget. I want that piece finished in two months," Jeev grins as he hands me my pipa case.

"I'll finish when I finish. Don't bug me."

"Show me what you have in two months. I do want to showcase a new work by our faculty for the summer concert."

"I hear and obey."

Then I lug my bag and pipa case and follow the crowd through Check-In and Departure. That Jeev plans to have the orchestra perform my new composition next summer is an accolade of sorts from the maestro, and I don't want to let him down. I pause to check that my passport and air ticket are in my bag, and look at the crowd milling around in the departure lounge of San Francisco's airport, wondering if I'm going home or leaving home, surprised that my heart still feels pulled both ways. There's the awkward Singapore urchin girl who had to keep quiet, and be careful not to jeopardize the Chang family's reputation and the American citizen who'd married and divorced, composed and taught, and marched with thousands to protest against war, and violence against women and children with no fear of arrest and incarceration. Sighing over my ambivalence about who I really am sometimes, I join the queue to board the plane. My pipa and I go through the usual security check. As the light seeps out of the San Francisco sky, my plane takes off. I sit back, waiting for the Seat Belt sign to go off, suddenly relieved. A weight lifts from my shoulders. I've been living as a free woman in Berkeley these past thirty years. Free from family ties and obligations, free to pursue my art and passion in music. I smile at this realization, thinking of poor Jeev ensnared by his Japanese carp, a sweet, young violinist from Tokyo. The fool's so besotted with the girl who loves ornamental fish that he spends hours at the aquariums with her even though it bores him to tears.

I kick off my shoes, and loosen my seat belt as guppies, angel fish and gold fish swim before my eyes. When the air steward comes down the aisle with drinks, I reach for a glass of white wine and gulp it down, hoping it will kill the fish. What do you do with the memories you want to forget? I should've asked Dr Forrest before I left. I sink into my seat, eyes shut, as the greenish light of a fish tank floods my mind.

*

"Look, Boy-boy, over here. Peacock-tails. Aren't they beautiful?"

"Yes, Ping Cheh-cheh."

A shoal of flitting peacock tails swam past an image of the three of them – Uncle Chang, Boy-boy and her, their three faces peering into the watery darkness, their eyes concentrated on the fish.

"My friend, Weng, could catch them with his bare hands."

"How?" Boy Boy asked.

"Like this. Still as a stork. Then whoop! He catches the fish. Look, tiger barbs with orange and black stripes. And over here – the electric blue tetras."

"How come you know their names, Cheh-cheh?"

"Ping Cheh-cheh takes the trouble to read books. You should be like her."

"Papa. Let's buy some fish. Please, Papa, please. "

"Okay, okay, but first, we'll visit Mama in hospital to see your new baby brother."

"Is Mama still sick?"

"No, she'll be home in a few days."

On a sudden impulse, Uncle Chang called in workmen the following week. They built a large shed next to the swimming pool in the back garden. Thirty fish tanks were mounted on steel shelves, and five more were placed on the floor of the shed. While Ah-ku was cloistered in her bedroom for a month during the traditional post-birth confinement, Uncle Chang took her and Boy-boy to the shops to stock the tanks with exotic fish. Every night, after dinner, the two of them pored over magazines, discussed the different species of fish they would buy, and argued over the merits of different brands of fish feed, the quality of the sand and rocks and fresh water weeds. "It says here the arowanas need a very large tank with a strong cover. They can grow up to more than eighty to ninety centimetres, and leap two metres into the air. And the water must be filtered, soft and slightly acidic. They're carnivorous. Eeeek! They eat live shrimps, earthworms, bloodworms and centipedes."

He peered over her shoulders as she read, and laughed at her seriousness as they chose porcelain windmills, bridges, pagodas, and other knick-knacks to enhance the fishes' environment.

"Aiyah! You people have ruined my back garden!" Ah-ku

shrieked when she came out to the garden with the baby at the end of her confinement. "Dah-ling, why do you need so many fish tanks? You mustn't listen to Ping. The neighbours will think we're running a fish shop here!"

"So you're the fish shop proprietor's wife now. Miss Kok will call you, Ah-soh, Ah-soh!" he teased, but Ah-ku was not amused.

"Who will feed the fish and clean the tanks when you're busy, eh? Don't expect Kan Jieh to do it. She's busy with the baby."

"I'll feed the fish and clean the tanks, Uncle."

"That's what you say now. It's school holidays. Let's see how long you last after the holidays are over. Talk is cheap, Ping."

Throughout the month long holiday in December, she spent many happy evenings with Uncle Chang and Boy-boy inside the shed feeding the fish and cleaning the tanks. She made sure that Ah-ku had no reason to complain when school reopened the following January.

Chinese New Year came and went, and the weather turned hot and dry. Feeding the fish plus schoolwork, piano lessons and trying to get to her weekly pipa sessions with Chong Suk took its toll over the next few months. Some nights she was too tired to visit the fish shed after dinner.

By August, her uncle's construction projects were also keeping him out late. He was overseeing the building of several Chang Brothers' cinemas in the new public housing estates in Jurong, Toa Payoh and Bedok. Chang Brothers International was also developing several ventures overseas. Often he came home late, too tired even to play mahjong.

"There's a smell coming from the back garden. That girl! I knew this would happen sooner or later," Ah-ku said to Kan Jieh.

The weather had hit a long dry spell. Temperatures soared in the afternoons. The shed had a zinc roof, which heated up quickly during the day. By noon, the inside was like an oven.

"The gods! The stench is getting worse and worse! It's coming into the house. Mrs Tan next door has phoned to complain.

Ping! Ping!"

Ah-ku gave her a severe scolding. The tropical fish started to die in great numbers. Even though she cleared off one lot of dead fish each day, more would die the next day while she was at school, and their white bloated bellies would remain floating in the tanks till she returned in the evening.

"Let them stink up the whole place. Didn't I say this would happen? Didn't I? Kan Jieh, this stench will kill the baby if not me."

"Madam! Choy! Don't say such an inauspicious thing! Kit Boy is sleeping."

"We'll clear out those tanks! Today. Now. Now. I can't stand it! Call the gardener in. Tell him to remove the dead fish and scrape off the green stuff in all the tanks.

Hundreds of tropical fish, goldfish, Japanese carp and the highly prized arowanas were placed in large red plastic pails of clean tap water. While Kan Jieh looked after the baby, Ah-ku took charge in the shed. With the help of the gardener and the maid, she spent the day scrubbing and hosing the thirty five tanks till they were squeaky clean, and filled with clean chlorinated water from the tap. "Aaah, this is better. The air still smells in here. But it's much cleaner."

She couldn't wait to surprise Uncle Chang. But when she proudly dragged him to the fish shed, a horrible sight greeted them. All the carps and goldfish were floating with their bellies up, and his five prized arowanas that had cost him thousands of dollars had died. And those in the tanks were struggling.

"But we just cleaned the tanks! I swear it, darling! We didn't do anything else!"

"The chlorine in the tap water killed them."

Dinner was eaten in silence that night. Even Boy-boy knew he had to keep quiet. After dinner, Ah-ku retired upstairs with Kan Jieh and the children, and Ping stayed in her room while Uncle Chang remained downstairs, in front of the TV all night. Near midnight, Ping heard him switch it off and the back door opened. She knew he was going out to the shed. She sat up in bed and waited for him to come into the house. She glanced at the clock. 12.40 a.m. She crept downstairs.

The back garden was bathed in moonlight. The swimming pool shimmered with greenish silvery lines. The shed was dark when she went in, except for the glow of his cigarette – like an angry full stop in the shadows. He didn't turn around although he must have heard her. As her eyes slowly adjusted to the gloom, she saw again his prized arowanas, Japanese carp and goldfish, their white bellies floating in the tanks. She made her way to the low bench and sat down beside him, struggling to frame her apology. It was her fault. She should have been more diligent. The silence deepened as she sat next to him. He continued to pull on his cigarette, and would not look at her.

"Uncle," she placed a hand on his knee.

"Ping!"

At the sound of Ah-ku's voice, she stood up at once.

"What are you doing here? Go to bed!"

Her uncle did not turn around, but went on smoking, a curl of blue smoke rising above his head. Arms akimbo, blocking the moonlight in the doorway, Ah-ku's eyes watched her like a hawk. She edged past her, but Ah-ku followed her back into the house.

"Don't think I'm blind. If I ever catch you alone with Uncle again, I'll send you away. Immediately. I mean it. A fly flits by. Male or female, I can tell. You're not a child any more. You know what I'm talking about."

18

Cars stopped. Pedestrians scrambled onto the covered walkways. Coming down Sago Lane – Dead Man's Lane as the Cantonese called it – was his father's ragtag band of old men playing the funeral dirge, their erhus wailing and the cymbals clanging. Weng slipped behind the pillar of a shophouse. His father had never talked about his other job, the one he did when there was no carpentering job for him in the boatyard. His old man had been coughing a lot at night, great heaving coughs that seemed to wrench out his lungs. Yet, here he came blowing the flute, his face set and impassive like the rest of the musicians, who looked like the sad clowns from a Chinese opera in their ill-fitting blue jackets, and hats blown askew by the wind. Weaving in and out of the crowd on the walkway, Weng followed the band till they reached the main road and boarded a lorry that would take them to the cemetery. When the lorry drove off, Weng's face and the muscles of his neck relaxed as though they had tensed up all this while. A momentary sense of relief coursed through his limbs. It made him question himself. Was he ashamed of what his father, a music teacher, had to do to make ends meet?

But playing in a funeral band was nothing to be ashamed of, he saw himself arguing with Ping. Why was he so eloquent inside his head but tongue-tied in her presence these days? A ravine separated those playing the dizi in the shacks by the river from those who tinkle on their pianos in large houses, he thought. Is that why she hadn't come for pipa practice these several weeks? His father had not said a word about his pupil's absence. Weng suspected snobbishness was keeping her away. He feared she might stop coming to the association altogether. Beyond the confines of the river and Chinatown, their music making and friendship was out of sync with the rest of their lives. His friends ragged him for hanging out with a rich girl. Her friends swooned over the Beatles and rolled their eyes, What? Listen to Zhao Jun's Lament on the pipa? Please spare us!

But the following week, Ping turned up at the clan association.

"Hi!"

"Hi," he muttered. Her cheerfulness grated on him although he couldn't think why.

"Aren't you pleased to see me?"

"What's there to be pleased about? You've changed."

"Aiyoh. Blame Mother Nature, lor."

She'd deliberately slipped into Singlish but he refused to be amused. "You've missed several practice sessions."

"Want to punish me, meh?"

"You sound false talking like this."

"So? Cannot, ah?"

"Look, stop it. I know you play the pipa only when you're free. And only because your Ah-ku forbids you. It's the attraction of the forbidden fruit, isn't it?"

"Wong Fook Weng, what's eating you today? I just got here. Isn't it enough that I lie through my teeth to come? Three or four times a month I lie to her. You think it's the attraction of the forbidden – what?"

He broke into a grin. The withering look she gave him was reassuring. He opened the cupboard and took out his gift. "I made it last month so you can practise your fingering at home when you can't come."

"Oh, Weng!"

The catch in her voice, as she held the plywood pipa cut-out in both her hands, made him forget the nights he had lain awake worried about her absence.

"You've even drawn the entire fret board in detail with all the struts and strings. I can pluck the strings and make music," she giggled and began to strum it as though it was the real thing. "Can you hear? Can you? It's producing music that only the two of us can hear."

He was smitten by the way she said 'the two of us.' Her honey brown face glowed and smiles fluttered like butterflies on her lips as she ran her fingers up and down the struts he had so painstakingly drawn.

"Do you like it?"

"Oh, Kor, need you ask?"

He turned away, and pretended to search the cupboard for her pipa. He hoped she hadn't seen the flush on his face as the heat rose from his belly to his ears.

"Gosh, Weng, I'll feel like a music thief when I practise on this cut-out at home. Like… like I'm stealing music from Ah-ku, but she doesn't know it. Why didn't you make this for me earlier? Then I wouldn't feel like I've stopped playing for months and months."

"Earlier, you didn't have to practise every day."

"You mean now I have to? Why?"

"You'll know when Pa comes."

"Tell me now, please! Please!"

"Wait, lah! I want to tell you first how I got this idea to make you a wood cut-out. Want to hear it or not? I'd read about it in a Chinese newspaper. When the Cultural Revolution started in China, many Chinese musicians were forced to work in the countryside. The Red Guards destroyed their instruments. So they secretly made wood cut-outs of their instruments, and practised on those to keep their fingers supple. They even hummed the music to each other so they wouldn't forget. Hummed and played entire solos on the wood cut-outs. They didn't give up."

"Wow, such passion and commitment."

"You said it. Practise, practise, practise. You missed six weeks."

"Ya, ya, don't nag. The teachers are loading us with tests and more tests. Exam year. Don't you have to slog in night school?"

"Ya, but I don't stop practising."

"I'm going to give up the piano."

"Still pretending to play it?"

"What do you want me to do? Tell Ah-ku I play the pipa? She's very insistent. Anyway it's only an hour a week. And I do want to learn how to read music."

"That's bullshit. It's a status symbol thing. Rich girl from rich family. Must learn the pi-an-no."

"Don't talk rot."

"A fact is a fact. Just listen to yourself. Your speech has changed. You don't speak Cantonese like before. You sound posh."

She yanked the pipa out of his hands and stalked off. She ignored him, and proceeded to tune her pipa, which was old but his father had mended the crack in its woodwork and re-conditioned it. Since then her pipa had acquired a distinct lisp when she plucked its strings. He took out his bamboo flute and played the first bar of her favourite folksong, Xiao Bai Chuan. The Little White Boat.

Her eyes lit up, and she broke her icy silence. "How's work?"

"As usual."

"You haven't told me anything about your job."

"What's there to tell? Work is work."

"Have you applied for the Poly yet?"

"Must you ask me about studies each time we meet? No study, no friendship, is it? Must I go to the Poly? Do I have to?" he bristled.

"It'll be a waste if you don't. You're very good at math."

"And you're very good at preaching. Poly needs money."

He bit his tongue; he shouldn't have said that. Life was simpler when the two of them were poor.

"Pa's been in and out of hospital. He was in for four days last month. The doctors found two spots in his lungs. But he's out now."

"The medical fees…"

"We manage. Pa's teaching pipa, and charging fees now."

"But who in Chinatown can pay?"

"It's a problem, isn't it? Those who can pay don't want to learn the pipa. They want to learn the pi-an-no."

"Please, let's not argue."

"I'm not arguing. A fact is a fact. Even you learn the piano."

"I've no choice."

"No choice? Not choosing is also a choice."

"You…"

"Ping."

"Uncle Chong Suk!"

Weng noticed the shock on her face. His father had grown very thin and sallow, and looked tired.

"Please accept this small gift, Uncle Chong Suk. It's a box of your favourite sausages from Hong Kong. How are you?"

"I'm fine; you shouldn't waste money like this, Ping."

"Not a waste. You're my shifu."

"Chieh." His father waved her words aside, but his eyes had lit up, pleased and embarrassed by his pupil's respect. "Don't buy me anything next time."

"Pa, I'll take the sausages if you don't want them."

"They're for your Pa!" She wrested the package from him, and gave him a playful box on the arm. He grinned, and knew that she'd forgiven him.

"Stop arguing you two. Come, Ping. To work. To music. Good to have you back. Come. Sit over here. Have you tuned your pipa? Good. When you're ready, play me that piece, Zhao Jun's Farewell to her Emperor."

Weng knew she was tensed as she sat down. Her left hand was grasping the neck of the pipa too tightly. Her fingers were pressing the frets too hard as she plucked the taut strings. Relax, he tried to signal to her. She'd forgotten his father's words. A pipa player's hand must be soft as a woman's holding a cup, her fingers curved around the pipa's swan-like neck in a half embrace as though caressing her lover. Her anxiety was not a good sign. He knew she wanted to play well for his father. Her shifu. He saw the twitching of her lips when she made a slip. A few discordant chords spilled out. She tried again and failed again. The fingering for Zhao Jun's Farewell was intricate, its spirit challenging, and its tone elusive and hard to hold for long. Each section had a hill that her fingers failed to surmount. Her pipa hesitated and her fingers slipped. Her playing sounded hollow and lacked intent, personality, tone and colour. Yet she struggled on. And on. Her persistence moved him. He raised his dizi to his lips and waited for a cue. As her playing faltered once again, he slipped in, his bamboo notes gliding like a drake to encircle the faltering mandarin duck, bolstering her phrasing and rhythm till her fingering grew assured, and their music harmonised. For one dizzy moment, he felt they were gliding like a pair of mandarin ducks in the lotus pond.

She looked up at him, and he caught the light in her eyes that revealed more than gratitude. But dare he trust his eyes? It could be his imagination or the light, or just the way she was playing. She faltered again, and he suppressed a groan. She was woefully out of practice in her fingering technique. When her pipa stopped, he kept his eyes on the floor. He couldn't bear to meet her eyes till the last hollow note had stopped vibrating in his head.

Pa opened his eyes. He had always listened to his students with his eyes closed, his face giving no hint of what he thought. As a teacher and parent, his father was hard to please, and rarely praised his students and children. Ping was his most promising pipa student, but tonight, he was brutal to her.

"Your playing has no soul," he snarled.

It sounded like a death knell to Weng. Nothing could be worse than a player with no soul.

"Pa, Ping will improve if she practises every day."

"Not good enough."

"She's your best student for the clan's concert."

"I said she's not good enough."

"Pa…"

"Weng, it's all right. I understand your Pa."

"No, you don't. You have no knowledge of his Pa."

His father's gaunt face was flushed as he fixed his eyes on his pupil.

"His Pa is dead. This is his shell. His Pa could have been an accomplished pipa player in an orchestra in Hong Kong. Or a trained music teacher if he had had your good fortune."

A loud racking cough made his father pause to catch his breath. Then he continued, "Things would have been different if his family had the money. But his family was poor. He had to chop wood. Dig earth. Look at these hands. These hands have chopped and cut. Heaved and hoed. Not music. Do you understand? Not music. These hands are a coolie's hands. Hard and calloused. Look at your hands. And these fingers. Slender and supple as bamboo. Such fingers can pluck music out of the sky. A pity. A great pity. They lack fire and sinew. Without fire, music has no passion. Without sinew, your playing has no discipline. Heaven lights up our soul just once, Ping. If we fail to feed the flame, it dies. Look at me. I'm a spent candle."

His father got up and left.

Ping said little before she went home. That night, Weng was worried that she would give up the pipa. But what he feared even more was that she would stop coming altogether.

19

She stayed away from the clan association and concentrated on her studies in the months leading to her 'O' Level exam. Except for the occasional phone call, Weng left her alone. Only when her results came out, did he dare to call her.

"Weng! I haven't heard from you for eons! Since you went into the army. What's the camp like? What's the food like?"

"Very bad. I miss you."

"Me too. I just got my results."

"That's why I call. How did you do?"

"What do you think?"

"C'mon, tell me."

"Eight distinctions."

"Wah-lau! Congrats! What subjects are you going to take in Pre-U?"

"Haven't decided yet."

"Take math."

"I'll be hopeless at 'A' Level math."

"Ni de mathematics hen hao," he suddenly switched to Mandarin. "Math has an inexorable logic absent in the human heart. It's possible to imagine a musical universe expressed in mathematical equations. Ni zhi dao ma? Do you know?"

She laughed. "Oh, Weng, you're different when you speak Mandarin."

His English speech had remained fractured and choppy like discordant notes that jarred her ears, yet when he spoke Mandarin, he was fluent and showed that he had thought deeply about things.

"Have you heard Mr Lim, my former math teacher? You got brain or not? Got qualifications or not?" he switched to Singlish. "You got brain? Good! Up the ladder to success you go. Can get a scholarship. Climb faster to the top. Exam results. Very important, one! You don't play-play! Exams come, your brain still sleeping? You fail. Then how? Education is competition."

Then he switched back to Mandarin. "Compete. Compare. Who's fair? Who's dark? How much? Which school? What grade? Where do you live? In a house or flat? How big? Three rooms or five rooms? HDB or private landed property? What's your father's occupation? Manager or labourer? Your mother's qualification? Graduate or non-graduate? That's what Singapore cares about."

He was chuckling over the phone, his voice warm, and his laughter generous. He was genuinely happy for her. And that made her happy for herself. She wanted to hug him.

"Weng, your math is so much better than mine. If your English improves, you can pass the subject and go to university instead of the Poly."

"What? Polytechnic not good enough for you, is it?"

"That's not what I mean."

"Then what do you mean? So much blah about English. Can't speak proper English, can't earn a living, is it?"

"You know I didn't mean that. You're not being logical."

"Snob."

"Weng!" the insult stung her.

He hung up, and she had no way of calling him back. There were no phones in the squatter huts down by the river. The gulf between his world and hers seemed greater than ever.

20

Home for the weekend, he slept in his old camp bed under the raintree, a regular NS bloke in his army fatigues, marking time waiting for the day when he would ROD and see the last of Inche, his foul-mouthed sergeant, the tanks, the night marches, barbed wires and his gun. She's closer to you than your fucking girlfriend! *Understooded?* The sergeant had barked. Yes, sir! the recruits yelled. How he hated life in the barracks.

Did Ping miss him? He pictured her sleeping in air-conditioned bliss in the large house with the Mercedes. Was she thinking of him tonight? He smiled at the stars peeping among the leaves, pleased with his father's news that she had returned sheepishly one day to the clan association, and had been practising hard since.

"Hey, Weng, back from camp? Long time no see!" a neighbour called out to him.

"Ya. What's new?"

"Hey, your family didn't tell you?"

"Pa said it's only a rumour. The government hasn't said anything official yet."

When he came home the following week, the rumour had ballooned and burst over the river, and blasted every squatter hut, hawker stall, and boatyard, although some still refused to believe it.

"Who said? Who said so?" they asked. "Did your grandfather say so?"

"It's orders from high up, very high up."

"Sure or not? When?"

"Wait and see, lor!

That same night, it was reported on prime time news on national radio and television. Three thousand five hundred and fifty-nine unlicensed squatters and their families, two thousand five hundred and thirteen hawkers would be evicted from the river by next year. Next to go would be the farmyards, charcoal yards, backyard factories, boatyards, bumboat operators, boat coolies, and their families – the culprits who dumped tons of filth into the river every year, the newspapers reported. 'A National Disgrace', a newspaper headline screamed. The river had become the city's sewer, flowing right smack through the heart of its prime commercial district. The stench and filth must be cleaned up and its businesses and inhabitants moved somewhere else. The Public Works Department would embark on a study and draw up plans for the re-development of the river basin.

"See! I told you! Didn't I say to apply for a flat? But no, you won't! Now we're evicted! Some families already got Quit Notices! Soon we'll have no roof over our heads!"

A huge quarrel blew up between his father and stepmother.

"Look here. I'm not stupid. I know why you won't leave this river! Still mourning her after all these years! I've given you three girls! Three children! I've washed and cleaned and cooked and slogged. Is that not enough for you?" his stepmother wailed.

After a few days of this, Weng was only too glad to go back to the army camp.

*

A petition was organised by the Squatters' Village and the Water Transport Workers' Union. Every head of household signed it, many laboriously writing their identity card number and name in Chinese characters for the first time. Those who could not write printed their thumbprint on the petition. Over a thousand names.

"Now we wait for Tua Pek Kong to answer our prayer. Be patient," Mr Lee, the union secretary, counselled the villagers. "We will not move. Let them send in the bulldozers first."

"The Hungry Ghost Festival is coming up, Old Lee. We'll pray and feed the ghosts who hunger for this shit hole, hahaha!"

Chong Suk maintained a determined quietude amidst the din. Tonight, he was glad to be out again under the trees with his pipa, away from the chatter of his wife and daughters in the hut. He stroked his pipa gently, savouring his solitude. A warm breeze brought a whiff of the river's mud. His neighbours, Lau Goo the carpenter, and Lau Ong, Ah Tek and Ah Lim, who worked on the bumboats, called out to him. They brought out their stools and joined him at the river's edge. Their children followed, and sat on wood crates away from the adults to talk their children's talk. His wife came out of the hut with three sticks of incense and stuck them under the raintree to appease the river's wandering spirits. The smoke kept the insects at bay as the men's voices rose and fell like the river's waves, punctuated by roars of laughter as Lau Ong and Lau Goo regaled them with the day's happenings on the boats. Ah Tek passed his pack of cigarettes round, and as the rest lit up, Chong Suk's gaze returned to the shimmering body of water, gleaming like a black eel with the lights from the bumboats anchored along the bank. On such a moonlit night, the river is a beauty to behold, he thought, and his pipa began to sing softly.

The women brought their stools and mugs of tea to join the men, and the talk soon grew loud and boisterous. Chong Suk stopped playing and joined in their loud arguments, and even louder laughter and teasing.

"Aye, don't know how long we can sit like this before we have to move," Lau Goo sighed. "Hey, old Chong, play us something cheerful."

"Yeah, a cheerful song to celebrate the moon."

"Uncle Chong Suk!"

"Look. Noodle Ting is here with his parents."

Chong Soh's smile was wide and welcoming.

"I know why you're here, young man. To ask for Ah Fong's hand. Isn't that so, young dog?" Lau Goo guffawed, and slapped Noodle Ting on the back.

"That's so," Noodle Ting blushed.

"Wah! Good news, Chong Suk! Good news, Chong Soh!"

"We've been waiting for this wedding feast for a long time! So what do you say, Chong Suk?"

"Ah Fong's mother," Chong Suk turned to his wife, "what do you say?"

"Ah Weng's father, whatever you say, whatever you say," Chong Soh beamed. "You're her father. Let them marry, lor. Marry before we have to move out."

"True, true. If we're kicked out of here, we might never see our neighbours again."

"Choy! Choy! We will always see our neighbours!"

"Leng-leng, ask Ah Fong to come out. Say her parents-in-law are here."

"I think she knows, Pa."

"Tell her to order coffee from the shop. Drinks on me!" Chong Suk laughed. "To welcome our in-laws to be."

"The first wedding in our family, we have to do it well. It's your eldest daughter's wedding, old Pa."

"I know, I know, old Ma. We'll marry our daughter off in style. A big wedding dinner with the proper ceremony. See, see, Ah Ting's parents are laughing at us. You're all invited to the wedding, my friends!"

They drank their coffee, at ease with each other, all thoughts of the redevelopment momentarily banished.

21

On the night of Ah Fong's wedding, Weng thought the riverfront was the happiest place in the city. The Double Happiness Restaurant was wreathed in festive bridal red. Bright red lanterns and strings of vermillion lights twinkled and glittered in the teacups and wine glasses set out on bright pink tablecloths and red double-happiness paper napkins. Weng looked across the room. He caught his father's eye and gave his old man the thumbs-up sign. His father had refused to wear the jacket that his stepmother had rented for him for the wedding, but as a concession to his eldest daughter, he had agreed to wear a shirt and tie. Now the sight of his old man in a long-sleeved white shirt and a dark blue tie made him smile.

"You look like a rich towkay, Pa."

His father scowled. "This thing is strangling me. Why people want to tie it round their neck I don't know."

Outside the restaurant, part of the road had been cordoned off for open-air dining. Several tables were reserved for their neighbours and their families, his father's friends, the men who used to work with him in the boatyard, the fish suppliers and buyers from his aunt and uncle's fishball stall, and their families.

"Must we invite their families too?" Fong had grumbled, worried about the extra expense. "Yes, yes, got to invite," his stepmother had insisted. "They invite us; we invite them back. Relationships must have this to and fro. When we marry in our village, the whole village is involved. No family marries alone."

The restaurant was beginning to fill. Guests arrived, pumping his parents' hands and teasing the bride and groom at the entrance. Waitresses in red samfoo jackets hurried round the tables, serving pu-erh tea to the women, and three-star whiskey and XO brandy to the men. Judging from the smiles, the men were impressed with the quality of the liquor.

"Our Noodle Ting must be doing well."

"Chong Suk's daughter is marrying well."

Fong, usually rough and boisterous, looked demure and resplendent sheathed in a red silk qipao embroidered with blue and green sequins shaped like a phoenix in flight.

"It's specially tailored for her, mind you. It's not rented," his stepmother announced to all and sundry. Fong had insisted that her groom should wear a white suit with a red tie to match her outfit. Poor Noodle Ting. Hot under the collar in the glare of lights, his brother-in-law swore he'd never wear another suit again. A sudden commotion at the entrance made Weng turn. A white Mercedes had drawn up outside the restaurant.

"Why, it's Ping! Welcome! Welcome! So glad you can come!" His stepmother immediately took possession of her.

"Congratulations, Auntie. This hongbao is from my Ah-ku for the bride and groom."

"Aiyah! No need, Ping! No need! Your coming is enough! Thank you! Thank you! Mrs Chang has done us a great honour by sending you! Mrs Chang is so very kind! So very gracious of her to give our family so much face to let you come. Ah Weng said he sent you the invitation card, but we didn't hear from you so we didn't expect you to come. Who would've thought that a member of the Chang family is here at my daughter's wedding tonight? A great honour, a great honour!"

His stepmother was speaking louder than usual. It was obvious that, like the proverbial Cantonese mother in the Hong Kong movies, she wanted their guests to know that Ping was from the wealthy Chang family.

"It's a very simple dinner, Ping. My son-in-law had wanted to host it in a bigger restaurant. But I told him better to save his money for his business. He runs a big noodle stall in the Chinatown market now, you know. Aye, things have changed for us and for you too. Look at you, a young lady chauffeured in a big car! Mr Chang Soo Beng is treating you very well!" His stepmother's voice rose another octave higher.

"You're very lucky. And you're bringing us good luck! You have to sit with us at the main table. Like family. My son-in-law is very generous. He insisted on this eight-course dinner with shark's fin, abalone and suckling pig for two hundred guests. Two hundred! Luckily, I asked for a small restaurant, if not, there'll be even more guests. Come, come. You must meet my son-in-law's parents. Mr and Mrs Ting, this is Miss Ping from the Chang family who own the warehouses in Boat Quay."

Weng was sorely tempted to cut in, but he restrained himself. This was his stepmother's happiest day; he should not spoil it for her, but he was cringing inside.

"Miss Ping is from the Chang family who own the warehouses and businesses up and down this river. Our house is built on their land, you know. Ping grew up with my son, Ah Weng. They used to play together as children. Now where is Ah Weng?"

"I can't stay long, Auntie. My uncle's car is coming back for me soon."

"What? Your uncle, Mr Chang Soo Beng, is coming?"

The question, loudly uttered, excited the guests.

"You heard that? You heard that?"

"What? Heard what?"

"One of the biggest landlords on the riverfront is coming to the dinner."

"Chang Soo Beng is coming."

"Waah! True or not? A lot of face for Chong Suk and Chong Soh! The Chang brothers. Always with MPs and VIPs."

"Ya, especially the PAP, the Pay And Pay Party!

Loud laughter and guffaws greeted this moniker for the People's Action Party.

"Not my uncle, Auntie. The car is coming."

"Hush! No matter, no matter, Ping. Sit down. Please eat. Please eat, everyone! To eat is good fortune! Eat, everybody! Eat and drink your fill tonight! Don't be shy. Help yourselves! Where is Ah Weng? He was here a minute ago. Kum, go and look for your brother. Tell him Ping is here."

"Hoi! Ping!"

"Auntie Molek!" Ping hugged her old friend.

"You know this girl, Molek Ee?"

"Know her? Mrs Chong Soh, I've known her since she was knee high."

"We saw you getting out of the car. Waaah! So rich and precious nowadays."

"Mrs Leeee! Uncle Ah Chek!"

"Yes, that's me, your trishaw uncle." Ah Chek pumped her hand up and down.

"How are you, Uncle Ah Chek?"

"Fine, fine. Nothing torn; nothing broken. Still in one piece. Still plying my trishaw. No bones broken yet."

"Choy! Choy! Nothing will break you. You'll live to a ripe old age. And we might as well tell you, Ping. We are as they say an old couple – old man, old wife."

"Oh, Auntie Molek, I'm so happy for you both, Uncle Ah Chek."

"Thank you, Ping, thank you. You must come and visit us."

"Fatt Chye left the coffee shop. Did you know? He stole from the till. So Old Kim kicked him out."

"Poor Kim Poh. How's she?"

"A shadow of her former self. Thin as a stick."

"Hush, talk about happy things tonight. It's a wedding

you're attending."

"Ya, ya, my old wife. I just want to ask Ping about her Ah-ku. How's our Miss Yoke Lan?"

"Chek! She's Mrs Chang now. How is she, Ping?"

"Sorry, Uncle. Sorry, Auntie." Weng grabbed her hand. "I've got to introduce Ping to my brother-in-law." He pulled her away from the group and took her to the rear of the restaurant.

"I've met your brother-in-law."

"How else could I get you away? I didn't think you'd come."

"I quarrelled with Ah-ku over this, but let's not talk about it. You look – hmm, you look very nice."

A wave of warmth rose from his belly to his face. He was awfully pleased, ridiculously so, and tried not to show it. He had rented the navy blue suit, and knew that his white shirt and tie of red and blue stripes matched it well. His hair was brushed, and he had slapped on some aftershave. "I pulled you in here to ask a favour."

"Granted. What?"

"I've brought your pipa from the association. Pa desperately wants to play his pipa tonight. So I've secretly asked his friends to urge him to play. I've brought my flute to accompany him. Will… will you join us?" When she looked hesitant, he quickly added, "You're his best student. He's very proud of you. He doesn't show it, but he is. He's not been well but don't ask him about his health. Will you join us?"

"Uncle Chong Suk is my shifu. I'll be honoured."

"Good. Dinner is about to start."

When the waiters brought in the first course, the men from his father's clan association burst into a rousing rendition of a traditional Cantonese wedding song that drew loud applause from the guests.

"Hey, Old Chong! Why don't you play us a tune? Give us a song!"

"Ya, a wedding song!"

"Come, come, father of the bride, play us a song!"

"Ya, play us a song, Noodle Ting's father-in-law."

His father stood up, his face florid with drink, joy and illness.

"Family, friends, clansmen and neighbours! Thank you! Thank you for gracing this joyous occasion. Tonight is the happiest night of my life. My eldest daughter, Fong, is marrying a good man. The best noodle maker in town!"

"Hear, hear! To their happiness!" the guests raised their glasses.

"Play your pipa, Old Chong! Music! Let's have music!"

"Ah Weng! Bring your father his pipa!"

His father looked around the restaurant, eyes bright with unshed tears of joy. A moment came, fleeting and bright, when a man stood before his family and friends, his woes suspended, his failures forgotten, and his iniquities forgiven. This was his father's moment. He handed the pipa to his father. Resting the instrument on his lap, his father sat on the raised dais in front of the curtain with the Chinese character, 'Double Happiness', sewn in bright red satin. The waitresses filled the women's cups with more tea and the men's glasses with more whiskey. Their guests fell silent and expectant. His father struck the pipa's fret board and launched into Joyous Spring Comes to the Valley filling the restaurant with the laughter of children and the chatter of young maids. His pipa trilled with the chirps of sparrows and golden orioles flitting in the bamboo groves. Weng joined in, blowing gently into his dizi, careful not to overwhelm the pipa's joyous melody.

Waiting in the wings, Ping came out on cue, and a ray of sunshine brightened his father's face. Reassured, she plucked the strings of her pipa lightly like a child skipping beside her teacher, lithe and graceful in her fingering, yet firm in her strumming. Her practice had paid off. His father's playing was strong and assured, and his pressure upon the strings was like a gentle lover's hand. The pipa's poetry evoking the immigrant's dream of plenty and harmony brought the house down.

"Encore! Encore!" the guests shouted again and again.

"Another song! Another song!"

The riverfront had never seen the likes of such a performance. Such beautiful music by a father and son, teacher and pupil ensemble. No father in the annals of Squatters' Village had ever performed at his daughter's wedding, and no father-in-law had ever performed for his son-in-law's family.

"A first, Old Chong! You scored a first!"

"Encore! Once more! Once more!" his friends urged him.

"No more! No more!" his stepmother stopped him.

Coughing and wheezing, his father hugged his beloved pipa. "Thank you, my friends! Thank you. If I drop dead tonight, I die a happy man!"

"Choy, choy, choy! What a thing to say at your daughter's wedding. You're drunk, old man!"

"Drunk? Ah Fong's mother, I'm happy! Not drunk! Not drunk!" He coughed into his handkerchief, and wheezed, "Aaah, Ping, you played well."

"Yaaaaaaaaaaaaaaaaam…!" The guests held their glasses high above their heads, their voices rising to the beams till the entire restaurant resounded in one voice, "SENG! To Success! Yam Seng! To Success and Happiness! Yaaaaaaaaaaaaaaaa…m Seng!"

He seized Ping's hand. "Let's go. They won't miss us." Squeezing past the crowded tables and running children, he shouted in her ear above the roars of Yam Sengs. "I've already told Pa I'm taking you home!"

"But my uncle's car is here."

"Send it away; send it away!" he laughed, happy and reckless as he pulled her towards the backlane. Behind the restaurant and shophouses, the deserted lane was hushed, bathed in a pale silver light. A full moon hung over the rooftops like a silver medal. "Remember what we used to do?" he whispered, his eyes shining with mischief. He was intensely aware of the warmth of her hand in his, and the rub of her shoulders against his forearm. "Remember? Cheap veg! Cheap veg, ho!"

"Ten cents! Twenty cents!" she cupped her hands and joined in.

"Cheap veg! Cheap veg! Oi!" Their voices rang out in the cool night air.

A man stepped out of the shadows, zipped up his fly and hurried off.

"Look, we frightened the poor guy. He was peeing," she giggled in his ear, her lips gently brushing his earlobe.

"Fishball! Big balls!" He yelled after the man. His heart was full. Oh how he'd missed her, he wanted to tell her. He was absurdly, ludicrously, incredibly happy. They'd performed so well with his father. "It means a lot to Pa. Thank you."

"I should thank you for inviting me to perform with my mentor. Come. Let's celebrate. Race you to the other end!" She sprinted away like a gazelle down the lane.

"Wait!"

He started after her. She was a good runner, fast and graceful, her slim legs gleaming in the silver light, but she was wearing heels. He was gaining on her. When she heard him getting close, she ran faster. He lengthened his strides, increased his speed and sprinted after her. Stretching out his arm, he caught her by the shoulder and spun her round. His arms encircled her waist and his lips brushed against her cheek. Panting, her breath coming hard and fast, she rested her head on his shoulders, one hand pressed against his heaving chest. He could feel the pounding of her heart. He shut his eyes and kissed her, inhaling the heady fragrance of perfume in her hair.

22

So here he is again. Same time, same date, same spot. Weng sighs. What does he get out of it? The same question each year, and each year he can never come up with a satisfactory answer. Each year, he's here at the riverfront to play his flute. A personal commemorative event, he explains. The small groups of old men seated here and there on the stone benches, and those boys and girls holding hands… ah well, they're here to pak-tor, out on a date. Not to listen to him, he assures the police officer. He's not disturbing the peace, but nevertheless, the officer gives him a warning.

He'd started coming here soon after his return from the Shanghai Conservatory of Music. Since then, he had not missed a single anniversary of the river squatters' protest. On this day, each year, he comes to the river in the evening, and as though by coincidence, his former neighbours and fellow squatters, old men in their sixties and seventies now, are here too, sitting on the stone benches, enjoying the breeze.

He looks around. This evening, some of the familiar faces among them are missing. They must have passed on, or perhaps they are too old or too infirm to come this year. The number who comes is bound to diminish. When the last of them dies, what happens then? Will he return? Ah well, he'll cross that bridge when he comes to it.

This year though, something new has happened. The denizens of the Internet have claimed him. The bloggers, the Facebook, Twitter and YouTube users have taken note of his annual performance. Yesterday, he'd stumbled on a blog with a photo of him and the caption: Silent Flautist Strikes with Great Soundscape at the Riverfront. Another blog: Lone Flautist at Boat Quay. Unlike the early years, when no one had paid him any attention, many youngsters these days try to talk to him, but he keeps his distance and silence. He of all people should be aware of the draconian law on public peace and order. So he has not spoken to nor acknowledged their presence, nor the presence of the old men, his former neighbours. Neither has he made any reference to his annual performance at the river to the press. Yet each year, the crowd of listeners grows a little larger, a little younger.

Tonight, the young crowd looks like they number close to a hundred. He has no idea where they come from. The music schools that have mushroomed all over the city, perhaps. The young people are sprawled on the grounds in front of the Asian Civilization Museum. He takes out his flute. Poor ignorant kids. They don't know what these old men know but can't articulate. Illiterate and resigned, these former squatters and coolies have neither the skill nor the will to speak the language of prosperous Singapore. They know neither English nor Mandarin. Yet these masters of the Teochew and Hokkien dialects know like the back of their hands the histories of lives left out of the sanitized history lessons taught in school. Ack! What can he do for them other than to play his flute? He is, after all, a flautist. He will play for these former squatters, the nameless grass growing by the roadside that was pulled up and removed. He has to commemorate their protest. Here's to the grass we step on!

Two thousand nine hundred and fifty-nine squatters and their families.

Five thousand hawkers and their families.

Several thousand boat builders and boatmen working on the bumboats and tuakows and their families.

Several hundred backyard factory operators, workers, coolies, and their families.

Vegetable gardeners, chicken farmers, duck farmers and their families.

And eight thousand pig farms, pig farmers and their families.

A memory recalled is a memory snatched from the jaws of defeat.

He will not forget the misery of his father crouched among the pots of withered chillies in the corridor of their new Housing Board flat. Nor the duck farmer who couldn't find another job after the family's eviction from the river. Nor the vegetable gardener, a father of six, who got drunk every night on the compensation the government paid him. Evicted from his land, the man lost his bearings. Grew violent and beat his wife and children every night. The desperate wives of these desperate men brought in mediums from the temples to exorcise their husbands' troubled spirits. Over time, these men turned grey, wrapped themselves in a cocoon of silence and tobacco smoke and withered away. Sallow and thin, you could see them sometimes eking out the dregs of their lives in the coffee shops of the Housing Board estates. How many former river men have drowned themselves in drink and depression? There are no national statistics. Just a few bloated bodies caught under the barges dredging the riverbed.

He walks over to the railing; flute in hand, unable to begin. Who is he trying to deceive anyway? The years have mellowed him. The good life on this golden sunny island has added flab to his waistline. Where once he would have fired a salvo of words into this crowd, he now plays the flute. He begins, breathing all the life of his being into his dizi, and the haunting air of Fishing Boats Over the Horizon rises above the city's traffic. The young people, lolling on the lawn, stop their chatter and sit up. The old men on the stone benches turn their heads and gaze out at the river, memories and cataracts clouding their aged eyes.

"What song is this?" a Malay girl asks her Chinese boyfriend.

"A folksong the Chinese school students used to sing."

"How do you know?"

"Google lah."

"Send me the link. Can Bluetooth or not?"

Part Four

Dark Waters

23

It was the Year of the Horse when the troubles began. The Lunar New Year had brought unusually hot, dry days. The lanes along the river were carpeted with brown leaves and the bright yellow blooms from the angsana trees. The sight cheered Weng a little. In the evenings when the air had cooled, he and his father took their rattan chairs out to the raintree by the river. While his father drank his tea and strummed his pipa, Weng played his flute. The men from the neighbouring huts gathered round for a smoke and chat. Their wives complained, but soon they too drew close, bringing out their stools and bowls of melon seeds and groundnuts to crack while they talked.

"Looks like the year of the horse is going to be bumpy," his father said. "The fengsui masters have been very circumspect in their predictions. They said the horse would defend the island's prosperity, but they also said we must guard against disasters."

"Ack! Trouble is brewing on the riverfront. You can bet on it," Lau Ong added.

In the middle of the year, the riverfront was in the news. The lightermen had gone on strike. Undeterred, boat owners and shipping companies like Chang Brothers Private Limited hired non-union coolies to break the strike. Fistfights erupted. One night, a warehouse belonging to the Chang family caught fire. Although the fire was put out immediately, a smouldering resentment billowed like smoke over the squatters' huts and boatyards. Political tracts started to appear in the village. Posters, handbills, pamphlets and dead leaves littered the lanes and roads. The broad trunks of the angsana trees were pasted with all kinds of accusations, announcements and manifestos written in Chinese. Dark rumours abounded.

"Beware. The ISD blokes in charge of security have sent their men to infiltrate our unions," one poster declared. Not long after that, the authorities suspended the night classes organised by the Water Transport Workers' Union. Mr Lee and his fellow teachers were questioned by the police, and detained for two weeks for investigations.

Weng was fuming when he read the news in camp. He had been one of the many poor boys who had benefited from these night classes, he told the investigating officer when he visited Mr Lee at the detention centre. The man took down his statement.

The rising tension of these brittle days wore out his father who fell ill. The boatyard owner dismissed him. His father, who was a hired hand working part-time, had no compensation. His fellow workers in the boatyard went on strike. Other boatyards joined in.

Stuck at home, his father grew pale and vague, and secretive. The family was worried. It took his stepmother's tears and hot words, and nights of nagging and arguing before she finally ferreted out the Quit Notice, hidden under the mattress. But his father refused to quit his home, his vegetable garden and fruit trees.

"I don't want to live in a concrete block. I will die there."

"Fool! Die or not, you think it's up to you, meh? You think you're the government?" his stepmother screeched. "If I had known back then that you were going to be such a mule, I wouldn't have married you!" She stormed into her kitchen and banged her pots and wok in the middle of the night.

A second letter arrived the following month from the lawyer

of Chang Brothers Pte Ltd. The family's hut was squatting on the Changs' land. His father was advised to seek help from the Housing and Development Board. By then, his father was ill again, and the lawyer's letter was put away and forgotten as something too depressing to be faced. Two months later, a stern-looking rent collector arrived at the door of their hut, and handed his father the third notice. Weng was in camp at the time, and heard the story from his sisters when he returned home the following weekend. His sisters reported that when their mother heard the words, "Jail," and "Police," she'd fallen on her knees and begged the rent collector for leniency.

"Dia sakit! Dia sakit! He's sick! Not well!" She kept crying in Malay, "Tolong, tolong! Mercy, mercy, please!"

The Malay man was so taken aback that he kept shaking his head whether in disbelief or denial, his sisters couldn't tell. Finally, he gave the family a month's grace. After that, his father had to report to the lawyer's office in person to show proof that he had gone to the Housing Board to apply for a rental flat.

Relieved, his stepmother turned the incident into a personal triumph. Squawking to their neighbours, she proudly declared that it was only because of her pleading that the Malay rent collector had given them a month's grace and the Chang Brothers' lawyer did not throw her husband in jail.

"Listen to me, Ah Weng's father! This year is 1978! Yat-gao-chaat-fatt! Sure to prosper as we Cantonese say. It's our lucky year! Go and get a new flat. Move to a new life. Get away from here. In the year of the horse, we must be adaptable."

24

The Year of the Horse was a good year for Chang Brothers. The company's first air-conditioned cinema was built; "mainly because of my husband," Ping overheard Ah-ku telling Miss Kok and other mahjong friends. Pleading the need to study for her coming 'A' Level exams, Ping stayed home with Kan Jieh and the baby, Kit-boy.

Pleased that Ping was not coming with them, Yoke Lan took Boy-boy's hand and got into the car beside Chang, glad that she'd nipped in the bud whatever it was that went on in the fish shed that night. These days, she made it a point to accompany Chang to all his functions, a task she had neglected when she was pregnant. But no more. She had better look after her man. Who knew better than her that a man attending functions alone was prey for other women?

"Congratulations, dear. Things are looking up. Miss Kok told me there's a rising confidence in the city."

"What does Miss Kok know? The strikes along the river are still on. That will scare away foreign investors if the government fails to control them."

"You're right, the strikes will scare away business. Boy-boy, Papa is working very hard to earn money to send you and Kit-boy to school. Do you know that?" she hugged her son, seated between them in their new car, a chauffeur-driven white Mercedes provided by the company for all its directors.

"Papa. I will make lots of money for you."

Chang ruffled his son's hair. "Good boy. You know," he said turning to her, "I had to push my brothers hard. Second Brother dug in his heels. Refused to change the company's business, and move away from these bumboats and water transport trade on the river. Now they agree I was right. Mustn't just stick to our father's boats and shipping. Second Brother kept arguing what's wrong with the old way? The bumboats made loads for our old man, he yelled at me at one meeting."

"Aiyah, Second Brother. He's a stick in the mud." She soothed him. "Weren't you the one who insisted on this charity premiere?"

"They didn't want it at first. But I said, look at Hong Kong. They know how to link charity with business. Charity makes money look less crass, and that won over my three sisters."

She laughed. "So your sisters are directors too?"

"Sleeping directors but the three of them can overpower my brothers," he laughed.

"So who invited the Minister?"

"I spoke to the Minister himself. See that?"

They had reached the cinema. Chang pointed to a large, white banner over the entrance, ablaze with lights and lined with baskets of flowers. Written large in glossy red paint was the Guest of Honour's name.

"My old man used to say in Hokkien oo lai, oo kee – in business, you've got to grease the wheels of power; must have this to and fro between business and politics."

"Boy-boy. Can you remember what to say when the Minister comes?"

"Yes, Mama. I'll say good evening, sir. Welcome to my Papa's new cinema, sir!"

The proud parents laughed as they walked into the foyer, holding their son's hand.

"Mr and Mrs Chang, welcome! Welcome!" the cinema staff greeted them.

The foyer was filled with invited guests. His half-brothers were here with their wives; stout, portly men in their sixties who moved through the crowd with the confidence of ocean liners, while Chang, fit and slim, looked like a speedboat, half their size and age. Yoke Lan greeted her in-laws.

"Boy-boy, say hello to your uncles and aunties."

Her sisters-in-law, matrons in their fifties and sixties, filled her in on the latest gossip on mistresses and manicures garnered from their shopping sprees in Hong Kong, the capital of Cantonese fashion and cuisine. At the drinks counter, Chang was talking to some men looking uncomfortable in their business suits of varying shades of grey with a corsage of pink orchids pinned to their lapels. It was a good thing that the new cinema had air-conditioning. She remembered a time when a cinema in Singapore was just an open field with a man and a projector in front of a white canvas sheet, and people had to bring their own chairs.

"Oh, Mr Chang, sir. Here, let me do it for you."

Yoke Lan turned. The note of familiarity in the woman's voice was a little jarring. A young woman was pinning a corsage of pink orchids onto the lapel of Chang's jacket. She walked over and stood beside him.

"Miss Maria Sim, meet my wife. Miss Sim is my new secretary," Chang said.

"Good evening, Mrs Chang."

"Good evening, Miss Sim."

"Is everything under control then, Miss Sim?"

"Everything's A-okay, sir," Miss Sim launched into English, speaking rapidly from then on. The young vixen seemed to have deliberately switched from Cantonese to English; her laughter was coquettish, and her English speech was fluent and confident.

Yoke Lan felt herself floundering in the rising babble. People were coming over to offer their congratulations to Chang. Someone put a drink in her hand. She turned to thank the man, but when she turned back to Chang, he had left her side and had gone to the other end of the foyer with Boy-boy and Miss Sim. Boy-boy said something that made the two of them laugh. In that very moment, she caught sight of herself in the mirrored walls, looking pale and distracted.

"Sister-in-law, are you feeling all right?" Margaret took her hand. A doctor at the General Hospital, she was the most friendly of Chang's three half-sisters.

"You must exercise more and get rid of that flab," Mary, a deputy director at the Ministry of Education, was blunt.

"So how are you and Baby Kit?" Helen, the lawyer, asked.

"I am velly well, tank you." She didn't know what made her take the plunge into English. There was a pause, then a burst of hooting laughter.

"Not bad, not bad at all," Helen said in Cantonese.

"Do say that again!" Mary squealed.

Steeling her nerves, she tried once more. "I learn spik English now. Must learn spik more. So as not too shy to spik to you."

"Say speak, not spik," Mary admonished. "But don't worry about your pronunciation for now. Speak more; you'll learn faster. If you make mistakes, it's all right."

They meant well, her sisters-in-law, but they continued to speak Cantonese despite her attempts to speak English with them. Did they think she wouldn't understand? Or was it because they thought she was not good enough to join their club? Or was she just being thin-skinned? She forced herself to smile. Would it kill them to slow their English speech a little? Would it? Their rapid guttural sounds made no sense to her.

The air in the foyer was getting stuffy. People were moving towards the cordon of red ribbons. She saw Miss Sim carrying a silver tray with a pair of scissors. The guest-of-honour must have arrived. She looked around. "Boy-boy! Boy-boy, where are you?"

"Here, Mama."

She hugged him.

"Good evening, Mrs Chang. Nin hao."

Surprised that the bespectacled man had addressed her in Mandarin, using nin instead of ni to show his respect, she smiled. "Good evening, ni hao."

"I'm the principal of Bukit Secondary School. I heard from our chairman, Mr Chang, that you used to play the pipa in Hong Kong."

"That… that was a very long time ago, Mister…" her voice suddenly cold and wary.

"Please call me Tan. I've a great favour to ask, Mrs Chang. My school has many students from poor families. I was wondering if we could persuade you to play your pipa at our fund-raising concert? It will be a great honour for us. A very great honour."

"I… I have to consult Mr Chang. Excuse me, Mr Tan. The Minister is here. I've to go. I'll… I'll let you know soon."

*

That request and Miss Sim worried her all week. When she finally brought up the subject during breakfast one morning, Chang was almost dismissive.

"It's up to you. The government wants to promote Chinese traditional arts. So I mentioned that my wife plays the pipa."

She liked the way he said, "my wife", and lapped it up with her morning coffee. They were seated across the table from each other in the dining room, having a late breakfast, just the two of them, which was a rare treat, for they seldom talked these days; he was so busy. He held his coffee in his hand and looked at her.

"Mr Tan and the school committee are waiting for an answer. So what is it?"

She noted the impatience in his voice.

"If you want me to perform…" she trailed off.

"So I take it, it's a yes then. More coffee?"

She shook her head, dismayed that he did want her to play her pipa. She thought they'd agreed that her past was buried for good.

He glanced at his watch. "Look at the time." He pushed back his chair and stood up. "The Consultative Committee is meeting again tonight." He downed the last of his coffee. "I'll be home late."

"I know." She forced a smile, remembering Miss Sim's crisp voice on the phone yesterday: sorry, Mr Chang cannot be disturbed. He'd walked to the back of her chair, and touched her lightly on the shoulders. She didn't turn around, but sat quite still, and waited. His hand smelt fragrant. She wondered if it was the new aftershave that she had bought him.

"Don't wait up for me."

She heard the chauffeur greet him, then the slam of the car door and the purr of the engine as the car eased out of the driveway. She sat nursing her cup of coffee as vague fears surged through her. She'd come a long way from the river and from Sum Koo, the woman who'd bought her from her deadbeat pa after her ma's death.

*

The morning after the burial, she was lying in bed listening to the breathing of the bodies pressed against her. Her brothers were making funny chewing noises, grinding their teeth in their sleep. Eyes closed, she waited for the grey dawn and Ma's footsteps on the bare boards of their hut. But sharp as a knife, the memory of yesterday's burial sliced her heart.

"Wake up, Yoke Lan."

She opened her eyes and sat up. Pa had never called her by name before. His tone frightened her. There was something solemn and formal in the way he'd called out to her. She wanted to cry, but Pa placed a finger on his lips. She held back her tears, and followed him out of the hut.

The sky was dishwater grey. Her father tucked a newspaper-wrapped parcel under his arm. They walked down the streets in silence, past the boats and shuttered huts. She wondered who would give her little brother his bottle of milk while they were gone. "Hurry!"

He was striding down the silent streets, never once looking back. She had to run to keep up. Through a maze of streets and lanes they walked till she was dizzy with fear and hunger. Finally, he stopped, and knocked on the door of a two-storey house. A woman came out, took a look at her, and handed Pa a red packet.

"Go with Sum Koo now. Be good, and do as you're told."

He thrust the newspaper-wrapped parcel into her arms. "Here. Take it. Your Ma made it."

She hugged the parcel and watched him run down the road. Not once did he look back.

A few months later, the Japanese bombed Singapore, and her days turned into nightmare. Pa did not come back for her. Japanese soldiers visited Sum Koo's pleasure house, and the young women squealed and cried at all hours of the night. But when she cried, Sum Koo caned her. "Choy! Choy! Choy! How dare you bring tears and bad luck to my parlour! Go into the kitchen! Who'll come if they see you crying like this?"

Her tears eventually dried up in the long hot empty days. Sum Koo engaged an old man to teach her the pipa.

"Learn the pipa, girl, and you'll never go hungry," the old man whispered in her ear as he fingered her between her thighs. He held her hand and taught her how to stroke and pluck the pipa's strings. At night she took the quilt out of its newspaper wrapping, and covered herself with it. In her sleep, she cried out, Ma! Ma!

When the Japanese renamed Singapore as Syonan, she had turned six. Neatly dressed in a pink samfoo with red frog buttons at the collar, she sat holding her pipa primly on her lap the way Sum Koo had taught her.

"That's right. A pipa songstress must sit up straight and look pretty. Now, smile. Look happy. A happy pretty face attracts money. If the uncles give you money, what must you do?"

"Give it to you, Sum Koo Mama."

"That's right. You give it to me. Who feeds you?"

"Sum Koo Mama."

"Who clothes you?"

"Sum Koo Mama."

"Who should you obey then?"

"Sum Koo Mama."

"Good. Now play your pipa. Don't forget to smile. And please the uncles. If they ask you to sit on their laps, you sit. If they ask you to play your pipa, you play. Do you understand?"

"Yes, Sum Koo Mama."

25

The red and white sign with the outline of a house was the Housing and Development Board's symbol of home and hope, a symbol that Chong Suk failed to appreciate as he and Weng edged past the crowd in the lift lobby. He was wary of entering the government building, and of the government officials. The housing rules and regulations were incomprehensible to him even though he could read them in the Chinese translation. Everything here was written first in English, then in Chinese, Malay and Tamil. Fair enough, he thought, we have many who can't read the English.

"Excuse me, excuse me, don't push!" a woman shouted.

The lifts were packed. Most people were heading for the department that handled rental flats, rented out to families like his who could not afford to purchase a Housing Board flat even at a subsidised rate.

Weng took a ticket, and stood in a corner with his father to wait for their turn to collect the application forms, which must be completed in triplicate. The week before, a surly clerk had sent him back to the end of the queue after he had filled in the wrong forms. Their number was called, and they hurried to Counter 16.

"Who is the applicant?"

"My father."

"Your father is the chief applicant. Why didn't he turn up at the appointed date given last month?" the horse-faced woman behind the glass partition asked.

"My father was in hospital."

"Chief applicant must come at the appointed date. Next! Number 3881!"

"Excuse me, what do I do now?"

"Go to Counter 21. Take another ticket and wait your turn. Next! 3881!"

He explained to his father what the Indian girl had said as they pushed their way through the milling crowd to counter 21, which was surrounded by shoving bodies. Men were clutching files and envelopes containing birth certificates, marriage certificates, school certificates, proof of employment and so on and they were filling forms, and more forms, for everything had to be completed in triplicate. Whether buying, renting or selling, all must seek the Board's approval, and submit the correct application forms in triplicate, detailing everything.

"Everything? Even how many times we shit?" his father muttered under his breath. They were called to a different counter.

"Number in the family?" the Indian clerk asked.

His father mumbled a nervous reply.

"Number in the family?" the Indian clerk asked again in Hokkien. "You understand, uncle? I ask you, father, mother and how many children?"

"Four." Weng replied in English on his father's behalf.

"Four, what?"

"Four children."

He was given another form, which he had forgotten to fill in earlier.

"Must indicate how much each family member earns. Must write it down here. Total family income in one month. Must write down here. Write everything down. You understand? Write your name in block letters according to your identity card and birth certificate. Race. Tick the box here. Chinese, Malay, Indian, or Others. Check everything carefully before you submit. Wrong submissions entail further delays. Have you brought all the required documents today?"

His father looked dazed.

"Yes, yes," again he answered on behalf of his old man.

"Put them in this tray, and wait for your number to be called."

Long queues snaked through the crowded, air-conditioned office all morning. Out in the corridor, housing agents sweated in their shirt and tie, and waited for their clients. Behind the glass panels in the grey building, teams of stern-faced clerks checked and ticked stacks of brown files and manila folders secured with green strings. Mothers nursing babies sat in corners, mothers with wailing toddlers milled around and chatted with each other while their older children ran in and out of the public washrooms, flushing the loos, and turning on the taps. Old men sat hunched over their plastic bags, and looked lost as a barrage of announcements in quick succession in English, Mandarin, Malay and Tamil boomed over their heads through the public address system.

"When, ah? When will they call us?" an old woman asked.

"Wait, lah! Ah Mah, you wait. How should I know? You keep asking me also no use!" the young woman chided her grandmother.

Weng guided his father to a corner of the waiting room.

"Did you bring Ma's identity card?"

Chong Suk dug into his shirt pocket and handed over his wife's card.

"You tell that Indian clerk I married your ma in China, and your stepma and I were married here, both in the traditional way. We didn't go to the registry. No marriage certificate. We went to the temple and served tea to our parents. But the girls' birth certificates are in that envelope. They have my name and their mother's name. You remember to explain this to her, Weng."

"It's okay, Pa. We qualify for a three-room rental flat."

"Excuse me, mister," the Malay man held out a clutch of forms. "I already fill these forms. You know English? Can check for me or not? I already made copies and submitted, but so long already, they never call my number. I was here early – early this morning."

"Sama-sama, Inche. We're in the same boat, Uncle," Weng assured him. "We're also waiting for them to call our number."

"What's he saying?" his father asked, and Weng briefly translated what the Malay man had said.

"Always like this every day. Everything kenna wait. Same thing in the government clinics. See doctor. Wait. See nurse. Wait. Buy medicine. Wait. Go toilet, also kenna wait. Whole life, we Singaporeans wait and wait. Only when die, no need to wait."

Again, Weng translated what the Malay man said, and his father laughed. "Tell him, Weng, tell him, I also feel the same. Tell him we better laugh; if not, we die. Then you want to wait also cannot wait."

Weng told the Malay man what his father said, and the man laughed and nodded to his father. "Ya-lah! What to do?"

"What flat did you apply for? How many rooms?" Weng asked.

"Only two rooms. I rent, not buy. I got six children. My wife and me, we sell mee rebus. How to buy a flat? I got to feed so many children. One room also cannot buy. I so envy my brothers. They can buy a flat already. My family must wait, don't know how long. Maybe six years. Maybe ten years. Must wait for my children to grow up, lah! Then can buy a flat, God willing, ya. My uncle. He sells mee rebus also, but his house got burnt down in a big fire. His family. No place to stay. So he applied. One month only he waited. He got his flat. A three-room flat in Geylang Serai. Very nice. Got lift up to his floor. Got own kitchen and toilet. I susah-lah! So difficult. Kenna wait. I ask the officers when. They say wait, wait. I ask them, how long I kenna wait? My wife and I and our children are sleeping like sardines now in my parents' flat. Very difficult for my children. They sleep outside the corridor at night. Sometimes the neighbours complain when the kids make noise. But what to do? We kenna wait. Whole life in this country, we wait."

His father laughed, and that made the man laugh. Other men

joined in their talk and so two hours passed in the camaraderie of strangers. After they had handed in their forms and the clerk had checked that all the boxes were correctly filled in, Weng took his father to the Maxwell Road Market for lunch.

It turned out to be their final outing.

26

Ping hardened her heart and forced herself to focus on her papers. It was November, the month of monsoon rains, and her year end 'A' Level exam. Chong Suk's death had come right in the middle of several crucial 'A' Level papers, and a week of bad news. A column had collapsed in one of the Chang Brothers' cinemas, which was still under construction. Two workers had been killed. Her uncle was the man in charge, so Ah-ku went on a temple campaign to enlist the help of all the gods in the heavens to dispel the cloud of bad luck that had descended on him. Her superstitious fears rose to fever pitch with each new report of ongoing investigations and an impending government inquiry, while Uncle Chang grew ever more morose and short-tempered. The lamps and candles on the altar in the dining room were kept lit day and night.

"If you attend this Chong Suk's funeral, you don't come back here. Go and stay somewhere else with your books and exams. I'm serious. I won't have you bringing bad luck and death back to my house. Red thread or no red thread at the funeral, I won't take the risk".

Behind her anger, Ah-ku's eyes seemed on the verge of tears, and Uncle Chang had never looked so grave and ill before. Ping knew she couldn't go and it would break Weng's heart.

*

Weng hated the housing estate in Bukit Ho Swee. His Pa would've been alive today if they were still living by the river. The new twelve-storey blocks painted a uniform grey and beige made everything even greyer in the foul rain that fell all day. Their new flat was at the end of the common corridor. It had the same brown door as all the other apartments. The same aluminium gate. The same frosted glass windows that had so thrilled his stepmother and sisters when they moved in. He heard the doorbell's chime, and opened the door.

"Come in." His voice was dull and flat.

"Ping, come in, come in. Thank you for coming." His stepmother took her hand.

"Auntie Chong Soh, I couldn't come earlier. My exam…"

He saw the glisten in her eyes when she turned to him, but it made little difference to him now.

"How are you, Auntie?"

His stepmother started to sob. The least little thing set her off.

"Pa collapsed in the corridor outside, near his chilli plants," Kum said.

"I blame myself. I should've checked on him. He'd just returned from hospital. Now it's just the four of us in this big flat, Ping. Two bedrooms and this large sitting room and the kitchen."

The tinge of pride in his stepmother's voice irritated him. He watched, unmoved, as tears pooled in her eyes.

"Aye, this flat feels big and empty now."

His stepmother lapsed into a distracted silence. Outside, the rain grew steadily heavier. He knew Ping was waiting for him to say something, but he couldn't speak. The memory of his father's listless figure crouched in the common corridor outside their flat, gazing vacantly down at the car park below through the bars of iron railing tore his heart. Abruptly, he went into his bedroom and shut the door, and wished he could shut out his stepmother's voice.

"Ah Weng's furious with us over the funeral. But a three-day wake costs a lot of money. After the hospital expenses, moving house and Ah Fong's wedding, we're up to our neck in debt already. I didn't want us to incur more debt. I'm doing it for Ah Weng's sake. He'll be the one paying. I know he misses his Pa. Who do I miss? Who knows my grief?"

His stepmother's loud sobbing stabbed his ears. He flung open his door before Ping could knock.

"One miserable night in his coffin downstairs. One night for a man of his musical talent? One night! And she calls it a wake. Pa's friends didn't even have time to come to see him one last time. Is that all the respect Pa deserved?"

27

The most dreadful thing about regret is 'What if…?' The question plagued her. It kept popping up in her head. What if I'd gone to the funeral? Weng wouldn't speak to her. She couldn't rest. She lost sleep. Christmas and Chinese New Year came and went. Eventually, she visited the flat again but Weng wasn't there. He seemed to be avoiding her.

With exams over, school was over. A large chunk of her life was over. Her classmates had moved on. Even her best friend from school was leaving Singapore.

"What? You're getting married? Satvindar Kaur! Why didn't you tell me earlier? When did you meet him?"

"My parents met him and his parents. In Bombay. At my aunt's house last year. His parents live in Bombay."

"You've not met him?"

"We exchanged letters and photos, and spoke on the phone a few times."

"And you're okay with that? Why didn't they match you with a guy here?"

"The Sikh community in Singapore is very small. Besides, he's a distant cousin, and an assistant professor at UCLA. After our wedding in Bombay, I'll go with him and live in Los Angeles."

"And you don't mind?"

"I can't wait to go."

Everything was changing so fast, she felt her head spinning.

That night she packed away her textbooks and stuffed her files of notes into three boxes, and shoved them into the hall closet. Waking up the next morning, the space on her bookshelf stared at her. The empty space bewildered her. She felt as though she was gazing into the dark fissure inside her heart. Nothing had turned out the way she'd expected. She'd thought that, after her exams, she and Weng would be together… But now, they were so far apart… What was she to do? Would she ever be able to make amends? She remembered her final music-making day with Uncle Chong Suk. He was tuning his pipa when she arrived at the clan association. His face was wan and sallow, but his eyes were bright as a sparrow's. They began their lesson as usual. As if nothing had changed, as if he had not been ill, and someone else had not taught her during his long absence.

He played a phrase and she followed, playing the same phrase, as was their practice. There were no music sheets like those she had received from her new pipa instructor, who was formally trained in music. With Chong Suk, her learning had been by rote and imitation. But she had outgrown this method of learning now, and as they practised, she grew impatient, and started to sketch, tentatively at first and then with more confidence, the outlines of a new melody. Chong Suk cocked his head, and gesturing that she should continue, he closed his eyes to listen to her playing. Then he strummed two or three phrases that painted the faint sketch of her melody with bold tonal colours.

Surprised, she strummed boldly again as though it was a leitmotif. Chong Suk's face brightened. He added a clef here and a sharp there, light touches of musical details modulating yet never changing the melody or the tempo of her composition. The experience was exhilariating to them both, and she had the distinct feeling that her Shifu was pleased. If he knew that she had had lessons from another teacher, he gave no hint of that other than this piece of advice.

"Play with your heart. It's something no teacher can teach you."

That was as close as he came to acknowledging graciously that his pupil had outgrown him. She missed him as sorely as she missed his son.

*

One afternoon, her phone rang. She answered it.

"Can you come out now?"

His voice was raspy and hoarse as though he had a sore throat. He was waiting for her in his van at the end of Juniper Lane. His gaunt face was taut. She saw how the muscles of his neck tensed when she climbed in beside him. His eyes were even darker than before, and he looked older and thinner. She did a quick mental count; it was exactly one hundred days. Weng had observed the traditional minimum of one hundred days of mourning before coming out to meet her.

They drove through the city to a part of the river that was forested and secluded from the roads. No boats came up this far from the river mouth, and there were no squatter huts in the vicinity. They had come here sometimes as children to swim and fish in the river after school. At midday, the fish hid under the weeds; she remembered how he'd taught her to wade into the cool waters without frightening them and catch the guppies with a coffee strainer.

He parked the van in a grove of trees, but made no move to get out. Careful not to be the first to break the silence in the van, she waited for him to speak. Beyond the trees, the river was snaking in and out among the bushes. He had told her that his father used to bring him here to play his flute while his father serenaded his mother's spirit on the pipa. She wanted to reach out and hug him.

"Pa…" he began and stopped, his eyes still on the sunlit river,

"Pa taught me the flute, not the pipa."

A bead of sweat rolled down the side of his face and dripped onto his shirt. He wiped his brow with his hand, and gripped the steering wheel again as though it was a vital support to give him the strength to speak.

"The pipa… it was his favourite instrument… not… the flute. The pipa was his first love. The flute his rice bowl… the instrument he played at funerals. For… for the money."

He reached behind his seat, and pulled out a pipa case. Its handle was tied with a bright red string.

"Pa said to give his pipa to you."

"I…"

No other words came out. Her throat had constricted; her vision had blurred. Tears rolled down her cheeks as he thrust the case into her arms. It was so unexpected that all she could do was to stare at the shabby, black leather case.

"Open it," he said.

Hands trembling, she untied the red string on its handle. The black leather was worn and criss-crossed with a thousand minute cracks. When her tremulous fingers fumbled with the rusty clasp, he reached over and opened it for her.

"I… I can't…" she began, but he stopped her.

"Pa wanted you to have it. No one in the family plays the pipa. Except you."

She bowed her head, fearing what he might see in her eyes. An insect was flying around her ear. She tried to swat it away, but it returned, humming somewhere beyond her reach. His choice of words had shocked her. No one in the family plays the pipa, except you. What was he trying to say? Was he trying to tell her something? Blood rushed to her face. She felt hot. Her heart was pounding as she lifted his father's pipa out of its case. The elegant pear-shaped instrument was a joy to hold; it had weight and gravitas, and a sense of its own history. Her fingers curled around its swan-like neck, her arm suddenly stiff as she tried to suppress without success the choke that rose in her throat. She tugged at the red thread tied to the pipa's curved neck.

"Don't untie it. It's to ward off bad luck. Ma... she tied the red thread."

His tone was harsh when he said "Ma," and anger flashed across his dark eyes. He had not shed a single tear at the wake and funeral, they'd told her. She held the pipa against her breast, and inhaled the fragrance of its wood mixed with the lingering scent of her teacher's hands, the scent of a rough but passionate man who had faithfully plucked these strings, and taught her the meaning of commitment.

"Shifu," she wept.

Her fingers twisted the red thread. She was unworthy of the history and passion embedded in the grain of this beauty, whose giver's heart was so generous.

Weng sat dry-eyed, lost in thought, staring at the sun-lit river beyond the copse of bush and trees, his grip on the steering wheel, hard as before, lest if he let go, her sobbing would overwhelm him. She had no idea how long they sat inside the van. In silence. Then he loosened his grip on the steering wheel, and his hand reached out to hold hers. With her eyes closed, she was acutely aware of the rough texture of his palm on the back of her hand. The heat inside the van was making her drowsy. She listened to the soft humming, faintly tuneful yet indistinct. Was he humming? She opened her eyes a little to glance at him. Yes. She could hear the faint, soft notes from a piece his father used to play. She hummed it too. All of a sudden, they let go of their hands, and pushed open the doors on both sides and got out of the van. At the same time. Their synchronicity startled her a little. He took his flute, and she, the pipa. Then they walked in single file between banks of tall grasses that bordered the narrow winding path that led to the river's edge. A pair of stray dogs stalked them part of the way, scampering into the bushes when Weng shooed them away.

The air was cool at the water's edge, the grove of trees providing a welcome shade. Beyond the trees, out in the middle of the river, diamond splinters crested the small waves, and the span of sky above the river was a bright cobalt blue, its harshness softened now and then by passing clouds. The shrill chirping of the crickets had ceased the moment they arrived, leaving a green silence humming at the river's edge.

He stood with his back towards her, still as a stork watching for prey. His shirt was wet and sweat-stained. How sharp and thin his shoulders had grown. She wanted to kiss those shoulders, kiss the sharp edge of his shoulder blades, and plant the warmth of her lips on his back. He brought the flute to his mouth and blew a lone, sad note. It hung in the afternoon's air before it floated over the glittering waters to the other side of the river. A light breeze picked up other notes of his flute and scattered them among the rustling leaves above their heads. A flock of sparrows flew out of the bushes suddenly in a loud flutter of wings. She plucked the strings of her shifu's pipa, echoing the flute's plaintive cries as pipa and dizi played once again his father's favourite song, Xiao Bai Chuan, about a little white boat sailing the oceans, seeking home.

All afternoon, they played song after song from his father's repertoire, their music rising like incense on the riverbank. A bright blue kingfisher dipped its beak into the waters and flew up the trees. His dizi soared with the bird, skittering across the water, twittering in and out of the foliage until overwhelmed, he stopped, and her pipa had to carry on alone like a dragonfly among the waterweeds. Then he took up his flute again and shrilled to the wind in the trees, scattering the ashes of his grief.

Drained and exhausted, his bony shoulders heaving, he dropped his flute at last and choked on his tears. She put down her pipa and wrapped her arms around him, holding him tight against her breast. Gently, she turned him round, kissing his forehead, eyes and cheeks. His mouth sought hers, hungry and urgent, his tongue probed her deeply, and then deeper still. She heard his harsh indrawn breath, felt his weight on her, pressing against her breasts;

felt his hand on her hips, heavy and warm, slip between her thighs. A soft moan escaped her. She clung to him, relieved that she had not lost him.

28

Weng clings to the railing. His memories have been troubling him ever since Mrs Chang, unaware of his past with Ping, told him that Ping was coming back to stay with her for two months. Maybe he should have told her then. But why trawl up the past when the past is gone? Let it go; let it go; don't cling. That's the mantra he's struggling to live by.

The bamboo flute is smooth and cool in his hand. It's his first flute, that precious gift from his father when he was a sad, silent boy after his mother's death. Since then, he has acquired a large collection, including a specially crafted dizi that he uses for his concerts. But his first flute is still among his favourites, and the one that he plays each year to commemorate his parents' death and the squatters' protest.

All for the music. Because of his music he'd survived much, even prison. Playing that flute in his head was his sole comfort in those uncertain hours in solitary confinement when he knew not whether it was day or night or the next day.

A small metal sink and a metal pot sat in the corner of his cell, its walls damp and cold past midnight. The steel door with a peephole that could be open from the outside only had troubled his sleep. Every half an hour or so, an eye peered at him through the peephole. He padded to and fro in the cell like an animal, clad only in a pair of underpants and vest, and lost count of the days.

He longed for daylight, for the sun on his face and the smell of the river. The guards took him back to the freezer every few hours, where the air hit him like a block of ice. His interrogators wore thick leather and denim jackets while he shivered in his underpants. Their questions hung in the frozen air like an axe above his head. They were endless, those questions. No matter what he said, it was not the answer they wanted to hear. He missed his music, but they wouldn't allow his family to bring him his flute.

He offers silent thanks to the dead, and reels in his memories. The old men and youngsters are waiting for him to begin. A young couple stops to listen. His little flute has acquired a haunting tone over the years, lacquered with the memories of a lonely boy who is now a lonely man.

"Why is he playing here? Is this part of the Arts Fest or what?"

"Busking is not allowed, you know," he heard a woman complain.

"Shhh! Who cares? Just listen and enjoy, lah."

Part Five

Betrayal

29

I will make my peace the moment I reach Singapore, I promise. The flight crew are already walking down the aisle, checking safety belts, as the plane prepares for descent. Despite myself, eagerness rises as I press my face against the window trying to see what's below the clouds. There's another half hour of flying to go but I'm already imagining the island coming into view, a nexus of luminance against the dark sky, a spider's web of shimmering jewels. Soon, very soon, the lights of the apartment blocks along the coast will come into view, then the numerous ships and vessels crowding her harbour and hugging her eastern coastline, the iridescence of streetlamps and buildings growing brighter and brighter as the plane glides down. Soon, very soon, I'll land once again on the little fart that was ejected out of Malaysia's butt. It's a familiar, sick joke, I know, but it amuses me to pull down the self-importance of this so-called Renaissance city that I've read so much about in recent weeks.

I've been back only twice – just a stopover for a day or two on my way to somewhere else – but this time, my stay will be a whole two months and in the home of Ah-ku and Kit to boot. I am, and I am not, looking forward to it. What will we talk about in the days ahead, Ah-ku and I? Now that she's old and has mellowed, she needs me more than I need her, and I can't bear it. It makes me miserable.

I don't feel daughterly towards her; I don't know what to say to her – how to explain away the thirty years of not stepping into her home? I've already made plans to get out of the house every day to work in the library, to visit all my childhood haunts as part of the research for my work-in-progress, which I promised Jeev to complete by next year. And… and to attend one or two concerts by the Singapore Chinese Orchestra to listen to their principal flautist playing the dizi, but this will not be purely for research.

*

The shrill ringing of his phone stops Weng in the middle of teaching his master class. Damn. He's forgotten to change it to silent. He fishes it out of his trouser pocket and switches it off. Whoever it is will have to wait till his class is over. Two hours later when he switches it back on, there've been two more calls and a member of the Soka Association has left a message 'hospital…' he reads.

Soon his car is speeding down the expressway from Clementi to Changi, filtering to the outer lane where the cars seem to be moving faster. He has the sensation that he's driving uphill, blocked by the cars in front, their taillights blinking. Fragments of pipa music, Mrs Chang's laughter, and his various conversations with her whirl through his head. During their last conversation she was visibly excited, her eyes shining with little smiles in expectation of Ping's return.

– She's coming home. She'll be staying with me.

– I'll bring her to the association. We'll attend your concert, Ah Weng. She's a professor of music, you know, in America.

She'd gotten the women's groups in the Soka Association to help to raise funds for his ensemble at a time when not many had heard him play or knew anything about his music.

Changi Hospital is white and sprawling, crouched in a busy corner of Simei Estate, cars and buses clogging the road leading to its entrance. He had to wait several minutes for the other cars to move out before he could find parking.

30

"Kor, this came for you today."

His sister Kum handed him another letter from America. Weng took it into his bedroom, closed the door, and crushed the letter into a ball before stuffing it into the brown canvas bag with the other crushed and unopened letters, all bearing the stamp of Iowa, USA.

He'd punched the wall till his knuckles bled the day Ping left. After that all life had drained out of him. He'd crawled through each day much the same as the days before. If not for his studies at the Poly, his work in the noodle factory, and his nights in Ah Lau's coffee shop as Noodle Ting's secretary, he would've gone mad. The work kept him busy even though at times he hardly knew what was said or remembered what he did or ate. His heart was a dark cavern where the wind howled every night.

Each week, her letters came, and each week he crushed them into a ball, unread. What was the bloody point? She was gone. The day he returned from military training in Taiwan was the day she left Singapore. The loss of her was another blow, another death.

You must go, Weng, she said, when the army picked him for the three-month training course in Taiwan. It's your chance to get out of Singapore. A good opportunity grab it, she said. So many bloody things she said in those days, saying one thing and meaning another. But that hadn't mattered then because she loved him. She'd let his tongue taste the sour sweetness between her breasts, melt into wetness the valley between her thighs as she arched her back to meet his mouth.

On weekends he would drive his van farther upriver to a spot hidden behind thick bushes and creepers, and spread their mat under the raintrees. There they slept in each other's arms, his face buried in her hair, infused with the sweet-sour tang of lemon and sweat that drove him crazy. Not a whiff of love's impermanence had entered his head then. Hell, it wasn't love. Not for her. He could see that now. It was sex. She fucked him under the raintree. That was all. He turned from the window, and wrenched off his tee shirt.

*

Noodle Ting showed him the newspaper headlines: Immediate Removal of Illegal Structures At the Riverfront. Polluters to be Severely Punished. The government had announced a budget of several millions to clean up the foul-smelling waterway.

"Clean up the river for us? My arse!" Noodle Ting swore and picked up the phone. "Allo? Ya, ya, We'll be there tonight. Those bastards didn't waste time. They will revoke my licence if I don't move! All squatters will be evicted. Come on, Weng! An avalanche is on the way!"

Weng threw himself into the work of writing petitions and appeals on behalf of his former neighbours in Kampong Squatters, work that he had started when his father was still alive. Sometimes he skipped classes. It couldn't be helped. He had to go to Ah Lau's coffee shop. Every night, men gathered in the shop angrily waving the letters and eviction notices written in the four official languages – English, Chinese, Malay and Tamil – none of which the hawkers could read. Fluent in Teochew, Hokkien and Cantonese, none of them were literate in written Chinese.

"All them squiggles look like pig's intestines." Lau Pang handed Weng the pink notice from the Urban Renewal Department. "Ah Weng, what does it say?"

He stayed up till the early hours typing letters of appeal. Armed with a book that taught him how to write in the jargon of civil servants, his polite missives to the government agencies were peppered with phrases like: Dear sir/madam… With reference to the above mentioned… in lieu of… and regarding the aforesaid which… at the afore-mentioned date. His letters often elicited an official reply or extracted an extension of stay for a hawker's stall or squatter's family. Word soon spread, and people came to look for him in the noodle factory and coffee shop. Perhaps it was because of this that he, and not Mr Lee, was asked to read out Chairman Toh's speech when the latter had a sore throat on the night when more than five hundred gathered in front of the coffee shop.

He had never made a speech before. His audience were his former neighbours and his elders. They knew his father, mother and stepmother. Many had attended his sister's wedding. These men were the uncles he knew from childhood, the fathers and relatives of his friends, part of the extended family and community of folks on the riverfront. He was part of them, and they were part of him. Unlike Ping who'd removed herself to live with those in the gated houses in Juniper Garden, who played badminton with the man whose family owned the land and bumboats and warehouses on the river. He thought of his father's listless figure crouched among the pots of wilted chilli plants. A cold anger gripped him. He crushed the speech in his hand, and spoke from his heart.

"Uncles, do you know why Chairman Toh's throat is sore?" he yelled in Hokkien.

"Too much coffee, lor!" the men laughed.

"No, uncles. It's too much change. Change has grabbed Chairman Toh's throat and choked him dry! Like all of you here. You are choked. Right or not? Choked with anger. Choked with frustration. You shout till your throats run dry, but no government officer hears you. Right or not, Uncles?"

"Right, Ah Weng! Go on, go on!"

"Let me tell you. Change has jumped out at us. From the government! From the newspapers, radio and TV! Look at these official notices. Ya, hold them up, Uncle Pang!"

He waved the pink form that Uncle Pang shoved into his hand.

"Such notices make our coffee bitter. We who were born on the river have lived here all our lives. Some of you for generations. We're the river people. We work here, live here, and hope to die here. But today, this is not allowed. We have to move out. Last year, they evicted my family. Now, they're evicting you. The government people say we have turned this river into a rubbish dump. It's an open sewer. A national disgrace. They want to clean it up. Clear us out as if we're part of the rubbish. The riffraff who pollute this river. Squatters! Polluters! They shout at us from their newspapers, their radios and television. Their officers blabber facts and figures in parliament. Forty-four thousand squatters. Two thousand and five hundred unlicensed hawkers work in unsanitary conditions. They mean you, Uncles. They mean us. We are the unclean! The unhygienic! But we should question these people.

Question number one. If we are unclean, why do they come to the river to eat our cheap hawker food? If we are unhygenic, why do they eat our chicken rice? Slurp up our fishball noodle soup? Wolf down plates of our char kway tiao? Question number two. Did any of them die after eating our food? Did their wives and children become ill? Did they fall sick because they ate fried kway tiao at our hawker stalls by the river? Half of this city comes to the Singapore River to eat our food every day. If we're so filthy, why aren't people ill after eating our hawker food? But these people will not answer our questions. Their newspapers will not even ask these questions. Their reporters write very impressive sounding words like all unlicencsed individuals operating in unsupervised and unsanitary conditions near the river must be moved out. And that means…?

"Us!"

"Louder! That means…"

"Us! Us!"

"How many of us?"

"All of us! All of us!"

They cheered and applauded him. "Ho-ah! Ho-ah! Excellent! Excellent!"

Noodle Ting was beaming with pride. Weng was just as surprised. Had all these months of listening to the men's anguish given him a voice? So excited was he over his extempore speech that he did not notice a man in their midst, quietly taking notes.

*

One evening when he was not required to attend meetings, he drove his van to the busiest part of the river where the bustle and racket were loud enough to drive out thoughts of Ping. Perched on a crate, he watched the coolies unloading a cargo of rice from the bumboats. Bent under the weight of three or four sacks, they thumped from gangplank to gangplank. Their grunts and cusses like music to his ears; their gruff voices were hard as grit.

"Hoi! Shit head! No eyes ah? I could've fallen in!"

"Fucking asshole! You were in my way!"

A young coolie had nudged another out of his way. The older man had almost lost his balance on the gangplank. Had he dropped the sacks of rice into the river, heaven forbid, not only would he be sacked on the spot, he would also be in debt for life! His load safe on shore now, the older man let fly his pent-up fury. A fistfight broke out. Hardjaws and hotheads swiftly gathered round the two men. Eviction orders and the loss of jobs and livelihoods had set tempers flaring at short fuse on the riverfront.

It was the same in Ah Lau's coffee shop the following night. Tempers were short, and men shouted to be heard.

"Three of my boats! All half complete. The wood not yet dry. How the hell am I to move? The bastards!" a boatbuilder thumped the table so hard, it set the cups rattling.

"The dogs took away my licence!" a man yelled from the back. "Is there no law on our side?"

Weng sat next to Mr Lee, the secretary of the Singapore River Villagers' Association, a worried frown on his brow.

"Listen! The government will give all hawkers a stall in the new markets," Mr Lee announced.

"Hoi, Old Lee! You think the government is giving us a stall? So good, meh? Give! My arse! We got to pay rent! Pay for water. Pay for light. Pay for rubbish removal. Pay for licence! Everything is pay and pay! They give with one hand, and take away with the other."

"The moment we move out of here, we pay and pay! Here on the river, we don't pay for utilities!"

"Hear, hear!"

The men thumped their fists on the coffee tables. Some even stood on their chairs.

"Don't worry, Ah Weng. These meetings are good," Mr Lee said. "Help people to say what they think. Help us to represent them better."

"Mr Lee. Mr Toh. Please help me," Mrs Tan, a washerwoman and a widow, sobbed. "Where can I go with my three children? I can't afford rent for a government flat."

"Chang Brothers closed their warehouse." Old Li the boat coolie was the next to speak. "I got no job. I need work. Any work. My children got to eat, Mr Lee."

Men crowded on the sidewalk, arms folded, as they listened to the chairman of the Singapore River Transport Workers' Union.

"It's time we petition City Hall and let the Prime Minister know our problems."

"A march! Organise a protest march!" someone shouted from the sidewalk.

"No! One step at a time. Write the petition first. Then march!"

"Who will write the petition?"

"Ah Weng!" Noodle Ting yelled. "Stand up, Ah Weng!"

*

After the meeting, he drove to the river even though it was very late. He parked his van near the footbridge and got out. He took the brown canvas bag with him and started to walk. It was very dark, but he was familiar with the path, which went past the boatyard and the twakows and bumboats tied up for the night. He walked quickly till he reached the dark grove of trees and bushes that fronted his father's old vegetable patch.

Two weeks ago, he had returned to harvest the pumpkins, and the police had warned him off. He wondered if there were any more pumpkins among the creepers. Unattended, the vegetable patch had turned to wasteland. As his eyes got used to the darkness, he was surprised to find the place fenced, and his former neighbours' huts deserted. He took a torch out of the canvas bag and shone it through the chain-link fence. The hut that was his home had a gleaming new padlock. The lock brought a smile to his face. His family had never locked their hut. He didn't know that the run-down hut was of such value to Chang Brothers Pte Ltd. He moved along the fence until he found the path that led to the river's edge. Overgrown grass and creepers made it difficult to find his way at times. Once or twice he stumbled and nearly lost his grip on the bag.

The breeze had dropped, and the dark trees looked forlorn. The warehouses across the river were empty husks. When the moon came up, he switched off his torch and stood for a moment in its pale silver light. Then following a bend of the river, he walked till he reached the small creek. A sliver of moon was swimming in it. Here, he had taught Ping to catch guppies and mudskippers. Here, he had played his flute, kissed and held her in his arms. Here, they had spent long afternoons under that raintree arching like a huge umbrella over the creek. His hand tightened its grip on the canvas bag. A sudden rising in the back of his throat was choking him. He didn't want to cry. It was over for him and Ping. Over. He dropped the canvas bag and stood still, very still. He thought of his mother. The night she'd disappeared into this river, and wiped the tears from his face. He would finish what he'd set out to do. He fished the last envelope out of his pocket, tore it into two, and wrapped the pieces round a rock. He flung the rock into the creek, and shattered the face of the moon. Then he squatted down with his bag and shook out the rest of the crushed and unopened envelopes. He worked rapidly, fearing he might change his mind. He flicked the lighter and held the flame to the papers. He threw in some dry leaves and twigs, and watched them burst into flames. A blinding incandescence. A shout! A crashing in the bushes behind him. He whirled round. A powerful flashlight blinded his eyes.

"Put out that bloody fire!" Their torches on him, the two policemen beat the flames down with a branch.

"Why are you here ?" They demanded to see his identity card.

With a sinking heart, he searched his pockets. "I… I've left my ID at home."

One man kept the torch on his face while the other searched his canvas bag.

"Come back to the station with us."

*

Pak! The hard palm slammed into his cheek.

– *Are you a Communist?*

– *No.*

– *Answer: No, sir!*

– *No, sir.*

– *Are you working for the Communists?*

– *You asked me that yesterday.*

The hard hand slammed his other cheek.

– *What were you doing in the coffee shop all those nights? Don't try to lie. We have records of all meetings in the coffee shop.*

– *I was listening to people. Is it wrong to listen?*

The pencil case whacked his face, just missing his right eye. Dribbling spit and blood, he wiped them off with the back of his hand. His throat hurt. A glass of water sat on the table out of the reach of his parched mouth. The room was freezing cold. He was shivering on the block of ice in his underpants. The eyes of the man in a thick, black, woollen sweater stared hard at him. The implacable eyes grew larger and darker as the man pressed him for an answer. Suddenly the room was filled with eyes, and mouths shouting, *Liar! Liar! Liar!*

"No! No! No!"

"Ah Weng, Ah Weng, wake up. It's all right, my son, it's all right. You're home. You're safe. Thank the Lord Buddha, you're safe at home."

He opened his eyes, his ears ringing as if there had been an explosion near his head. He felt his stepmother's hand on his chest rubbing Vicks on him, felt the rising heat of the balm entering his body, and allowed himself to savour the sensation of flesh on flesh. The palm of his stepmother's hand was rough, a washerwoman's hand that had slapped him and held him when he was a child. Her face looking down at him was anxious. It pained him to see the crow's feet around her eyes. Her hair had grown white. He sat up.

"Will you eat something now?" she asked.

He started to eat the rice porridge she had brought while she sat on the chair next to his bed, her rough wrinkled hands on her lap. These days, his stepmother was less loud, less garrulous, less demanding. She'd made a great effort to accommodate his fluctuating moods. He turned to face the wall, ashamed of his sudden urge to cry; he cried so easily these days. It was as if he was trying to make up for all those dry months of steeling himself when he had to pit his hardness against the grey walls of his cell and the men who interrogated him.

He got out of bed and went into the living room. The same television sat on the same low table as before, next to the same brown sofa and the low shelf for shoes. The furniture had not changed, yet the apartment felt strangely unfamiliar as though he was a new tenant. A hush had settled in the flat. Kum and Leng had already left for work, and his stepmother was washing up at the kitchen sink. He walked through the tiny kitchen to use the bathroom and toilet. He showered three to four times a day now; the jets of cold water calmed him. He liked the privacy inside the bathroom, something denied him in the detention centre. There, he had to strip, shower, and empty his bowels, all done with a guard watching him. He remembered the kind Malay guard who had averted his eyes while he was showering, but his partner, the young Chinese bloke had stared stone-faced at his flaccid penis.

Put things behind you and look ahead, Noodle Ting had advised. He could resume his studies at the Poly next year, he thought. But he had no wish to do anything or go anywhere. Since coming home, he had remained indoors. Strangers made him fearful and nervous.

Shame, anger and self-loathing filled him. He felt paralysed. From the kitchen came the sound of running water from the tap. It cheered him to hear that. Reminded him of the sound of the river. Water is movement and freedom, seeping into the earth, infiltrating the cracks and crannies in the bedrock, turning into torrential streams that rush down mountains to flood the plains. His memories of the river when he was in solitary had given him strength. He recalled the countless times he had jumped into its cool dark waters with friends, fished in its creeks or just sat on its banks with Ping to watch the bumboats in the evening.

The demons in that detention centre had not overwhelmed him. With each passing day his spirit was growing stronger. His hand reached for his bamboo flute. He placed it carefully across his chest like an amulet to ward off evil, and shut his eyes, softly humming a song his father used to sing:

'Drop by drop, raindrops gather in a ditch;
Drop by drop, the ditch becomes a creek;
The creek becomes a stream, the stream becomes a river;
The river joins the sea; the sun shines on the sea,
The sea becomes a cloud, the cloud turns into rain;
Drop by drop, raindrops gather a ditch; drop by drop the ditch becomes…'

"How's he, Chong Soh?"

"He's sleeping now. He's had a nightmare."

His stepmother and Ah Por, the faith healer, came into his room, speaking in low, hushed voices so as not to wake him. He kept his eyes closed, faking sleep. They were at it again. He must be patient; they meant no harm.

"Sleeping is good, Chong Soh. Let him sleep but give me one of his shirts."

"Take this. He wore this for three days and slept in it too."

"Good. I'll use it. Give me something else; something he treasures."

"His flute. He used to play it with his Pa."

"Good. His spirit will come back faster when it remembers his flute. We can start now. Please light the incense and joss sticks."

There were just two of them today. On previous occasions – was it last week or last month? His sense of time was vague, merging past and present, day and night. On a previous occasion, a blur of faces had peered down at him. His stepmother and sisters were wailing and calling his name as though he were dead.

Ah Por began to sing softly. "Hoi-loi! Hoi-loi, come home, come home, my child. O wandering child. Hoi-loi to your Ma. Hoi-loi to your grieving Ma and family."

The old woman's cracked voice rose and fell like ocean waves, the rhythm and tempo of her singing making him feel light and sleepy.

"Don't cry, Ah Weng's mother,' he heard Ah Por's voice. "His spirit will return. Let him rest now. Let him sleep."

"My poor boy. He was just trying to help others."

"The government says white is black or black is white, who are we to argue? They say they're Communists. What can you do?"

"Ah Por, I know. People like us. We must keep our mouths shut and our heads down. The government says move, we must move. Take this flat. If not for me, Ah Weng's father would've been jailed. He didn't want to move. It's only because I fought him that we have this flat today."

"This flat sent Pa to his grave!"

"Ah Weng!"

"Get out! Get out!"

Anderson, Cavenagh, Elgin, Coleman, Read, Ord, Clemenceau. He recalled each bridge by its English name as he played his imaginary flute alone in his cell. His mind roamed the backlanes and alleyways in Telok Ayer, Pulau Saigon, Boat Quay, Clarke Quay, Robertson Quay, Alkaff Quay going as far as Kim Seng Bridge. He knew the nameless footbridges like old pals, the wooden planks and coconut trunks thrown across little streams and ditches. He crawled into nooks and recesses, wading into ditch and brook with her. Where hadn't he brought her? He had kissed her everywhere and loved her by the brook behind the Honolulu creepers and wild bushes where the crows nested at night. The pain in his chest ached. His throat felt dry as if a sticky lump of rice was stuck in it. It was the Changs who had had him prosecuted for trespassing on their land. The land where his family had lived for all those years. Where is justice?

"This came for you a while ago. Another letter from America."

A cold fury seized him. He ripped open the envelope in front of his stepmother, and tore up the letter.

31

Ping remembered her first winter in America as the winter of nosebleeds and desolation. The University of Iowa was buried under a thick blanket of snow. People retreated into their houses. The streets were deserted, and darkness fell in the afternoon. The city was white under a bleak sky, heavy with clouds. Snowdrifts were everywhere, and icy blasts chilled her to the bone. So desolate and alone, she longed for death every day. Her nostrils were clogged with crusts of dried blood, which she dared not pry loose lest she bled again. Breathing was an effort in the cold, dry air. The arctic winds mauled her cracked lips that no balm seemed able to heal. Her head felt heavy and dull under the thick woollen cap and scarf that covered her neck and ears. She wore several layers under her heavy coat, and wound a second scarf around her neck, but still she felt the ice-cold sharp teeth that bit her chapped skin. Her gloved hands were stiff, and her toes were frozen. She rubbed her hands and stamped her feet, and cursed the education agency in Singapore that had hurriedly arranged for her to come to the US. It should go to hell for enrolling her in a university in the middle of this frozen wasteland. Iowa City was dead in winter, hemmed in by miles of snow-covered emptiness under a leaden sky that pressed down upon her head. Most days, she felt she couldn't face the icy grit outside, and stayed indoors in the Mayflower Hall.

She stood at the window of her room, staring through the glass pane at the white field across the road. Six mad American boys wearing nothing but tee shirts and shorts had dashed out of the hall to chase a ball in the snow. Then just as quickly as they had dashed out, they ran back into the hall. Snow had begun to fall, the day growing dark as night although it was just three o'clock in the afternoon. She sat down at her desk, took out her journal and wrote: Four walls and a window. A room in a university dorm is the loneliest place on earth. Lonelier than a windowless cubicle in Chinatown.

But the Mayflower was well-heated and its recreation rooms downstairs were packed with loud, cheerful American students. The girls stopped their chatter whenever she approached. 'Hi, how're ya do'in?' they said. 'Have a nice day!' They smiled and turned away. An invisible wall separated her from them, a wall she could not scale in her current state of self-loathing. She did not know she was grieving. What had she done?

Her shoulders sagged. She moved with the lethargy of an old woman weighed down by a thick waterlogged quilt. The simplest of tasks proved insurmountable at times. Just getting out of bed in the morning, and pulling on her socks and sweaters required a Herculean effort.

The university's doctor diagnosed mild depression, and referred her to the college counsellor. But what could she say to the white American woman with the cherry red lips and bright smile? Regret was too late. Much too late. Why had she agreed to it? The Catholic nuns in the convent school had indoctrinated her well. Her guilt sat like a heavy millstone on her chest. She had committed a mortal sin, and Hell was what she deserved. She struggled through each day, and wrote to Weng week after dreary week, hoping for a reply. She longed for a card from him. Even a 'hello' would have sufficed.

Nothing came in the post. Not a word from Weng.

She wrote brief, cheerful letters home to Ah-ku, knowing that Uncle Chang would be the one to read and translate them for her.

Each week she dutifully dropped two letters into the mailbox, one for Ah-ku and one for Weng. They sank like rocks into the grey waters of the Iowa River.

– *After all we've done for you, do you want to bring shame to Uncle? Do you want to see his name splashed all over the papers because of you and that noodle boy?*

She struggled into her boots, lacing them up tightly, and pulled on another woollen sweater; then came the thick jacket lined with fleece. She put on her thick leather gloves and wrapped a woollen scarf around her neck, left the room and closed the door only to find out that she had to pull off a glove so she could reach into the pocket of her thick jacket for the key to lock the door. By the time she finished all these daily operations, she was sweating under the layers of misery and anger.

– *That noodle boy is up to no good in that night school. You think he's really studying? That school is run by Communists.*

Weng's not a Communist!

– *You can say what you like. But if you get mixed up with him... if the police find out that you're with him, you can forget about the certificate of suitability for university.*

– *It's your future. I don't care what you do with it. If you want to sell noodles all your life, go ahead. But don't you dare mess up your Uncle's life. After all we've done for you!*

She stood on the bridge for a long time, staring into the grey icy water. The Iowa River was nothing like the river she had left. The few ducks that did not make the journey south to warmer climes huddled by its banks, lonely and forlorn. Plagued by cold sores and nosebleeds, she struggled to shut out Ah-ku's hard voice. All for a certificate! But no such certificates were required in America simply to go to University. This was a free country; Americans could say and do what they wanted. They could protest against their government; they could even march for peace and free love.

But even so her heart ached for the bright lights of Chinatown, and the hawkers' stalls in Pagoda Street. Why didn't Weng write to her? One afternoon, she went to the library as usual – the only alternative to her dreary room. She took the lift to the top floor and sat at a table near the radiator. There she chanced upon a copy of a women's magazine. Someone must have left it there, for such magazines were not part of the library's collection. Idly, she flipped through the gaudy pages filled with girls in bikinis, and suddenly felt compelled to read on:

"The embryo in the first month is visible as a tiny piece of tissue. In the second month, the foetus is about two centimetres long. The face is formed. Limbs are partially formed. At about eight centimetres in the third month, the sex of the foetus can be distinguished. Limbs, fingers, toes and ears are fully formed. Nails begin to app–"

Her head reeled. The odour of stainless steel and disinfectant threatened to overpower her senses. Carefully, she tucked the magazine under her thick jacket and took the lift down. She remembered the saccharine music in the lift of the private clinic in the Hamden Park medical centre. The doctor's room was stylishly furnished in black leather and chrome, and smelled of mouthwash. She'd sat, stiff and silent, next to Ah-ku who was doing all the talking. The doctor looked professorial with gold-rimmed glasses perched on his nose, a yellow bowtie at his neck and black suspenders. His Cantonese was impeccable, but he switched to English when he turned to her. He was soft-spoken and matter-of-fact.

"It's a simple procedure; there're rarely any long-term side effects. You'll be under sedation, of course. You won't feel any pain. After it's over, we'll keep you here for observation. Just for half a day to make sure you're all right. An overnight stay is usually not necessary. If everything's fine, you can go home on the same day, and we'll give you some painkillers to take home with you."

She had sat with her hands on her lap, mute, unable to ask him any questions. Her mind had shut itself against further knowledge of the thing he was going to do.

– Why hadn't she cried out? Run away?

Back in her room in Mayflower, she switched on the study lamp, placed the magazine on her desk and pulled off her gloves, scarf and jacket. Next came the sweaters; one by one, she pulled them over her head and flung them on the back of the chair. She went to the bathroom and washed her face.

Ah-ku had heard her retching in the bathroom back in Juniper Garden, and she had had to tell her. She remembered the pallor on Ah-ku's face, and then her hoarse whisper:

– *Is it Uncle's?*

Too shocked to reply and weak at the knees, she had rushed into the bathroom and retched again.

– *Is it?* Ah-ku shook her shoulder.

She shook her head.

– *Then whose?*

She refused to answer.

– *You common roadside trash! I should've left you in the coffee shop with Kim Poh.*

She was seventeen, and a part of her agreed.

She turned on the tap and splashed more icy water on her face again and again. Then she sat down at her desk and opened the magazine with the smiling girl in the red bikini on the front cover. She found the page with the article, and forced herself to read.

"…a general or local anaesthesia is given to the mother. Her cervix is dilated, and a suction curette, a hollow tube with a sharp tip, is inserted into the womb…"

She felt nauseous. Her stomach heaved.

How could she have done that? How could she? Without telling him? Without talking to Weng?

Empty-eyed, she lay on the bed, staring up at the ceiling as fragments of a poem by Seamus Heaney came to her.

"An illegitimate spawning…

…a minnow with hooks

Tearing her open"

She imagined the young mother lowering her newborn, pink

and bloody, into the dark icy waters, its limbs still kicking as the girl-mother held it down till its mewling cries, like a kitten's, ceased.

Weng, Weng, her heart called out to him. Forgive… forgive m– but the word was stuck in her throat.

That night, she slashed her wrists.

Part Six

Spring Comes to Tea Mountain

32

When spring came, she began to take long solitary walks once again. The snow had melted and the ground was wet. The air was still very cold but not freezing. The lawns around campus were bathed in a pale green light as a weak sun shone on the grass growing between patches of melting snow. Passing the auditorium, a poster caught her attention. Master pipa player, Professor Chen Ma Xian from the University of California, Berkeley, was giving a talk at that very moment. She hurried inside and took the first empty seat she saw in the front row.

"Our body is in the concert hall now, but our mind, ahhh, our beautiful mind, it is wandering among the trees and mountain streams, walking, walking while we're here, plucking, plucking our pipa strings. That's how you should play. Play the pipa as if you're dreaming music or is it the music dreaming you, yes?"

The man on the stage laughed, and caught her startled look.

"Ahh, miss who has just come in. Huan yin, huan yin. Welcome, welcome." He was glad to see a fellow Chinese, he said. "You play pipa?"

She nodded and shrank into her seat, wishing she hadn't been so impulsive. Except for two Chinese women, the audience was white and American. She wouldn't have come in by that door if she knew it led to the front rows. She hadn't played the pipa for months, hadn't had the heart to touch it. But to get up and leave now would be bad form. Professor Chen held up his hand, and showed the audience his acrylic fingernails.

"In life and in music, we adapt to change, yes? Ahh, great big change. Revolutionary change in China. In the old days, pipa players used fingernails. Like this. Today, we wear acrylic nails. Like these. Acrylic nails changed our playing. Pipa strings also changed from silk strings to gang xian or metallic strings. This changed the tonal colours of the pipa. Listen carefully. Can you hear the difference?"

He played a few notes on the pipa with metallic strings. Ping sat up, mesmerised by the new sound. It had been a long time since she last heard such beautiful notes from the pipa. Not since Uncle Chong Suk's death.

"Pipa with gang xian has a brighter tonal palette. Listen again." Professor Chen played the pipa with silk strings. "You hear it? What's the difference?"

"The pipa with silk strings has more resonance."

The words had popped out before she realised that she'd spoken.

"Yes, Miss. Yes, yes, you in the front row. You said that? Please. Please come on stage. Come. Come. You made a very good point. Come. Come up please."

She felt her blood rushing to her face. She went up to the stage, and he handed her his pipa. "Qing. Please. Please play a few notes for us." He spoke in Mandarin.

Too shocked to refuse, she played the opening bar of a folksong. He recognised it at once, and proceeded to play the same song on the other pipa with the metallic strings. His notes had such a clarity and purity of tone and pitch that she was devastated. Her opening bar was like a string of mismatched stones; his was a string of jade and pearls.

"Music comes out of the silence in us. Seek the silence inside your heart and your music will flow. Please close your eyes and breathe in. Slowly, slowly… breathing in… breathing out. One, two, three, four, five. Listen to your breath. Listen with your inner ear. Breathing in. Breathing out."

He plucked a string on his pipa, and gestured to her to do the same. She was dismayed and wanted to leave the stage. She didn't want to be humiliated again. He was putting her on show. But his eyes held her and would not let her leave. He struck another note on his pipa, looked up at her and smiled.

"Play," he whispered. "Don't fear. Please sit down." He pointed to the chair beside him, determined not to let her leave the stage and wallow in self-pity after her miserable showing. He played a few bars, and looked at her expectantly. His eyes, warm and kindly, winked from under his dark bushy brows.

"Play. Try," he said.

"You can do it." A woman in the front row smiled up at her. A few people clapped. Her resistance crumbling, she sat down with his pipa, held it upright on her lap, and composed herself.

Uncle Chong Suk was dead. Weng was gone. What had she to fear if she played badly now?

She took a deep breath and struck the strings and plunged in, recklessly striking a series of chords with a flourish. The audience burst into applause. Professor Chen grinned at her. He picked up from where she stopped, and played a new bar of notes on his pipa with the gang xian or metallic strings. Clean, strong notes which she answered with a series of shrill birdcalls on the pipa with silk strings. His face breaking into a broad grin now, he responded with a new phrasing. She threw in two bars in rapid succession that sent ripples across the stage. This drew another big smile and a nod from him. His keen eyes urged her on. He added another new bar of notes to her ripples. They carried on in this exhilarating manner for some minutes until a certain rhythm was established between them, and she forgot she was on stage. She forgot the audience. She forgot the cold outside. She forgot her pain.

New sounds were gathering in her head like birds suddenly freed from their cages. She grew bold. She started to improvise, altering a phrase here, adding a note there to the familiar tune he was playing, then a series of notes that added a splash of colour and an undertone of playfulness to his musical replies as back and forth, they hit their pipas in a game of musical ping pong. Their musical sparring delighted the audience.

"Bravo! Bravo!" They applauded again and again.

"Stand up, Miss, and take a bow. They're applauding your playing and your courage." He took her hand and made her take a bow with him whereupon she burst into tears.

"I'm sorry, Professor Chen. I… I…"

"No need sorry. I saw hunger in your eyes. I know hunger and longing. I was starved in China during the Cultural Revolution. No pipa. No music. No life. Just the walking dead inside my camp."

He held up his hand. The lights dimmed. Silence descended on the audience. His pipa, steady and still, his fingers curled around its swan neck, then with a sudden flick of wrist, several chords lit up the auditorium like an incandescent flame. And then, there was nothing. A collective indrawn breath in the audience as the sound faded till all that was left was a palpable, expectant silence.

The lights came up. A thunderous applause rang out. In that instant, her life changed. She decided to leave Iowa City and join Professor Chen in Berkeley.

33

"Exceptions? Of course we make exceptions! If we don't, half of Berkeley would be empty. Look at the number of oddballs in this department, yours truly included."

A quick bow and he was up like a jack-in-the-box with a laugh loud enough to wake the dead.

"So! What took you so long to come? Professor Chen told me about you last semester. Great guy, isn't he?"

Tall and lanky, his light brown eyes were twinkling. Perched on his hawk-like nose was a pair of wire-framed glasses with one of its legs held by a safety pin. His curly brown hair was pulled back in a ponytail, and tied with a bright pink ribbon. He was wearing a pale pink and white floral shirt, candy pink jeans and white loafers. In Singapore, men did not dress like this unless they were pondans, she thought, squirming at her own use of the derogatory Malay word for gay men. The sign on his door said: *Peter Rajeev Acharya – Not Pete, for pete's sake! And not Jeeves, but Jeev.*

"Never maul an artist's name. A name is like a music note. It has a definite sound value. If it's two beats, give it two beats. Like Peter. Not Pete for pete's sake."

"Professor Acharya…"

"No, no, no." He flapped his long arms like a frantic stork. "See this sign? Read it. Jeev. Repeat after me. Jeev."

"Jeev."

"That's better. I see a sheepish smile and questions in your eyes. I know. I know. You're asking yourself. Hmmm... why this collocation of names? I'm schizo. See? This is America. Everyone has to have some kind of neurosis. You're nobody if you don't have one. So I'm a schizo and I play the cello. See? It rhymes. That's going on my next tee shirt. Now where were we? As I was saying, here in Berkeley, we celebrate talent and music. Scholars, ethno-musicologists, performers, composers, you name them; we welcome them. We've a large group of Bay Area musicians who provide specialised instruction. Our faculty specialises in European, African, Latin American, Middle Eastern and Asian traditions. Feel free to explore. Explore, experiment, excogitate and improvise. That's our motto."

He was unlike anyone she had met. She enrolled in the ethno music department, taking classes in music theory, music history, and the history of Western and Eastern music, as well as ethnomusicology and composition. Her focus was the pipa. She was hungry, and signed up for two classes on composition in the first semester alone. By the second semester, she had started to experiment with different sounds and instruments in relation to the pipa. Every music student in Berkeley was into experimentation. It was a challenging place to be. There was so much to learn. It left her no time for reflection or self-pity.

"Juxtapose. Counterpoint. Concord. Discord. Mix and harmonise. Practise. Practise. Practise."

She was lucky to get Professor Chen Ma Xian as her specialist instructor and mentor. He had been instrumental in getting her a place here. She lied to Ah-ku and Uncle Chang about the courses she was taking in the new university, in case they stopped sending her money.

That first summer in Berkeley, warmth started to creep back into her bones. For the first time, she noticed that the American sky arcing over the campus was vast and wide compared to the smallness of the Singapore horizons. Buoyed by the warmth of the Californian sun and the expansive atmosphere in Berkeley, something inside her began to thaw. She continued to write to Weng, but she no longer worried herself sick waiting for a reply. She knew none would arrive.

She talked to Sandy, her college counsellor, once a week and hurled herself headlong into everything to do with music to make up for lost time. Chen Ma Xian counselled patience, but his advice fell on deaf ears. He was years older, and she was young and ignorant. She read voraciously in the library, and led an intense albeit solitary life. All week, she attended lectures and practised for long hours in the music studio in the Asian Music Department. On summer evenings, she ventured outdoors with Uncle Chong Suk's pipa, and played it in a quiet nook beside a small stream in the gardens, far from the crowds and those scary types who sported dreadlocks, torn jeans and tie-dyed tees.

She saw Professor Acharya – no, Jeev – striding across the campus as though he wanted to fly, not run. The man was like a grasshopper. He had smashed her stereotypes of Indian men, university professors and cello players. She had thought cello players were paunchy middle-aged men with ponderous souls. This one was tall, lanky and wacky, and several times a day, she caught herself looking out for him on campus.

She revelled in the Californian sunshine. One weekend, she plucked up courage and took the bus into the centre of San Francisco, amazed by the tempo and music she found in its streets. The quick clicks of heels on pavement, the shouts of the hotdog vendors, the singing and fiddling of buskers, the clink of coins that passers-by threw into their jam jars and tin mugs excited her. The deep bass of the African-American singers and the mellifluous baying of saxophones in Mission cafes drew her for the first time to jazz and blues. The music was new to her. She realised that she'd been living in a music ghetto in Pagoda Street where the only offerings were from Hong Kong, Taiwan and China. American pop, jazz and blues that played over the radio and in the record shops back home had largely passed her by. Now on weekends, she stood mesmerised in Mission cafés and street corners as strong winds from the Pacific Ocean blasted open her eardrums with the strange new sounds of this American city. San Francisco had a beat and rhythm that drew her close, helping her to forget.

At first, she worried about her safety among the unkempt men with long hair and dreadlocks panhandling in street corners, trailed by half-starved dogs. Back home in Singapore, large posters in public places like the post offices had warned the public against such men with long hair. Foreign singers, musicians and tourists with unkempt looks were denied entry into the country. But over here in San Francisco, a bearded guy in a dirty saffron tee and torn jeans had given her a warm smile and a white daisy. She'd accepted his flower and laughed at her own irrational fears.

Another weekend, overcome by homesickness, she took the bus to San Francisco's Chinatown. Wandering into a park, she stumbled upon a plaque put up by the Chinese-American community to commemorate Courage in the Face of Humiliation, her guide book said:

"Do they think we Chinese are not made of flesh and blood? That we don't have souls? Should we allow ourselves to be treated like dumb animals and cargo? If China should become strong someday, I will have a big stone tablet erected at each Chinese trading port to commemorate how America had kept us in captivity. But I will have these words 'Please enter' carved on it to show the world that in spite of the unkind treatment accorded us by Americans, we Chinese treat others more generously. Such a response is far superior to killing or retaliating in kind."

Stirring words from a Chinese schoolteacher mistreated by US Immigration in 1903. She sat down on a bench in the shadow of Mai Zhouyi's courage, amazed at the distance the Chinese had travelled in America, and vowed she too would work hard and move forward.

She returned to the same spot every Saturday, and brought her pipa. Soon a group gathered whenever she played, drawn by the music of Southern China. A Dream of Red Mansion brought tears to some grey-haired men and women, who must have suffered like Mai Zhouyi but now sat sipping their lattes and cappuccinos on the sidewalks while elsewhere their American-born daughters, togged out in short leather skirts, rock 'n' rolled around town with their American boyfriends. Free and unconfined. She wanted to be like those daughters.

Later, she met a student from China who had come to the US to study.

"I like here. I not go back to China after my studies here," Miss Li Hoong told her in heavily accented English. "My husband is Chinese Army man. We divorced. I couldn't take it. Cannot overcome restrictions from Chinese culture. When I spik Chinese, I get forced back into old ways of tinking. Very limiting. Now I spik English. I date black men. You want to meet black man? I introduce to you."

Ping laughed to hide her unease. She'd never dated dark-skinned men before, and had to question her attitudes to race now. She remembered her own discrimination in Pagoda Street. Weng was the only one who never called her anything but Ping. She missed him.

*

"Darling, in Berkeley, you're free to re-invent yourself. No more bras!"

Nancy Miller-Lim of Chinese-German-Jewish descent flung her bra across their room and out of the window. Ping was flabbergasted, but Nancy laughed.

"Where were you in the sixties? Women burnt their bras in this country. We were bold. We were strong. We stood up as women. Didn't you know?"

Ping remembered some of her classmates singing 'I Am Woman', which had been a number one hit on Radio Singapore but it was nothing more than a pop song to them. The girls in her dorm here walked around braless and were practically naked at times. Unused to seeing so much flesh, she averted her eyes. Her dorm mates teased her mercilessly, but she refused to go braless to class.

Beneath their seeming flippancy, however, there was seriousness and passion. Nancy and her friends often stayed up late into the night arguing politics and philosophy. They questioned everything – the politics of music, dictatorial conductors in orchestras, university funding of questionable research, their Congressmen's voting record, their nation's fucked-up foreign policies, and the post-Vietnam War politics in Washington. She felt terribly out of her depth and dreaded going to those classes where she was the only Asian student. She was scared stiff of saying something inane that might be greeted by polite silence or a pained smile. She was not used to speaking up in class. Berkeley's students and faculty were justifiably proud that they had fought for free speech.

"The Free Speech Movement began right here. In Sproul Plaza," Jeev told her, his lanky frame sprawled on the steps beside her. She remained silent. Her heart was racing too fast for her to think of anything to say in response. "Come and have coffee sometime," he rushed off without waiting for her reply.

All that day, she floated in and out of the music department, humming… he remembers me… he remembers me… a nobody.

Stop acting like a stupid, self-effacing Asian fool, she scolded herself, and blamed Singapore's education system. Her years in school hadn't prepared her for debate and discussion. Fiddlesticks! Miss Vaithilingam's strident voice roared in her head. Be ready to take your place in the world, girls. Then came the next image – Ah-ku striding down Pagoda Street with a bamboo pole to hammer on the door of the flea-in-the-dog's-rear. No, it wasn't the education system – she had had strong role models. She looked up at the clear, blue Californian sky and shook her head. No debate and confrontation for her; it wasn't her style. But that afternoon, in class, her hand suddenly shot up of its own volition.

"Excuse me, Professor Murphy. It's wrong what you've just said." She could hear her blood rushing to her head, feel the hot flush spreading on her face. "The… er… the pipa is the queen of strings in the history of music. Since ancient times in China, empresses and courtesans, scholars in court, generals in war, and beggars in the street have played the pipa. High and low, the pipa reached every level of Chinese society. Can… can you say the same for the pianoforte in European society?"

Silence. Professor Murphy stared at her, and then he smiled. The cheers and thumbs-up from her classmates, and the grin on Professor Murphy's face astounded her. That afternoon, Jeev plonked down beside her again on the steps in Sproul Plaza.

"Just heard you gave ole' Murphy some cud to chew."

"I didn't mean to be rude."

"Na-ah, you weren't rude. You spoke your mind. That's what you should do. Are you enjoying his class?"

"His music history class is all about Europe. Not a word about Asia."

"Are you waving the Asian flag?"

One thing led to another, and another, and another.

Ahhhhhhh! She was screaming her head off on Halloween night when Jeev's car hit a hundred and sixty on the freeway. She clung to her seat until the car stopped.

Candle-lit shadows danced on the walls in the basement of his friend's house. Faces, with eyes outlined with kohl, called out greetings.

"Jeev! Who have you brought?"

A black girl dressed in black, strumming a guitar in the corner, put down her instrument and walked over. Her partner, a young white man wielding a stick, was hitting water-filled bottles to make music. And someone swaying in the shadows was beating a hypnotic rhythm on an African drum. Incense and cigarette smoke filled the room crowded with shadows.

"Hi. You're from Singapore?"

"Yeah," she said, trying out her newly acquired American drawl.

"Whash it like living under the commies?" a young man asked.

"We're not Communist."

"Hey, isn't China under the commies?"

"But I'm not from China."

"You bloody dimwit! She's from a tiny island called Singapore!" Jeev blasted the guy's ear.

"Where the hell is it, man?"

"South from Nam! Our guys went there for R & R during the war!"

"Oh, man! You're from R & R land!"

"What're you into?" Another guy asked her.

"The pipa."

"It's some kind of sitar? I'm into the sitar. Mind blowin'…"

"Shove it, Rob. She and I gotta go and do our thing." Jeev pulled her on to the dance floor.

"Does the pipa help to define you as Chinese?"

"Does the sitar define you as Indian?"

"Touché !" He planted a kiss on her lips.

All week, she was ridiculously, unbelievably, undeservedly happy, and relieved that he wasn't teaching her. They met every weekend. The next summer, he took her camping in Yosemite Park. Then he vanished at the end of the semester. She called his office again and again.

"No. No message," the girl said. She suspected that the girl was lying. She recalled Millionaire, the old geezer who had walked out on Ah-ku. *Damn if she'd let the same thing happen to her!*

The next weekend, she went to the flea market with Nancy and bought herself a black leather skirt and black leather boots. That night, she hung out at Mike's Place. From then on, all winter, she rocked and jived and twisted 'till she was half dead in that airless basement. To hell with Peter Rajeev Acharya! Nancy took her to other basements in other places. Under Nancy's tutelage, she coloured her hair yellow, sniffed, smoked and inhaled, and learned to strum her pipa like a guitar. Hey man, a new sound. New effects. Explore. Experiment. And why not? Jeev had encouraged her to be bold. She would show him what bold is. She tried out different playing styles, different drinks and different smokes till the contents of her stomach splattered all over Nancy's bed one night.

"Shite, Ping! I just changed those damn sheets!"

"SHUT UP! Bitch!"

Nancy left her sprawled on her belly on the floor. The streaks of yellow and green on brown staining the carpet were disgusting colours of failure. Failure. Such a beautiful word, she thought. Failure. And started to giggle. Failure. Failure. Failure. Singaporeans cannot fail. Achieve, we must achieve. She couldn't stop giggling. Dog's vomit, she threw up again. She gazed thoughtfully at the mess, lost among its myriad forms and shadows. She was exactly as Uncle Chong Suk had predicted. Just as Ah-ku had said. She lacked backbone. No fibre, no will, and no discipline. Howl! She started to howl like the bastard mongrel that she was. It would have been better if Ah-ku had whipped her. A common roadside flower, that's what you are, Ah-ku had hissed. Her whole inside heaved in protest. She retched again. Her breakfast had splattered into the sink. With head bowed, she had emerged from the bathroom, and admitted the fault was hers. The weakness was hers. The loving was hers. She blamed no one.

– *It's that noodle boy. I knew it. Does he know?*

– *If he really cared about you, this wouldn't have happened.*

– *A moment's pleasure. A lifetime of pain. Haven't I taught you anything?*

– *I gave you an education. Gave you opportunities I never had.*

– *I tried, Ping! Must you pull me down into the shit?*

Tears had welled in Ah-ku's eyes. She wanted to kneel and beg her for forgiveness. But Ah-ku had stood up. A hard glint in her eyes.

– Uncle Chang must never know. You're not to ruin his chances. Don't you care about him even if you don't care about me?

A lone saxophone wailed its lonesome reply down the corridor. The music rolled in under her door as she lay stoned on the brown carpet, staring at the ceiling, her finger tracing the music's counterpoint in streaks of red and gold. She retched again.

– What am I to do with you? Ah-ku had wailed.

Another spasm coursed through her guts and up the throat making her run for the bathroom again.

– Three months, you say you missed your period. That's twelve weeks. We'll go to the clinic right away. The doctor will wash it out.

Wash it out. Wash it off. The Cantonese phrase had a clinical ring. A cold metallic ambiguity that distanced the doer from the deed. Metal trolleys with black rubber wheels. Nurses in white. The wicked gleam of stainless steel trays with sharp scissors and hypodermic needles. A steel bowl with white gauze bandages. She saw them all and shook her head.

– What do you want then? Marry him and hawk noodles all your life? Is that what you want? Be a hawker's wife? Play the pipa and hawk your body? She was detritus left on a park bench, which the cleaners swept up at dawn, and stuffed into garbage bags. She strained to catch the sound of falling stars outside the window.

What time is it? Is it night or is it day? Had time stood still while she lay on this filthy floor in a pool of vomit? Oh, man, she'd sunk low, very low

How low, how low, the sax moaned, and her eyes closed.

Three clear notes woke her. Like three silver raindrops in the sky, they hung above her head tantalizingly out of her thirsty reach. She stuck out her tongue to catch them. Pearls fell with a rippling of strings. She caught their echoes and the sound of rain. Cool cleansing rain that washed away the demons of the night.

From the bowels of the building, a cello was braying, its music swelling like sheets billowing in the breeze. A rush of air blew into the room bringing a tropical storm that broke over her swollen head. It uprooted trees, and lifted the roofs of the brown huts along the river.

– *No!* She heard herself cry out. The storm subsided as suddenly as it had begun. Painfully, she pushed herself up and started to write furiously. Dots and dashes, breves and semi-breves filling page after page of her notebook. How long had she been sitting on the sodden carpet writing? Her arm was ready to drop when the doorbell rang and wouldn't stop ringing.

"Who the hell is it?" she yelled.

"Cello and pizza delivery!"

"Go to hell!"

"Please, Ping, open the door. I need to tell you… why…"

"I don't care!"

"I had to go back to India. My father died!"

She flung open her door, and fell into Jeev's arms.

Part Seven

Only Music Can Save Us

34

Eagerly, I press my face against the cabin window. At last. The island is coming into view. The pilot's voice over the intercom gives the height, ground temperature, local time and the usual warning about smuggling drugs. Soon, very soon, Ah-ku will be there, waiting for me, leaning at the rail, peering anxiously through the glass barrier, no doubt, with John or Kit by her side. Fool, I chide myself; the thought of her waiting for you is making you excited as a kid. Are you still yearning for her maternal love and affection? Stop being ridiculous. It's just the start of your sabbatical, idiot. But still my eyes remain glued to the window because our last phone conversation has changed things somewhat between us. Ah-ku had sounded different. More vulnerable, less hostile.

Outside the plane's window the lights below are coming closer, the buildings and lines of blue lights rising, and then with a bump, we're taxiing down the runway. The triplets in the front row, two girls and a boy, clap their little dimpled hands, bringing smiles to their parents' tired faces. I ease back into my seat and watch the young woman across the aisle take out her compact to dab the shine off her nose and prepare her face for disembarkation. When the plane stops, the clicks of safety belts and people standing up to open the overhead compartments fill the plane. Bags and parcels are handed to wives and girlfriends, and cell phones are switched on. Mine beeps at once. It's a Singapore number I don't recognise. I click open the message box and give a start. Hello, Ping. I will be meeting you at airport. Wong Fook Weng.

I read it a second time. Is this a joke? Is the message really from him? Why is he coming to meet me? Why didn't someone alert me? These questions rush past as I read the message again. Wong Fook Weng. He has signed off with the name I often see in the glossy magazines and brochures of the Singapore Chinese Orchestra.

I've kept in touch with the Singapore music scene as part of my professional interest, and the name of the orchestra's principal flautist and dizi player, well known in Asian music circles, has not escaped my notice. In fact, I've been quietly tracking his rise to fame. Is the use of his formal name an indication of the distance between us? A sign that he's coming to meet me on professional grounds? But who the devil has arranged for him to meet me in the first place? Where're Kit and John? Why aren't my brothers meeting me? Where's Ah-ku?

I sweep away the lock of hair irritating my eyes, and reach for the old leather case, strapped in the seat next to mine. Chong Suk's pipa is coming home with me for the first time. I step on to the moving walkway. The sudden tautness in my back and the weight of years in the old pipa case make me faint. Hurriedly, I step off the walkway, brush past the other passengers, and make for the washroom. I need time. Time to prepare myself and gather my thoughts. Calm down. Calm down, I whisper silently staring into the mirror above the washbasin. The anguished face of the seventeen-year-old banished to the icy wastes of Iowa is staring back at me.

On the night of my sudden departure, I had dashed into the washroom to escape Ah-ku's nagging.

– Remember, ah! I'm giving you a university education in Ah-mae-lica. At great expense. Make something of it.

– If you fail, don't come back

– I won't come back even if I succeed!

Locked in my memory, Weng and I are forever young, forever anguished, forever separated and betrayed. How are we to meet after all these years?

I walk out of the washroom slowly, hugging his father's gift in both arms like a shield as I go down the escalator and join the queue for immigration clearance. Why are Singapore's airport officers so darn efficient? At this moment, I wouldn't have minded another ten minutes of queuing, but I'm waved through quickly.

I scan the waiting crowd behind the plate glass, pick him out at once standing behind the barrier. I'm absurdly relieved. He looks nothing like the tuxedoed maestro in the glossy brochures. Clad in a white tee shirt, gray Bermuda shorts and black sandals, he looks like the Weng I once knew – tall, lanky and slightly dishevelled. Only older with a tinge of gray at the temples, and some tautness in his profile, some tension in his neck in the way he holds his head. He sees me, and waves. I raise my arm, not sure what I ought to say to him when we meet. I watch the bags coming down the conveyor belt, aware of the flood threatening to burst through my head. Luggage. Focus on the luggage, I tell myself. Carefully, I place the pipa case in a trolley. Then I pull my two bags from the carousel, load them onto the trolley, and head for Exit, pushing the trolley nervously in front of me as the glass doors slide open.

"Welcome home, Ping."

My hand is grasped and shaken. He takes over the trolley, and my eyes rest on his fingers. Still slender and long. I can't catch what he's saying. He's pushing the trolley through the milling, smiling throng, their muffled voices sounding familiar and yet different. Their disjointed words and phrases flit in and out of my ears, I can't seem to focus at all.

"…good flight…? Sleep… no?"

His dark eyes are gazing at me. They're smiling. I try to smile back.

"How long has it been?"

"What? Sorry…" His question catches me off guard.

"I said how long since we…"

"A lifetime, a lifetime," I answer as the smile in his eyes fade and an awkward, tentative expression spread like a shadow over his face. The silence of the years is sinking slowly into the space between us as we walk side by side, with him pushing the trolley, and I walking next to him wrapped in a daze of half-lit memories of a battered pram filled with vegetables, and a laughing boy and girl pushing it.

"How are you?" I manage to croak at last.

"Nothing broken; nothing torn. Still in one piece."

I almost trip over his answer and wonder if that was deliberate. His sudden switch to Cantonese has cut me to the bone and pulled me across the language threshold to home. But his face shows nothing; he seems unaware of the effect of his Cantonese.

"John and Kit. Where are they?" I ask, also in Cantonese, pleased that hanging out with the old folks in San Francisco's Chinatown has helped me to retain the language of my childhood.

"John and Kit? They… er… can't come. So I told them… I told them I'd meet… prepare you for… Your Ah-ku… she…"

The sudden blast shatters the rest of his words. My arms make a frantic grab for them. The room is suddenly turning, turning. My head is reeling. His hard grip steadies me, but I can't hear a word of what he's saying. His mouth is moving but I hear nothing. The sudden thunderous roar of jets has sent blood rushing between my ears making me gasp like a fish on land. The tightness in my chest is excruciating. My eyes are smarting from the pain. His grip on my arm tightens, and his anxious voice comes through.

"Steady now, steady Ping… wanted to prepare you… very sorry… I… idiot, idiot… I should've waited… waited till… "

A handkerchief is pushed into my hand. The sudden scent of musk stops the smarting in my eyes. I fight off the unruly horde of images and sensations hurtling like a pack of wild horses through my head. His words, his sweat, his snot when he thrust his grey rag under my runny nose just before he rang the convent's bell that fateful night, all came rushing back.

The glass doors slide open, and the blast of heat tells me that we're out in the hot humid night. He pushes the trolley with one hand, and with the other, he holds on to my arm as we make our way down the rows of cars. By the time we reach his car, my shirt is soaked from the humidity. He loads my two bags into the boot, and opens the door on the passenger's side. Then he hands me the pipa case. For a fleeting second, his eyes rest on its faded red string, the look of memory on his face but his mouth says nothing. He closes the car door and comes round to the other side. He gets behind the steering wheel, turns on the air-conditioning and straps on his seat belt.

"Ping… Ping."

"Eh?"

"Please belt up. Here. Let me help you."

But I push the pipa case into his arms instead, and strap on the belt myself. Without another word, he hands back the worn leather case, and drives out of the airport and on to the expressway, gathering speed as palm trees, raintrees and pink bougainvilleas whizz past. My eyes register these minutiae. Focus, Ping. Focus on what is in front of you, I tell myself. I keep my eyes on the lights of the cars in front. I sense his eyes on me. He has glanced in my direction twice. Does he see a middle-aged woman, tensed and withdrawn? Note the worry lines around a bitter mouth and the taut veins in her neck? Her hands clenched on the pipa's handle?

"How did Ah-ku…?"

But before I finish, my hand has already shot up to stop his reply. The red taillights of the cars are swimming in my misting gaze. I bite my lips. I don't want to cry in his car. My hands are taut. I relax my grip on the pipa and take a deep breath and exhale. Another deep breath. Exhale slowly… one… two… three… four … five… I count. My mind is floating out to the sea on the left. Away, away, floating far away, my eyes searching the dark expanse, searching the gaps between the lights of the far-off ships before returning to gaze once again at the red taillights of the cars in front. Focus, focus, I tell myself. Focus on the lines of cars slowing down at the approach to Benjamin Sheares Bridge. Watch how the city's towers rise before us like steel-clad warriors ready to do battle with the rest of the world. The three towers of the new casino, stand sombre and stiff like memorial tablets to the dead, holding aloft their tray of offerings to the city's ancestral spirits. The cars are going down the curve of the bridge. We are driving past dismal grey concrete pylons, their iron rods thrusting out of the earth's foundation like monstrous claws. The grove of green trees and casuarinas fails to lift the city's gloom. I dread what's to come as the cars grind to a halt at the traffic lights. I feel the hot breath of grief crouched at the edge of my mind, nostrils flaring, waiting to pounce the moment I take my eyes off the cars. Ah-ku is gone. What am I to do? Focus, focus on the now, focus, I repeat the mantra, my mind bobbing like a boat at sea robbed off its anchor. I'm abandoned yet again.

Where are the familiar landmarks of my childhood? Is this Rochor Road? Has his car gone past Rochor Road? Nothing looks familiar to me. The car weaves through heavy traffic. Ahead looms the brightly lit maternity hospital glowing with smug gaiety. Why is he taking this road? Is there a hidden message?

"Why did you come to the airport?" I ask pointedly.

No answer from him. Either he's pretending he hasn't heard or he's concentrating hard, guiding his car through the dense traffic snaking past the Newton hawkers' centre. He squeezes past the buses, and we are back on Bukit Timah Road. But where are the raintrees? Where are the tall, majestic raintrees that used to tower above the road and two-storey townhouses like open-armed benevolent kings? Now all I see are these hideous modern high-rises and thick hedges that screen off the monsoon canal where the two of us had once caught guppies during that glorious, glorious time when Ah-ku abandoned me in the coffee shop.

*

Weng steals a glance at the silent woman beside him, slumped in her seat, as if all life has drained out of her. It's his fault. He shouldn't have opened his mouth. Their first meeting, and he has fouled it. What an idiot. He'd dreamt of this meeting, planned for it – had even rehearsed what he would say.

Out of the corner of his eye, he sees her staring at the apartment blocks as his car turns off the expressway and enters the public housing estate.

"This is a new town… built by HDB… er… the Housing and Development Board."

When she remains silent, he turns back to his driving, his parched mouth filled with the acrid taste of burnt grass. As the silence in the car balloons, he realises that she's miles away. He can't reach her. He shouldn't have spoken. He keeps his eyes on the road until at last he turns into the car park and stops.

"Er… Ping. We're here. The wake is in the pavilion over there, behind this block. Can't see it from here. It's… er… sandwiched between two apartment blocks. Residents use the pavilion for weddings and funerals."

She lets him help her out of the car.

*

I'm in a daze. He's talking again, guiding me down the path, his words flowing around us like flotsam in the thick muggy air. Heads turn as we walk into the pavilion. The crowd's stares are unnerving. Their eyes are trained on us as we walk down the rows of white plastic chairs, their voices buzzing like a hive of angry bees, their furious wings beating against my eardrums. I'm surprised to see such a large crowd. There must be more than a hundred people here. The whole place is ablaze with light from the white fluorescent tubes on the ceiling. Large grey industrial fans are whirring above our heads. I can't hear what Weng is saying. Hand on my arm, he's guiding me towards the white-draped altar, but I'm dragging my feet, fighting the impulse to run from him. Run from this shining white blaze and mob of gawking strangers. But the photograph next to the altar stops me. I stare at the portrait of Ah-ku propped up on an easel, arrested by her bright smile and bright pink lips.

A tabernacle of dark polished wood sits in the centre of the altar, a white candle lit on either side of it. A bronze bowl rests on a small red cushion. Beside it, a wooden stick, a plate of four oranges, and a white vase with a single yellow chrysanthemum. The starkness of the altar shocks me. It looks terribly bare. So different from the clutter of traditional Chinese altars with their ornate red candles, joss papers and sticks of incense, three cups of tea and three cups of rice wine, and platters of roast pork, roast duck, a whole steamed chicken and pyramids of rice cakes and fruit.

Weng nudges me gently towards the casket but dread slows my steps. The brain knows what to expect but the limbs hang back. I see Kit and John standing near the casket, their heads bowed. The heavy odour of lilies and chrysanthemums overwhelms me. I feel faint. My legs are heavy; my movements sluggish, but my mind is flitting frantically, beating its wings like a frightened bird trapped in a small space, looking for escape. In the sudden dark that swarms the eyes, I trip. Weng's grip on my arm keeps me on my feet. I glance at the face in the casket and turn away. Relieved. It's not Ah-ku. Not her. A cold blast blows through my chest. The sudden hollow in my rib cage feels as though a surgeon had yanked out my heart and lungs.

"I'm glad you could make it. We've been waiting for you," John says.

Dressed in mourning white, he looks haggard and worn out. His hair has greyed since we last met briefly at the Changi Airport a few years ago.

"The members of the Soka Association are waiting for us. We've got to start the service now. Come."

My two brothers wedge me between them in the first row of white chairs, John on my right and Kit on my left. John's wife, Liz, and their two sons join us; the six of us make up Ah-ku's family. There are no relatives. None of the aunts and uncles and cousins is here. I'm not surprised, for Ah-ku has cut them off long ago.

A solemn-faced gentleman in a white shirt and dark trousers bows before the altar. He opens the doors of the tabernacle, bows before it with great reverence, and lifts the wooden stick to sound the bronze bowl. Once. Twice. Thrice. The chatter in the pavilion subsides. The man's sonorous voice rises like a solemn bassoon.

"Nam... myoho... renge... kyo... "

Each vowel is given its full weight and value as it rolls from his mouth and down the rows of seats over the heads of the crowd like a sorrowful roll call to honour the dead.

"Nam... myoho... renge... kyo... " the crowd intones after him.

The incomprehensible words rush towards me like a tidal wave, the voices churning up a swelling surf. Breakers pound against my head. The intensity and repetition of the chant stir ripples of shock through my nervous system, already stretched and exhausted after sixteen hours in sleepless flight. At times, the strange words hit against my temples like hailstones. I shut my eyes against the onslaught, but it's impossible to shut my ears. I turn around in my seat. Search for Weng in the crowd; relieved when I spy him at the end of the last row, chanting like the rest. I turn back to the altar and close my eyes again. There's a crackling static in my head. A mallet is pounding on my skull. I fight the impulse to cover my ears, and clasp my hands tightly. A headache looms, threatening to explode into a migraine.

"Nam... myoho... renge... kyo! Nam... myoho... renge... kyo! Nam... myoho... renge... kyo...! "

– Lord, have mercy! Christ, have mercy! Lord, have mercy! Christ, have mercy! I haven't stepped inside a church for years, but the words come unbidden. I turn back to look at Weng again. He's still chanting, his eyes trained on a distant spot beyond the pavilion, unaware of my predicament. I'm struggling, floundering in the sea of foreign sounds, longing for things to end when suddenly the gale subsides, and the loud voices drop to a peaceful murmuring.

"Nam… myoho… renge… kyo… oo"

The bronze bowl chimes three times. The man who led the chanting rises from his seat. He bows before the tabernacle, and with great reverence, closes its doors. When he turns to bow to us, the mourners, I'm shocked. Tears are streaming down his face.

My own eyes are bone dry.

35

I haven't moved from my seat, all night, and haven't been able to eat a bite of supper. I'm dismayed that Weng had left after the prayer service without telling me. A sea of strangers had surrounded us as soon as the service was over. So many had come forward to offer their condolences, and there was such a hubbub during the buffet supper that I felt we were at a social gathering instead of a wake. It was way past midnight before the last of the mourners left although it seems strange to think of them as mourners, since none of them is family. All are members of Ah-ku's Buddhist association, the name of which I've forgotten. The pavilion feels strangely empty and quiet now. There's just Kit and me, and he's keeping himself busy, stacking and re-stacking the white chairs at the far end of the pavilion.

I watch him, wondering if he knows we're half siblings. Probably not. Ah-ku would have taken that to her grave. I close me eyes and take a deep breath. The quiet of the late hour and the cool night air is beginning to soothe my frayed nerves.

John has gone up to the flat with Liz and their two boys to catch some sleep before they take over the next watch at four a.m. I've volunteered to take the first watch with Kit since sleep is out of the question anyway, thanks to my jetlag. I haven't forgotten the importance of keeping watch throughout the night during a wake, a Chinese tradition that has remained unbroken for over two thousand years. The family has to protect the deceased's body. Stay close by as the soul has not yet transited into the netherworld. It's hovering around. It could get lost if it can't find its family. To leave Ah-ku's body alone and vulnerable in the coffin is simply inconceivable.

My heart feels nothing. I would like to cry but I can't. I can't bring myself to go near the coffin again. My reluctance shocks me. It's not fear or superstition that's keeping me away. Nothing of the sort. I simply don't want to see that face in the casket. It's not Ah-ku's face; it's a mask that the mortician has painted on. I miss the funerals of my childhood when wakes were social events. Tables were set up for mahjong and card games, and friends, relatives and neighbours would talk and gamble all night 'to keep the dead company'. Old aunts would tell stories about the deceased, and Taoist monks would lead the family in keening for the dead so that Yen Lo, the Emperor of Hell, would know just how much the deceased was missed. So much grief, guilt and atonement had filled the air at those traditional funerals. Whatever material goods the deceased had lacked in this life, his family would burn a paper version of them for him in the next life. I had watched many such bonfires of paper houses, and chests of paper silver and gold with Weng. Remembering them makes me wish that he hadn't left so quickly after the prayer service. Why didn't he stay?

When another scene from our shared past breaks into my head, I stand up, grab a broom and dustpan, and walk over to Kit. He looks up, smiles, and continues to stuff used paper cups and plates into the bins. I start to sweep up the bits of food, sweet wrappers and soiled napkins blown onto the floor by the overhead fans.

"Kit."

"Eh?"

"Didn't the old aunties used to say no sweeping during a wake?"

"We Buddhists are not superstitious. Ma said grief should not be a display of dirt."

"Did Ah-ku really say that?"

"More than a hundred times."

The smile on Kit's face is enigmatic. I can't tell if he's relieved or pleased that we're talking after my long silence.

"Ma said many things. She used to preach, you know."

"No, I didn't know. Just like I didn't know that so many people knew her."

"We didn't expect so many to turn up tonight. This being the first night, the obituary is not out yet in the papers. Tomorrow morning it'll be out. We can expect a bigger crowd tomorrow night. Ma's been a lay leader in the Singapore Soka Association for many years, you see." He turns to look at the smiling face propped up on the easel beside the altar.

"What's Soka?" I ask.

"It's a Buddhist organisation that started in Japan."

"Oh? No wonder the prayer service tonight is so different from the funerals in Chinatown when Ah-ku and I were living there."

"You and Ma lived in Chinatown before?"

"Didn't Ah-ku tell you and John?"

"Nope. Ma didn't tell Kor and me."

I'm not surprised. Ah-ku would've erased that past. Just like her to delete what she didn't want to remember. But tonight is not the time to tell Kit.

"What was that strange phrase you people kept chanting?" I ask him.

"Oh, it's *Nam myoho renge kyo*, the fundamental law of life and the universe. It's expounded in Nichiren Buddhism."

Vaguely, I recall Ah-ku trying to tell me about it on the phone in her usual strident, belligerent voice, which had immediately caused me to shut my mind. We start sweeping again, Kit on the right and I on the left side of the pavilion, pushing our brooms under the chairs and tables.

"Kit."

"Eh?"

"I noticed you still call John, Kor. Big Brother?"

He looks at me, puzzled. "Habit, I guess. Also being Asian, you know."

He smiles his enigmatic smile again. I ignore the slight condescension in his "being Asian, you know." Perhaps it's not intended as a slight. Perhaps I'm just being ultra-sensitive tonight. He thinks I'm American, of course.

Kit switches off the fans overhead. The sudden cessation of the whirring blades brings a sudden silence broken only by the swishing of his broom as he sweeps peanut shells, melon seeds and sweet wrappers into his dustpan. He empties dustpan after dustpan into the large black garbage bags that the casket company has provided. And I do the same. When we finally put away our brooms, it's almost two in the morning.

"Coffee?" he asks.

"Yes, please. What day was yesterday?"

"Thursday. Ma died on Wednesday night."

I pull my chair closer to the table as he pours coffee from the flask that Liz has left for us.

"I was still flying over the Pacific, watching a Jet Li movie …" My voice trails off to a whisper.

He throws a quick glance at me and gulps down his coffee, almost scalding his throat.

"How did she…?"

"Heart attack."

He sits down heavily, and puts down his cup.

"I'm sorry Kor and I couldn't tell you the details earlier tonight. Too many people. Too many things to see to."

He rubs at the frown between his brows and sucks in a deep breath, and fixes his eyes on the stray cat curled under the chair.

"A nurse at the hospital told us a passer-by … he'd found Ma on a stone bench… in the park… in Tampines… her head bowed … her arms hanging by her side. He called Emergency…

the ambulance came… the paramedics tried… they tried to revive her… but… but she was gone."

He frowns again and tries not to think of his mother dying alone on a stone bench with no family to hold her hand.

"Is this what the Buddhists called karma?" I ask.

"I don't know," he gives a shrug and heaves a sigh. "The Soka members said that Ma had gained the final merit. Said she's attained Buddhahood because she was on her way to chant the Lotus Sutra."

"It's a comfort if one is a believer, I suppose."

He looks at me, and turns away, trying to hide the stab of resentment on his face.

"I… I'm sorry."

"No, don't, please. It's not your fault. I… er… I'm certain that Ma didn't want to die so soon. She was… she was waiting for you to come home to celebrate her birthday. Ma had insisted that we should wait. Wait for you to come back. But the night before you were due to arrive, Ma called me on my cell phone. I… I was the last person she spoke to."

He, the child Ah-ku had accused of making her life a misery from the day he was born. He was the other millstone around her neck. We certainly have something in common, but tonight is not the time to tell him.

– Kit! Pain! Pain!

– Ma! Where are you? Ma! Ma!'

"I called her mobile phone again and again, thinking that she might be in the MRT and the train had entered a tunnel or no-signal zone. Ma was often slow in answering, sometimes rummaging in her handbag and not finding her phone. Sometimes, she couldn't even hear it ring. She was deaf at times. So I didn't worry at first. I waited a while, and then called her again. When that failed, I called our neighbour and asked him to knock on Ma's door. The guy reported that no one came to the door; the flat was in darkness. That was when I started to panic. Had she fainted inside the flat?

Had there been an accident? She'd shouted, "Pain! Pain!" I phoned Kor, and he shouted at me for not phoning him earlier. We took turns to call Ma's mobile phone every few minutes all night. Finally, a woman's voice answered me."

Kit's voice is hoarse and cracked by now from strain and lack of sleep. I reach for the flask, and replenish his cup of coffee, and he drinks it thirstily.

"We were asked to go to Changi Hospital at once," he continues. "Kor, Liz, their two boys and I, we rushed to the hospital. Where did the passer-by find our mother? Kor asked the nurse. Tampines, the nurse replied."

Kit looks as though he's going to cry. He takes another gulp of hot coffee, and mops his brow.

"Ma had told me; she'd told me that morning. Just before I rushed out with Dave to beat the morning traffic into the city. She was attending a Buddhist youth meeting that night. She must've said, Tampines. Could she have said, Tampines?"

His eyes appeal for help.

"Could she ...? Did she say Tampines? Are you sure, Kit? Maybe she said something else," I try to comfort him.

He searches his memory once more, and gives up.

If only he had listened that morning, maybe... maybe he could have found her before ... no, he cannot bring himself to continue. "I... er... I'm sorry. Your first night home. Your first extended visit home after so many years. I – I'm sorry to burden you with this." The nurse had told him not to worry. Said death was instantaneous. When the paramedics found her, her body was very relaxed. She was seated, hunched forward, her arms hanging loosely by her sides. There was no pain.

How did the nurse know? She wasn't there. Those words had done little to comfort him. Nevertheless, he repeats the same words to me now, watching my face pinch up, and my eyes reddening. But no tears would come.

"Go on, Kit."

"We had to leave Ma overnight in the mortuary. The doctors had to determine the cause of death. Ma had never been seriously ill before. Never had to stay in a hospital."

He fights the rising tension in his back, like anxiety or anger, but it's neither. Some reaction he has never felt before. He remembers the two male attendants, their dark faces stern and impassive as they ordered the family to leave and shut the door. Why had he allowed it? Allowed them to strip and clean the body?

"Kit. Kit."

"Eh?" He shakes his head as though rousing himself from sleep.

"What's the cause of death?"

"The death cert says hypertensive ischaemic heart disease.'

"What's that?"

"A massive heart attack." He gets up to switch on one of the overhead fans. "Did Ma tell you she accepted Dave, my partner?" he asks, changing the subject abruptly.

"About Dave? No. No, she didn't." I look at him. "Is he the guy seated next to you during the prayer service?"

"Hmm, that's him. If she hadn't accepted him, I would've left Ma… like… like you."

"I didn't leave her, Kit. She packed me off to Iowa; she literally threw me out."

36

After a night of restless sleep, my head feels heavy and my heart is numb. Lying curled on my side in Ah-ku's bed, I wonder if I'd just heard her voice as I was drifting out of sleep. Was it a shout from a neighbour's flat that woke me up? Or an echo in the walls? Could it be a part of me, unwilling to accept death, is hoping against hope to catch something to confirm that the body in the casket is not Ah-ku's? She's still in my head. I can't forget the strident voice, the tone and words calibrated when provoked to cause maximum hurt to its listener. Why my brain chooses to remember such fragments of encoded pain, stored in the memory cells only to burst open like livid pimples during moments of shock and grief is beyond my comprehension. Is this how others remember the past, or is it just my perverted brain?

Turning to lie on my back, I notice the signs of age and decay in the room – the lumpy feel of the mattress, the peeling paint and stains of brown seepage on the ceiling, and a faint, stale odour in the bed linen that reminds me of the windowless cubicles in Pagoda Street. Could it be from a weak bladder, or a declining memory that forgot some unwashed laundry stashed away somewhere in the room? Among the smells is the reek of old Chinese newspapers. It seems to be coming from under the bed. I roll over to the edge and peer under it. A penumbra of grey dust on the floor shocks me.

Ah-ku was very particular about cleanliness. In Juniper Garden, the maid had to sweep and mop and polish daily.

I sit up, and pull up a corner of the mattress.

"Oh my god."

Chinese newspapers yellowed with age are tucked under it. Did Ah-ku shove them there after she had read them, and then forgot them? Or was the old lady trying to shore up her sagging mattress? Why didn't she ask Kit or John to buy her a new mattress? If money were needed, I would've wired more over. If only I'd known about the state of this bedroom. Not the kind of place I'd imagined Ah-ku to be living in. It's certainly not the opulent boudoir she had been used to as the mistress of the house in Juniper Garden. Not the room for a woman who loved her baubles and bling. I still remember how Ah-ku had once drawn her bedroom curtains and crawled under the bed with Miss Kok and Mrs Tan so the three of them could compare the brilliance of their diamond rings in the dark.

How she must've suffered here. The furnishing in this room is so basic. Below the window, two wooden planks on four orange bricks form a bookshelf. It holds three framed photographs, a stack of Chinese books and magazines, and several tin boxes. The dressing table, pushed against the wall, has a chipped Formica top, and its mirror is water stained. A box of loose powder, a small pink plastic basket with several lipsticks, two hairbrushes, a red plastic comb, and two rows of tiny bottles of free sample perfumes neatly arranged. The sight of these makes the heart ache and brings a lump to my throat. I pick up one of the samples. Ah-ku used to wear expensive French perfumes that came in fancy bottles with gold tops and tassels. I put the sample bottle back. Yank open the drawers and cupboard doors. Hanging inside the wardrobe are the pant-suits I had sent over from San Francisco's summer sales. I reach in to stroke the fabric. The suits feel warm as though they still retain the warmth of the body they'd once clothed, still exude a faint and slightly heady mix of body and perfume. I draw closer.

Before I realise it, my face is nuzzling among the pant-suits.

– *O god!* I pull away at once. Slam shut the cupboard door. With quickening breath, I stride towards the window. Part the curtains, and wince in the sudden glare. Everything is dazzlingly white outside. The buildings are sharp-edged with hardly any shade. What time is it? I look at my watch. Ten in the morning. The sun is already high in the sky. My eyes are tearing from the glare of glass from the neighbours' windows. I draw the curtains and turn back to the darkened room, panting a little from the effort to calm my nerves.

I pick up one of the photographs on the bookshelf. Ah-ku is shaking hands with a Sikh Indian man in a grey suit and a red turban. Another shows her with several women wearing sun hats in a park, and a third has her dressed in a traditional Chinese qipao, playing the pipa with a group of elderly men and women. A sigh escapes my lips. Ah-ku had carved out a life for herself after Uncle Chang's death, a life that I knew nothing about. I've no memory of her complaining about her bedroom. The old woman had complained about everything else but not this. Not this. Why? I want to cry.

I put on the white tee shirt and black cotton drawstring pants that Liz has laid out for me on a chair. It's the traditional mourning attire that family members have to wear throughout the wake and funeral.

As I leave the bedroom, I notice that the other bedroom door is closed. Kit and Dave are still asleep. I'd liked Dave the moment Kit introduced him last night.

"Here, better put something into your stomach. Call it breakfast," Dave had smiled. He's Eurasian, he said, with bloodlines from all over Europe and India. Scot, Portuguese, maybe French on his grand-pappy's side and Indian, Malay, Chinese and Javanese on his grand-mother's side.

"Oh yes, I'm a full-blown chap jing, all mixed," he'd laughed. He had brought them noodles. "You like fried prawn noodles? You do? Good. Fried prawn noodles, Hokkien mee. Best eaten with fresh sliced chilli and a dash of freshly squeezed lime if you want a kick," he said before turning to Kit and kissing him on the cheek. Kit blushed a beetroot red.

Coming back to the flat at four this morning, it was Dave, not Kit, who told me that they've been together for more than three years before moving in to live as a couple. I was surprised but not shocked. What shocked me was Ah-ku's silence. Throughout our countless phone conversations across the Pacific, not once did Ah-ku mention Dave and Kit. Was it a case of what's not said, doesn't exist? Was the old lady ashamed and disappointed by her younger son? So many secrets. It makes me wonder.

I go into the kitchen and make myself a strong cup of coffee, and take it into the living room, still puzzling over Ah-ku's reticence about Kit and Dave. As I sit down at the small dining table, all at once I'm back in Juniper Garden where the large round dining table could seat twelve, sometimes more. Ah-ku would often squeeze in a couple of extra guests at her big, noisy steamboat dinners, urging everyone to cook their sliced fish, marinated slivers of chicken and pork liver in the steaming pot of soup at the centre of the table.

– Do you miss those dinners you hosted for Uncle Chang and his friends? I'd asked her once, hoping to provoke her, but she was adamant in not remembering.

– I don't dwell on the past. Why keep asking me about such things? If you want to remember those days, you go ahead.

But the past caught up with her anyway. The rambling phone call we had recently showed that Ah-ku couldn't escape her past.

– I can't sleep. He keeps appearing in front of me when I'm alone.

– Who appeared…?

– Who else? Your uncle! He keeps disturbing me. All these years, he's never entered my dreams. Now suddenly, I dream of him every night. So I pray for him. I chant prayers for his soul. But these past few days, I can't chant. I keep forgetting my words! The pain in my heart is pulling… pulling…

– Where's your pain? Left side or right side?

– *... pulling so tight... and...*

– *Did you see a doctor?*

– *What for? The doctor treats me like an old granny. Western doctor, Chinese doctor, all ask me to relax. Let go, Ah Por. You must let go. Let go! Let go! How to let go? If I know, then I don't have to consult them! So easy for these doctors to talk. If that's how they become doctors, I can be a doctor too. Just tell people to let go. But my memories won't let me go. They're pulling me. All night they haunt me. Not a moment's peace in my whole life. Not even in my old age. I ask Heaven. Why? Why? He left me. He jumped off the bridge. No goodbye. No will. Just left his shoes on the bridge. And a mountain of debts. A big hoo-ha in the newspapers. I had to sell everything. Everything! I didn't know where to hide my face. That's why I don't want to remember. Remember for what? More pain? More heartache? More shame? What for I think? Think near; think far, life is still the same.*

– *That was a long time ago ...*

– *One woman after another, your Uncle went after them. How do you think I felt? You left me. He left me. John has left me for his wife. These days, I'm waiting for Kit to leave me too. Come home, Ping. Come home and stay with me this time. In the end, you're the closest I have.*

That threw me into a panic. Ah-ku had never spoken to me like this before.

– *I've –I've got to put down the phone. The battery has run out,* I lied.

For years, Ah-ku had held me at a distance. And I, in turn, had kept her at arm's length, the unforgiving ocean between us. Even when Uncle died, Ah-ku didn't want me there. She had deliberately phoned me at the last minute when it was too late to fly back for the funeral. She wouldn't, just wouldn't let me be part of her family.

– *The funeral is tomorrow, no time for you to come back...*

I'd flung the phone across the room, screeching: "Bitch! Bitch!" Jeev had to calm me down.

"Everything she does, is just to hurt me. Why does she do it?"

"Because you let her..."

"Rubbish!" I yelled. Yelled my head off at Jeev.

No more! I decided there and then. No more! Something

had changed.

It was too late to fly home in time. Even if I could've caught a flight that same night, it would've been too late. When I reached Singapore two days later, Uncle Chang had already been cremated and his ashes scattered in the sea. Ah-ku hadn't waited for me, hadn't allowed me to perform my final duty. So I took the next flight back to Berkeley.

Since then, I'd never stepped into Juniper Garden again. And after the house was sold, I didn't visit the family's new apartment. Our contact was limited to meeting at the airport during my stopovers.

37

My mood brightens the moment I step into the brilliant sunshine in the ground floor lobby. I take a deep breath. My heart feels hollow as if something vital has been sucked out of me in the bedroom. I wonder if Weng would come to the wake, and hope he will. Surely he can't be avoiding me. You don't drive all the way to pick up someone at the airport for nothing. Especially someone you've refused to meet for eons. Every action has an intention, unless it's a reaction, says Jeev. Weng is far too serious to act without an intention. But perhaps he's just being kind. There's been a sudden death and the family is distraught. It's only natural that as a fellow member of Ah-ku's Buddhist organisation, he would offer to meet me at the airport. Nothing complicated there. I mean nothing to him. Nothing.

The lobby's sunshine has dimmed. An old man shuffles past with a plastic bag of coffee dangling from a red plastic string. I watch as he sits down on a stone bench and drink his brew with a straw. It's been a long time since I last saw hot coffee being carried and drunk this way. It reminds me of Old Kim's coffee shop where the coolies used to drink their takeaway coffee out of condensed milk tins tied with a raffia string. Plastic bags have replaced the tins.

"Gao-jah, Ah-chek. Good morning, uncle," I greet the old man in my rudimentary Hokkien, a dialect I haven't used for years.

"Gao-jah," the old man looks up. "Want some coffee?" He holds up his bag with a toothy smile.

"No, thank you, uncle. You drink and have a good day."

I wave goodbye, suddenly comforted, as though the hoary spirit of the Guardian Earth God has welcomed me back. The ground floor, aptly called the void deck, is deserted. I wonder if Ah-ku had sat alone on a stone bench like the old man. Perhaps fighting the loneliness she so vehemently denied. Once or twice I'd tried to probe, but she was incensed. What's it with you? Always asking this and that! I've no time to be lonely!

Ah-ku's pride will not admit to vulnerabilities. That's what makes that last phone conversation all the more disturbing. I shake my head, trying to shake off the persistent fly hovering at the edge of my mind. Something is threatening to break through. Something more than a headache, or worse, a migraine.

"Good morning, Aunty Ping."

"Oh, good morning, James." I try to sound cheerful. Perhaps the severe throbbing in my head will subside soon. "Morning, John."

"Good morning."

He looks like he hasn't slept for days. His eyes are dark pools, devoid of expression, and his unsmiling face with the high cheekbones is grim. For a fleeting moment, I think I'm staring at Uncle Chang on the night the fish died and Ah-ku had stood with arms akimbo in the doorway. Shaking off the dark shadow, I walk resolutely towards the altar. But a bad memory, once surfaced, cannot be dismissed so easily. Like a pendulum it swings back and forth. The harder I push it away, the faster it returns to mock me. Defeated, I stand at the altar before Ah-ku's smiling face. The eyes in the photograph stare out at me. Palms together, I quickly make the obligatory three bows of respect, and return to the table.

"Did you manage to sleep?" John asks.

"Not much." I feel tired and drained.

"Dad!" James calls from the other side of the pavilion. "Where to put this table?"

"In the corner." Turning back to me, John says that he has bought dim sum for breakfast. "Some siew pao, pork dumplings and siew mai. Also fishball noodles and sweet bean curd. I don't know what you like. Please help yourself."

"Thanks." The throbbing in my head begins to subside. "Come and sit with me, James. We haven't really met, have we?"

"No, Aunty Ping." The teenager sits down beside me with a bowl of noodles. "Can I get you anything?"

"No, thanks. My stomach is still asleep." I watch the boy eat his breakfast with an enviable teenage appetite, digging into his soy sauce noodles with his chopsticks. "How old are you, James?"

"I'll be fifteen next month."

I remember how Ah-ku had complained incessantly about the boys after Liz and her two sons from a previous marriage had moved in with John.

– Those two boys! Their mother didn't teach them any manners. John is stupid. I don't know what he's thinking.

– He's a grown man, Ah-ku. You can't…

– Don't you lecture me! I'm not like other mothers. I don't cling to my sons. If he doesn't want children of his own, it's his lookout. His karma.

"You've got some great biceps, James. Do you lift weights?"

"Sometimes. I'm captain of my school's junior soccer team."

"Wow, that's great. Where's your mum?"

"Liz will be here later. She's helping me to attend to some clients." John hands me the Straits Times. "The obituary is on the second last page. Coffee or tea?"

"Coffee, please."

He makes us a cup of instant mix each, and settles down to read the papers. I make no attempt to engage him in polite talk; his mind seems to be on something else.

A truck pulls up at the entrance to the pavilion.

"Delivery! Ten floral wreaths," the driver shouts.

Minutes later, another truck arrives to deliver a large pile of colourful Made-in-China blankets. Each blanket is embossed with large Chinese characters in black satin that are messages of condolences and sympathy for Mr John Chang, Senior Vice-President of Zenith Realtors, and his family. Soon John is busy on the phone thanking all those who have sent wreaths, sympathy blankets and banners.

Meanwhile, more vans arrive with banners, baskets of flowers and floral wreaths. John directs the workers from the casket company to tie ropes between the pavilion's pillars to hang up the sympathy blankets, and shows them where to place the wreaths.

"One hundred and three, one hundred and four. Wow! One hundred and five sympathy blankets, Dad! Any more and the ropes will give way."

The slim line of a smile appears on John's face as he turns to me.

"It's a scam, you know. The casket company phoned my office yesterday and took orders from all my colleagues. They even called up some of my clients."

His phone rings again, and he turns away, texting and taking yet more calls, making arrangements for more chairs and tables for tonight's buffet supper and prayer service.

I walk down the covered walkway with James, admiring the wreaths of white roses, tropical ferns, yellow chrysanthemums and lilies-of-the-valley on large wooden stands lining both sides of the covered walkway. Several more wreaths are added to the ones flanking the altar. By the time the men have finished hanging up the sympathy blankets and banners, the colourful display has attracted a small crowd of curious neighbours and passers-by.

"Aunty Ping, Dad says these banners and blankets are not part of the Soka Association's kind of funeral. But his friends don't know about Soka."

"I guess they don't. These banners belong to traditional Chinese funerals. Like the kind I saw as a kid."

"Really? Tell me more."

"On the day of the funeral, there would be a procession from the home to the main road. One or two Chinese bands would play.

Coolies were hired to carry the sympathy banners and blankets. These were strung up on tall bamboo poles so everyone could read the names and messages. The bands and the banners went in front of the hearse. The family and mourners walked behind, wailing loudly. The louder the better. It means you're more filial. Their friends would carry large umbrellas to shelter them from the hot sun. The funerals always took place in the late morning or afternoon when the sun was hottest. Don't ask me why."

"Wow, I've never seen such a grand funeral."

"Perhaps you never will. Customs have changed. Funerals are simpler now."

By lunchtime, so many wreaths and banners have been hung up around the pavilion that it looks as if someone important has passed away. People on lunch break are also beginning to stream in to pay their last respects.

"Who are they?" I ask Kit who has come down with Dave to help John.

"People Ma has helped. She was very active in the Soka Association for many years. Ever since I was a kid."

As we watch, a woman accompanied by a little girl bows three times before Ah-ku's photograph. Oblivious of those around her, the woman kneels, chanting, *"Nam… myoho… renge… kyo… "* as tears stream down her cheeks. I would like to go over to comfort her, but the woman is so wrapped up in her own sorrow that it would be rude to intrude. Watching the woman, I'm aware of the hollow cavern inside my heart and wonder at my lack of emotion.

"Hey, babe, I didn't realise that your ma is respected by so many," I overhear Dave's comment, and suddenly something hardens inside me. Ah-ku's sole ambition in life is to be respectable and respected by others.

"Lunch is here! Come and eat! Ping!"

Liz walks in with her younger son, Joe, carrying boxes of chicken rice. Her long hair swept back and held by a white clip, Liz takes charge of the meal.

"Come, Ping. Eat first. We've got to eat. Visitors will understand. I'll go over and explain to them. If we don't eat now, we won't have time to eat together later today. We've got to eat as a family now. Hey, Kit. Dave. Come and eat. This is Ping's first day home. Let's eat together."

She hands out the styrofoam boxes of rice, plastic forks and spoons.

"Sit over here, Ping. Joe, you sit up straight, can or not? Don't slouch. James, pass the chilli sauce. Who wants more chilli sauce? Dave, you want chilli or not? Ping, can you take chilli? This chicken rice is very good. I drove all the way to Tiong Bahru to buy. So eat. Eat more. I bought extra."

Loud, energetic, and used to taking charge, Liz reminds me of a younger Ah-ku. Could this have been the cause of their conflict? Two strong women living together in a small flat, fighting to take charge of the same man, a husband to one, and a son to the other, it spelt conflict. But when I questioned the wisdom of having three generations living under one roof, Ah-ku was riled.

– I don't expect you to understand. You're a foreigner now. That woman is twisting my son round her finger. But she forgets. Nothing can come between a mother and her son. Who's closer – a mother or a wife? A wife, you can change like a dress. A mother will be your mother forever! You can't change the one who carried you nine months in her womb.

– But, Ah-ku, husband and wife can be naked with each other. Can you be naked with your son?

– Choy! Choy! Choy! You've a dirty mind and a poisonous tongue! I don't expect you to understand, Ping. You've never been a mother.

– And whose fault is that?

The silence at the other end was loud. There were no more phone calls from Singapore after that for nearly four months.

"Ping, you're not eating."

"I am, I am, Liz. Thank you for buying the mourning suits for me."

"Everyone in the family must wear black and white. Come. You must eat. Last night you didn't eat."

"Liz, I… I'm grateful that you include me in the family."

"What're you saying? You are family. Now that Ma has left us…" her voice trailing off, "I… I… I've been feeling lousy. We … we shouldn't… shouldn't have moved out and left… left her alone," Liz sobs into her napkin.

I place an awkward arm around Liz's shoulders and wait for her sobbing to stop. We've met only twice, and each time, Ah-ku had done all the talking.

"I'm so sorry. Please eat, Ping, eat. Drink more water. Thanks." Liz accepts the tissue, and dabs her eyes. "I'm sorry. I kept thinking and thinking last night. We shouldn't have moved out." She cries again.

John returns to the table with a cup of hot tea. He places it silently in front of his wife, and sits down. No one has the appetite to eat. The two boys quietly clear away the half-eaten food and plastic spoons, and John makes some coffee. He has not spoken a word. I sense his misery, but I don't know what to say to bridge the distance of years between us. We drink our coffee in silence. After a long while, as though in answer to a question, John tells me that Kit has gone with Dave to fetch Kan Jieh from the old folks' home.

"Kan Jieh?" I frown.

"Don't you remember her? Kan Jieh, our old amah."

"They're here already."

Liz wipes her eyes and hurries to the front of the pavilion to help a frail, silver-haired woman walking towards us with the aid of a walking stick.

Everyone stands up to greet the old amah. Peering through her thick granny glasses, Kan Jieh's eyes light up.

"Why it's you, Miss Ping. Aiyah, it's been a long time. But I recognise you. I never expected to see you again. Aaah… such a long, very long time. You were just a girl when you left." Shaking her head in amazement, the frail old woman sits down. "Only seventeen, only seventeen when you left. Look at you now."

"Kan Jieh, please, have some tea."

"Thank you, Boy-boy."

James and Joe start to giggle. What? Their stern-looking stepfather is Boy-boy? They draw closer to the table to listen to the old amah.

"How are you, Miss Ping? I heard from Madam that you're a professor now. She was so proud of you, you know. So very proud of the three of you."

Kan Jieh's gaze on John, Kit and me is fond and proprietary as though we are still her charges. Her white hair coiled into a small bun at the back of her head and held in place by two jade and gold hairpins, Kan Jieh is still wearing the hairstyle that marks her out as an amah jieh from Southern China, women who'd vowed to stay single, and loyal to their sisterhood of amah jieh. I notice that Kan Jieh is pointedly ignoring Liz, but I'm not surprised. The old amah's loyalty, as always, is with her Madam.

The whole family rises to accompany our amah to the altar of her beloved Madam. When John sounds the bronze bell, we kneel dutifully while Kan Jieh remains standing, hunched over her walking stick, lost in thought. Older than her mistress, tradition dictates that she must not kneel.

"Aye, Madam is gone to her rest. Nothing is sadder than white hair bidding farewell to black," Kan Jieh dabs a tear from her eyes, and allows Kit to lead her back to her seat.

"You're so tall now, Kit boy. To think I bathed and cleaned your bottom, and before that, it was Boy-boy's bom-bom."

A loud chortle explodes from James and Joe. Liz glares at her two boys. John, stiff and tight-lipped, offers Kan Jieh another cup of tea.

"Thank you, Boy-boy. Pu-erh tea is your mother's favourite tea."

John is silent, wary and distant. I wonder what's troubling him, but that will have to wait. The old amah is in the mood to reminisce, and duty, custom and gratitude for all the years of her faithful service dictate that we should listen to her. She expects no less. Having had a hand in bringing up Kit and John, she's like the family's grand old aunt who must be accorded due respect.

"Aye, so you're a professor now, Miss Ping. Who would've thought in those days that this urchin girl from Chinatown could rise so high?" Kan Jieh laughs softly, shaking her head as she peers out of her black, plastic-framed glasses that make her eyes look larger than they are.

I shrug off the comment. For want of something to do, I join the others in shelling the plate of groundnuts on the table, and wonder aloud why unshelled nuts are served at a wake.

"The customary plate of sweets is to sweeten bitter sorrow, and the red threads are to ward off bad luck and the evil eye. What are groundnuts for?"

"For eating," Dave grins.

"But why groundnuts?"

All eyes turn to Kan Jieh, but the old amah's attention has wandered off.

"Tor-dau, tor-dau, jiak lau-lau. Groundnut, groundnut, eat them up. Eat them up for long life," Liz recites a familiar Hokkien rhyme. "We used to sing that as children whenever we ate nuts. Maybe that's why they're served at wakes and funerals. So those who attend will be blessed with long life."

"Is that true, Kan Jieh?" I ask.

"Madam would've gone to your graduation and wedding, you know, Miss Ping."

"What?"

The amah raises her hand to stop the rest from interrupting.

"If you'd asked Madam a third time, she would've relented. She was ready to relent. But you didn't phone again. She was hurt. She didn't say it, but I could tell she was very hurt that time."

A tremor runs through my hands as I try to shell a nut. Tor-dau, tor-dau, jiak lau-lau. The Hokkien rhyme keeps repeating in my head. There's something soothing in these childhood rhymes, something comforting in the movement of fingers shelling groundnuts. I tear open a nut and crush the shells under my palm. Uncle Chang was the only one who'd bothered to phone me. I take a deep breath. The volcanic rumbling in my head subsides, but I can't let the old amah's comment pass without saying something.

"Ah-ku refused to meet Jeev. The man I was going to marry. My graduation and wedding were on the same day. How could Ah-ku say she would attend one but not the other? It's an insult to Jeev. And to me. She might as well not come."

"Ack! We say stupid things in anger, Miss Ping. Madam sent you overseas to study. Why wouldn't she want to attend your graduation?"

"She never cared about me like that."

"Madam was proud, she was proud of you."

But I can't recall a single affectionate gesture from Ah-ku. I can remember as though it were yesterday her harsh voice and cold looks. I glance at Kit and John. They don't even know that I'm their sibling. And that's the other knife, isn't it? That Ah-ku had thrust into my heart and left it in there to fester.

"I was her bastard daughter, Kan Jieh."

The crackling of groundnut shells stops. I turn to Kit and John.

"Ah-ku was afraid no man would marry her. Afraid your father would ditch her if he knew. I was forbidden to call her Ma. Did she tell the two of you? Did she care enough about me to tell you two that I'm your half-sister? Did Ah-ku tell you, Kan Jieh? Did she? Did she?" In my agitation, I've risen from my seat.

"Please sit down. Please." John sounds weary. "Ah-ku, Auntie, Ma. It's just a name. What does it matter what you call her?"

"You're wrong, John. Dead wrong. Names do matter. It mattered when I was a child who wanted her mother to be a mother. Damn it, John. You have a mother and father. I don't even know who my father is. I had to see a shrink for years in Berkeley. Did you know that? My life was a mess."

"Ping, our mother is dead."

Liz reaches over the table to take my hand. I pull away. I regret my outburst. I'd wanted to bring this matter up only after the funeral, after everything is settled. Kan Jieh has closed her eyes and seems to have drifted off. My outburst has meant nothing to her. She does not understand English. She wakes up with a start, coughs, and pulls up a corner of her white samfoo blouse to dab her eyes.

"Madam, aye, Madam. Always full of dreams. She told me all she wants is a house with a garden and a mango tree, and a husband who comes home to her every night." A soft peal of laughter follows this revelation, and Kan Jieh steers our talk back to Cantonese. "Madam used to sing. Yan-yan wei ngo; ngo wei yan-yan."

"Everyone helps me; I help everyone," Kit translates for Dave.

"That's how Madam, that's how she wants to live. Do you children remember the mango tree in the back garden, near the swimming pool? The mangoes. They used to hang down like green lobes. I was with her when she planted that tree. Aye, aye, my heart aches. Who would've thought she'd go before this old bag of bones? Don't mind me, Miss Ping. I'm an old woman rambling on and on."

"Call me Ping, please, Kan Jieh."

"Nay, I'm too old to change how I speak. One foot in the grave already."

"You've got many more years, Kan Jieh."

"Ack! Who can tell when we die? Such things are written in the book of Fate. It was fated that I should work for Madam. I was her landlady first before I became her amah," she chuckles seeing the surprise on our faces. "It was I who rented half of my coolie fong to her in Hong Kong. That was how we met. Even though a coolie fong was cheap, she couldn't afford to rent the entire room in those days. Even three meals a day was a problem for her. Sometimes she had to borrow money from me."

"I didn't know this."

"Aye, lots of things you don't know, Miss Ping. You stayed away a long time. Far too long." Kan Jieh wags a finger as though she's speaking to a naughty child.

The others have stopped shelling nuts. John looks as though he hopes there will be no more bombshells, but like the rest he's resigned, for the old will talk whether the young wants to listen or not. And his two boys are listening in rapt attention, and have not moved from the table since Kan Jieh sat down. He reaches for his wife's hand and Kan Jieh continues.

"Aye, we were not like mistress and maid, Madam and I. She told me to call her, Yoke Lan, but I wouldn't have it. Not proper, I said. I was very particular. Call me proud. We, amah jieh, we plait our hair and know our place. We know our duty in public. But in private, she and I were very close. We spoke like relatives, Madam and I. She confided in me, and I in her."

The pride in the old amah's voice is palpable, coming from that charmed place that I recognise as love, trust, or loyalty, and I'm filled with envy. And pain.

"Aye, Miss Ping, what am I to do now that she's gone? I've no family, no relations here. She was the only one. Inside my heart, she was my goddaughter. But I never told her. Aye, these old eyes see, and this old heart feels." Kan Jieh weeps softly.

Kit asks if anyone would like more coffee.

"Black, please. Make it strong," Dave says.

He returns with two white plastic cups of instant coffee, and hands one to Dave, and the other to me. "Drink it. You need it."

"Thanks." I'm touched by his gesture. Perhaps our talk the night before had done something. Created a bond perhaps. But I fear disappointment; I dare not hope or think further.

"Ack! Thank you. Those were the first words Madam made you say. Do you remember, Miss Ping? The first day when you came to live with us, she made you say thank you to me."

"How can I forget? Your madam treated me like an outcast."

"For that you must blame your father."

"I've no father, Kan Jieh."

"Your father was Indian, Miss Ping."

38

Leaving his car in the parking lot, Weng takes his flute and strides across the park to the tunnel under the road and out to the trees near the Asian Civilization Museum. He turns left and walks across the bridge to the Fullerton Hotel, the grand old dame that used to be the city's premier post office. But the dame is hemmed in now, towered over and dwarfed by the multi-storey office blocks and banks. He strides down the sidewalk, past the shuttered bars and restaurants of Boat Quay and then on to Clarke Quay, trying to shake off the restlessness that's keeping him awake. It's impossible not to think of her now that she's back. He stops at the spot where the creek used to be, where the two of them had fished and swum and kissed before he made a bonfire of her letters, before the creek was filled up and built over, before the quays were prettified for tourists. He inhales and exhales, and tries to slow down his breathing to ease the tightness in his chest and the tension in his back.

For weeks past, he's lain awake, listening to the rumble of memories roaming through his nights like dogs foraging in the dump. An old man's sigh emanate from the pit of his belly. He marvels that he can still feel like this at his age. In his basest moments, he had hoped she would be grey and ravaged, with bitter lines skirting the corners of her mouth, but time has treated her kindly. Academia has given her gravitas. She has done well in

America; she's still superior to him. So where does that leave him?

– *O, you poor whining sod! Have the years squeezed you dry?* He berates himself. His wife had left him, childless. Jia-yi, the recipient of Shanghai's highest music award, loved the piano more than she wanted a child. Pregnancy was out of the question; it would have impeded her promising career as a concert pianist. Singapore was only her stepping-stone out of China into the arms of the beckoning world. Their divorce was inevitable. Since then he had had other women as he made the rounds of music festivals and competitions, gaining his share of glowing reviews and recognition from Hong Kong, Beijing, Taipeh and other cities. He took what he could and left when he couldn't bear another night of arousal between expert hands under the sheets of a cold hotel bed.

– *Fool, you're trapped in the past; it's futile to yearn for what's lost.*

Yet here he is, back at the river again, unable to face down his insomnia in his silent, empty flat now that she has come back. They have spoken, and in all likelihood, they will speak again. The thought of speaking with her again is making his heart pound faster than a marathon runner's. The drive from the airport to the wake had been as painful for him as it was for her. Their brief exchange of words was a disaster. The hours of planning what he'd say had come to naught. He'd lacked tact. He was too eager and anxious, and spoke too fast and too soon in breaking the bad news to her. The shock made her retreat into a shell he dared not break. Her face was a mask.

He looks at his watch. Three a.m. Why the hell has he come to gaze at the dark waters again? The river can't answer his questions, nor soothe his heart, and neither can Ping, even if he were to confront her. But what is there to confront after all these years? She was so young back then, and so was he… and yet, her abrupt departure from his life all those years ago has discoloured his relationships with all the women who came after her. None of them had measured up, and that's what's eating him. He gazes out at the poor river. Gone are her crooked, winding inlets, ditches, creeks and streams that led to nowhere and everywhere. Gone are the ducks and sun-browned urchins who used to swim here, where he had waded in, holding Ping's hand, eyes intent on the mud banks, searching for catfish, aware that her hips were rubbing against his, her palm resting warm and snug in his as the red setting sun lit up their eyes and set the wild grass on fire. He remembers the pall of humid air, the smoke from the cooking fires in the squatters' huts that had hung thick and tense above them. The air was sizzling with the fragrance of fried ginger and sesame oil when she kissed him hard on the lips.

"Hai! Hai! Hai!" He yelled into the wind.

The river rippling black and orange in the moonlight warned of dangers unknown. At dusk, he'd watched its serpentine waters slithering into the deep undergrowth and recesses of the creeks and swamps upstream, disappearing into the unfathomable darkness. Hai, who fears the serpent these days? It's a toothless little grey worm now carrying boatloads of tourists. The times have changed; Ping has changed. She isn't the girl he'd kissed on the riverbank. He'd best leave her alone. She needs to grieve, and then she will probably leave again, go back to America.

– So stay away from her, old man. Don't be an idiot. Your time in prison should have taught you all about wretched hearts and betrayal. What are you hoping for? Love? The desire to love is all there is. Damn it. All there is.

He raises his flute to his lips, but a sudden night bird's cry startles with a flutter of wings. He falters.

– Play! Play with your whole heart. Heaven lights up our soul just once. If we fail to feed the flame, it dies. My son, in choosing the flute, you've chosen to be with humble folks. The scholar plays the pipa; the boatman plays the flute. Play it, Ah Weng, with all your heart.

He hears his father's voice urging him on.

Has he lost his fire? Once he had spoken out loudly and passionately. After his incarceration, not a single comment on politics has emerged from his mouth in public. No, he has nothing to say these days. The same gods are still worshipped in the same temples. On nights like this, he wants to flee this island's golden cage. His flame will die if he doesn't leave. But if he does leave, it will affect his music, which is born out of this gilded cage. Out of this constant tension and contradiction in the city, and in him.

He raises his flute to his lips once more, and rips the night's silence with the trill of A Lone Hawk's Cry.

39

Kan Jieh looks at me sharply, and reaches for my hand. Holding it firmly, the old amah traces the lines across my right palm.

"You see these lines, Miss Ping? Your destiny is in these lines. Your birth was an accident."

"Why didn't Ah-ku tell me? Why did she tell you and not me, Kan Jieh? How did she meet my father?"

"Aye, Miss Ping, your generation asks too many questions. My generation and Madam's ne'er questioned our elders like this. My poor Madam…"

Kan Jieh's eyes grow distant. Outside the pavillion, the sky is a brilliant blue. The fierce white afternoon heat and high humidity has bathed us in sweat.

"After her mother died, Madam's father, that good-for-nothing, sold her to Sum Koo who owned a brothel. When the Japanese bombed Singapore, and the gwai-lo English left, Sum Koo's brothel prospered. Her pipa singsong girls earned her thousands of Japanese dollars. But Sum Koo was a fool. She thought the Japanese devils would be in Singapore forever. She hoarded Japanese dollars. Kept them in a tin under her bed. 'When this war is over, I will live like a queen,' she said. Three years later, the English gwai-lo won the war, and returned. Sum Koo went mad. Overnight her Japanese dollars were useless. Not worth anything.

And the English gwai-lo, they closed down her brothel. Her pipa singsong girls ran away. Everything fell apart. Sum Koo beat Madam. Beat her every day. Times were hard, you see, very hard, after the war. Sum Koo had no money. She had to marry a noodle hawker. She made Madam work at the noodle stall. That was how Madam met your father, Miss Ping."

"You're very sure he's Indian?"

"Why else would Madam say so if it's not so? He went to the noodle stall every night, and every night he bought a bowl of fishball noodle soup from her. He spoke Cantonese. He'd grown up with Cantonese neighbours. Every night, he left a small piece of peanut cake on the table for her. He'd noticed that sometimes, poor Madam was so hungry that she ate the leftover noodles in the bowls, and Sum Koo smacked her. Madam was fifteen. The young man was very handsome, very kind, treated her like a human being, and not a dog."

"Did Ah-ku tell you all this, Kan Jieh?"

"She told me everything, Miss Ping. How she met the young man secretly after Sum Koo and the noodle hawker had gone to bed, and how they'd planned to elope. But one night, he was not at their usual meeting place. Night after night, she waited for him but he never went back to the noodle stall again. Nine months later, you were born."

Kan Jieh's eyes are fixed on me, the bastard daughter. A choked cry is stuck in my throat.

40

The pavilion has filled up like the night before. Packed with members of the Soka Association, the three hundred chairs that John ordered are not enough. Latecomers have to stand in the aisles and at the back. I take my seat in the front row next to Kit, John, Liz, Dave and my two nephews. How stiff and awful we look. Such a pained gaze in our eyes. Kan Jieh is the only one who appears at peace, counting her prayer beads quietly, oblivious of the crowd. A sudden resentment against the old amah seizes me. Ashamed, I scan the faces behind me; it's not Kan Jieh's fault that Ah-ku had taken her secret to her grave. I spot Weng with a group of elderly men at the far end. Relieved, I turn back to the altar where Mr Tang is leading the prayer service again.

"Nam… myoho… renge… kyo…" the crowd chants.

The loud whirring of the electric fans adds to the din. Inside my head, a trapped fly is desperate for escape.

"Nam… myoho… renge… kyo…"

Three hundred voices intensifying in tempo and pace the throbbing in my temples. I can't sit still. I keep shifting in my seat, keep turning around to make sure that Weng is still here, keep wondering if he will leave as soon as the service ends. It's a struggle to push away the thoughts that are crowding in. I'm buffeted about like a boat in a storm. I look to Weng as a ship looks to its anchor.

He's the only one who knows me, now that Ah-ku is … is … I can't bring myself to say the word. Focus. Focus. Focus like these Buddhists, I tell myself. Don't think. But how not to think? Ah-ku's smiling face is out there before me at the altar. How to look at the face and not think? I've kept Ah-ku at arm's length. I close my eyes. The chanting is wearing me down.

"Nam… myoho… renge… kyo… Nam… myoho… renge… kyo… "

Sonorous voices pound against my brain, their sound waves vibrating like taut steel wires stretched between my ears. My heart is like a clenched fist in my chest. I think of my wasted years. I had married in a fit of madness. How else can you explain it? It was over in less than a year. Jeev and I managed to drag it out for another five, but that was more out of pride and a refusal to admit defeat. I had wanted a child, but I did not tell Jeev. Neither did I tell Ah-ku. I did not tell her about my divorce either, or about the men who came after Jeev. Those forgettable affairs that meant little to me. The longest had lasted a year or two perhaps. I can't remember, and don't want to remember. My energy was channelled into teaching, composing and performing the music I tried so hard to shape. I had to work hard, harder than others to prove my worth in the new country. This too, I told no one. Especially not Ah-ku. Told her nothing about my new life in America. Didn't tell her when I was featured at last on ABC's radio and TV programmes. Didn't tell her when I received invitations to perform in concerts in San Francisco, Boston, and finally New York. I'm good but not good enough. Not a maestro of the pipa the way Weng is a maestro of the dizi. But I have my consolations – an academic position as a musicologist in a prestigious university. My battle for recognition has been hard won. It's not over yet. The pipa is so little known in the US. My music is what Americans have always labelled as "ethno" or "Sino" or "Asian" – exotic sounds that thrive at the margins of western orchestras with their grand pianos, cellos and violins.

"Nam… myoho… renge… kyo… Nam… myoho… renge… kyo… "

Relentless in their repetition, the swelling tide of voices, waves of dissonance and discordance swirling around in the screaming, maddening sea of sounds threaten to overpower me in its turbulence, in its thrashing, clamouring, chanting, intoning, invoking, its surging upward and forward of the sea's roar. My eyes desperately seek the one face in the crowd that can save me. His eyes meet and hold mine. Startled, I turn back to the altar.

I try to focus on Mr Tang's back, conscious of the nape of my neck turning warm under the gaze of his eyes behind me. The warmth is rising to my ears. I imagine them reddening. Alarmed, I suck in my breath. There it is again. I heard it – the faint lilt of a dizi. Reluctant to turn around again, I close my eyes. The faint, almost inaudible notes float past like petals in the undertow of the chant. Light as a red silk thread floating in the roaring waters, the unexpected strain of dizi music buoys my spirits. The tension in my shoulders eases; my ears open like a cockle shell. I hear the musicality of the rhythmic chant. Begin to marvel at the variations of pitch and tempo in the melodic repetition of the Buddhist mantra. It seems to dance in my ears now seemingly familiar, now unfamiliar yet strangely soothing. Intrigued, I dig into my tote bag under the seat and take out notepad and pen. Scribbling as fast as I can, I try to capture the musical qualities of the chanting voices, scribbling notations, trebles and clefs in the hope that my black dots and dashes will capture the music I failed to appreciate earlier.

"Nam… myoho… renge… kyo… oo…"

Ebbing in diminuendo, soughing to a soft *"kyo-oooo"* like a breeze, Mr Tang's rod strokes the bronze bell, and the crowd falls silent. He bows before the sacred scroll and closes the tabernacle, turns to the family and bows. I notice the glistening wet in his eyes again, and wonder what Ah-ku had done to stir such sorrow in the man. But there's no time to ask. A long queue has already formed, snaking its way to the altar. People are already pushing back their chairs, standing up, talking and smiling and greeting one another as they wait patiently to offer their condolences and gifts of 'white gold' to the family. The white gold or money is placed discreetly inside a white envelope to help the family to defray the cost of the funeral. Better than going to the pub to drink a beer in honour of the dead as they do in Berkeley. I stand up, looking for Weng in the crowd. But there's no sign of him.

Relatives from Liz's large family and several strangers come up to me. A teary-eyed young woman shakes my hand. "Aunty Chang," the young woman tells me, "had stayed up with my dying father all night, praying. My father had lung cancer and could not pray. So Aunty Chang prayed for my father," the young woman sobs.

A man in a wheelchair tells everyone that it was Aunty Chang who had encouraged him to help out at the Soka youth group. "I was drowning in self-pity and contemplated suicide after my accident," he says softly in Mandarin, his eyes reddening as he speaks. "But Aunty Chang was full of faith and encouragement. She never gave up on me."

"Aunty Chang used to bring packets of noodles for my brother and me after my father left us. Sometimes she gave us money for school." The teenager's eyes well up as she recounts how Aunty Chang gave her money one day to top up her bus card when her mother lost her job.

These stories prick me like thorns. Am I supposed to gather them and weave them into a crown for the dead? Why are these people telling me? Is this part of the rituals of a Buddhist wake? I turn to Liz.

"No need to understand, Ping. Just listen. There's nothing we can do. It's the customary practice. You never know what people will say."

41

I let myself into the apartment; disappointed once again that Weng had left without speaking to me. Is he avoiding me? We'd stopped talking so abruptly the other night. I stretch out on the sofa and close my eyes. I've had no rest the whole day. What with all the coming and going, the greeting of strangers, Kan Jieh's bombshell has left me exhausted. Kit's flat is a haven. Fifteen storeys above the madness in the pavilion below where the crowd is tucking into yet another obligatory buffet supper.

My cell phone buzzes. It's Jeev. Suddenly I'm relieved, and pleased to hear his voice from across the Pacific.

"How're you doin'? Have you eaten your first ten course meal yet?"

"Jeev, Ah-ku… she passed away before I reached home."

"No. Oh no. It must have been such a shock."

"It's hard to take it in."

"I'm so sorry… "

"I didn't get the chance to…"

"Say goodbye?"

There's a long silence before either can speak. I couldn't bring myself to tell Jeev all that I'd heard about Ah-ku.

"About the music…"

"Don't worry about it. Take your time. Take all the time you need. Some things you can't rush. Mourning is one of them. Call me if you need anything. Anything. I mean it."

Jeev, dear Jeev. I'm touched by his concern. Years after our acrimonious divorce, we've finally become good friends through music.

I get up from the sofa and go into the kitchen. Pull open the fridge door. Seeing a jug of water with a slice of lemon in it, I fill a glass and drink it all at once, the icy liquid searing my parched throat. Then I refill the glass, and go into the bedroom.

The smell of old newspapers is still pervasive even though earlier I've removed all the newspapers under the bed. I put the glass down on the dressing table, and start to pull out the albums on the bookshelf. Quickly, I flip through their pages of snapshots of Ah-ku with Kit and John when they were little, playing in the garden of the big house, paddling in the swimming pool, or riding their tricycles. There are photos of her and Uncle Chang at official dinners and cinema openings, several albums of these in fact, but not a single photo of her as a child or teenager. Restless and despondent, I return to the sitting room, and my gaze falls on the low black altar. A small black tabernacle similar to the one in the pavilion is its centrepiece, and there's a white vase with a wilted yellow rose, a bronze bowl, a wooden rod, a string of beads and a prayer book. So this is where Ah-ku fights her demons. Did she ever think of the man, my father, I wonder.

I step out into the balcony and look up at the sky. A lace of clouds has veiled the moon. The front door opens, and John comes in with a large box. If he notices my red eyes, he gives no sign of it.

"I must count the money," he mutters.

"Everybody has left?" I ask.

"Almost." He puts the box down on the dining table.

I close my notebook and join him as he empties out a heap of white envelopes from the box.

"White gold," he says, and starts to open them.

He has worked out a method and likes things to be organised.

First, he extracts the dollar notes from each envelope, and smoothens out the creases before setting them aside in neat piles according to denominations of twos, fives, tens and fifties. I sit across the table from him and start to open the envelopes too. We work in silence, and the piles of red, blue and mauve notes on the table begin to rise. When each pile is high enough, he pushes aside the envelopes and counts the money in each pile. Then he records the amount in an accounts book while I watch him. That done; we tear open the other envelopes and repeat the process. There must be more than four hundred envelopes, he reckons. For almost an hour, we work without speaking. When half of the envelopes have been opened and the money duly counted and recorded, he rises from his seat and stretches his arms. "Coke?" he asks.

"Yes, please." I stand up to stretch my arms too while he goes into the kitchen, and returns with two cans of diet coke.

"Cold." He hands one to me.

"Where's Kan Jieh?"

"Resting in one of the deckchairs. Liz has asked her to stay the night, so she's sitting up with Kit and Liz for the first watch."

"You and I will take the second watch then?"

"Yes. Four a.m. James and Joe are asleep in the deckchairs too. They'll join us if they can wake up. And, oh, Weng. He said he'd come tomorrow. His ensemble group wants to play for Ma."

"Oh?" I'm surprised. "He's going to play his dizi? How did Ah-ku know him?"

"Weng's also a member of the Soka Association. He used to give her free tickets to his concerts."

I say nothing. We return to the envelopes and the counting. The mindless work soothes us. Tearing open the envelopes, taking out the dollar notes, smoothening away the creases, counting the money and recording each sum and tallying the figures in John's book. He looks as if he wants to say something to me, but doesn't know how to begin. He wipes his hands with a tissue. The dollar notes have left a sticky film of dirt on them. He wipes them a second time with a wet tissue, and coughs.

"Cheh. Many things happened while you were away."

I must have looked startled for he quickly added,

"Not your fault for not being here. Things happened. Pa went bankrupt."

He wipes his hands with another wet tissue again. "Pa… he… he couldn't take it." He starts crushing and stuffing the torn-up envelopes into a plastic bag. He talks better when his hands are doing something.

"It's… how shall I say it? It was very difficult for us. For as long as I remember, Ma was one angry woman. She scolded Kit and me every day. Not joking. We got scolded every day. That was our boyhood. This afternoon, I listened to Kan Jieh. Tonight, I listened to what the Soka people said. All very good things about Ma. She has done a lot for other people. She visited them when they were ill. Encouraged them when they were down. You know, it might sound strange to you…"

His voice trails off as he stuffs the last of the envelopes into the plastic bag, twists the top and knots it tight.

"…she'd never said a word of encouragement to Kit and me. Never listened to us. Just scolded us. Left, right and centre. Called us millstones round her neck. Burdens on her back."

He drinks more coke, and pushes himself to go on, his hands restlessly flipping the pages of the accounts book.

"Everything I did was a failure to her. In her eyes, I didn't do well. I had problems with my job. I could never meet her expectations. My job – it's not good enough. My wife – she's not good enough. My sons – her grandsons – not good enough. Sometimes, she'd say to me… my friend's son is working overseas or my friend's son has bought a big house. When I worked hard and slogged like Pa, she also complained. Don't be like him. Work, work, work till he forgot his soul. Forgot his own family. If she thinks I behaved like Pa, she scolded me. Not like Pa, she also grumbled. I couldn't take it. I had to move out. I always failed to meet her expectations.

I don't know why. Even this funeral," he downs the last bit of coke, "this funeral, I failed her too.

"The day… the day her body returned from the undertaker, I… I wasn't here to receive her and the casket. Kit was the one who did it. Actually I, the elder son, should've closed her coffin. But…" he licks his dry lips, "I wasn't back in time. The auspicious time for closing the coffin was fixed. The undertaker couldn't wait. I had gone to the newspaper office to place the obituary. Coming back, I was stuck in a traffic jam on Orchard Road. My taxi was crawling. So I failed her yet again."

He crushes the empty can, goes into the kitchen, and washes his face at the sink. When he returns to the table, I'm silent. I would like to say something, anything to comfort him, but no words come to my aid. I push my list of figures towards him. They are the sums of money I've counted. He tallies my figures together with his, and records the final sum into his accounts book. Then we tie a rubber band around each bundle of dollar notes, and he stuffs the whole lot into a large envelope.

"I'll lock it in Ma's drawer. Tomorrow, there'll be a larger crowd than tonight. It's the last night of the wake."

"Have you ordered more chairs?"

"Yes. Six hundred. Tonight we have three hundred chairs and they're not enough. Liz has also ordered a buffet supper for six hundred. The service will be longer tomorrow night."

"More chanting again?"

"It must be strange to you."

"Very strange. I've never seen such a wake."

"Ma used to chant very loudly. Every morning and evening. Ah well! We got used to it." He goes into the kitchen with the plastic bag of torn envelopes.

"John, I… er… er… thank you for…" my voice breaks, and I can't go on.

He says nothing. He looks me in the eye and nods; he understands what I'm trying to say. Something has been rekindled between us.

"Another coke, Cheh?"

"No, thanks. I just remembered something else. Whenever Ahku was furious with me or you or Liz or the relatives, she'd phone me and yell: Don't think without all of you, I'll die! Got family, I can live. Got no family, I can also live. With or without family, it is all the same to me. I have nothing to fear. Hundreds will mourn me when I die!"

"She told you that?"

"Many times."

"She also said that to me and Kit."

A smile slowly spread over our faces. My phone rings. I answer it, and turn to him. "I called for a cab earlier. It's here."

"Where're you going?"

"The river. I'll be back for the second watch."

"But it's very late."

"I need to clear my head."

He nods. Neither of us has to mention it. Our old amah has triggered an avalanche.

"Call me if you can't get a taxi back."

"I will."

42

Hemmed in by banks of thick clouds, the pale watery moon is a distant orb above the sleeping city. Office blocks tower above the river mouth, shrunken by landfills. The city's hunger for land has eaten up parts of the river. The placid ribbon rippling darkly between the grey concrete embankments is much narrower now than the broad, meandering, congested, teeming, busy waterway of my childhood when the expanse of blue sky arcing over the river mouth was wide and high. Instead of bumboats and twakows crowding its banks, now it's the pubs and restaurants that pack the riverfront. Fortunately, due to the lateness of the hour, these establishments are closed. Grateful for the absence of noise, traffic and pedestrians, I walk on. Unwanted memories crowd into my head jostling for attention as I stare uneasily at the iron structure ahead.

Built by colonial engineers from the grimy city of Glasgow, Cavenagh Bridge was originally meant for traffic, but now it's a footbridge, spanning the river where it's deepest at high tide. A ghostly grey in the streetlamps' glow, the bridge is stirring a sense of unease in me. It beckons, yet intimidates. Feelings that have dogged me all day like some cloying spider's threads clinging to my eyes are rising, and my eyes are welling at the thought of Uncle Chang alone on the bridge on a night like this. Why did he take off his shoes and place them side by side before he climbed these railings and jumped into the waters? That he chose to leave his shoes and enter the next world barefoot has remained a mystery. Ah-ku had mentioned those black leather brogues only in passing, but to me, the black shoes are an indelible image of Uncle Chang's last hour on earth. The final full-stop that marks the end of his life.

His memory returns with such force now that I think I'm seeing his shoes on the bridge. I move closer. I know my mind is playing tricks. But the sudden urge to pay my respect at the spot where he'd jumped seizes me. I've got to do it. I must do it. I should've done it years ago, in spite of Ah-ku. Yet I hesitate, immobilised by a childhood fear of unhappy souls. She would not approve. She'd deliberately left off phoning me till it was too late to attend the funeral and cremation. Years of cold war had ensued between us as a result, and my grief, finding no outlet, had turned to ice. Frozen memories of badminton games and visits to the fish shops were locked away. And the fish shed with its dark interior.

– *No, not this, not this memory.*

My hands tighten their grip on the railings; my body tenses. Small brown leaves shimmering in the river's small eddies of currents and pockets of movement are stirring up the liquid mix of half-forgotten scenes. Odd moments in Juniper Garden jump out at me. They flicker and shine like passing headlamps in the fog. In the momentary blinding brightness, the glimpse of arms startles me. Uncle Chang's arms were around me. I see myself leaning against his chest, sobbing.

– *Because of the fish. Because of the fish*, I insist before Ah-ku's silhouette looming in the doorway, the moon shining behind her.

There's no denying what happened in the fish shed that night. A nascent incandescence at once innocent and dangerous had flared in me. A blinding shaft had speared my heart. I catch a glimpse of white on the bridge. Is that him? His lanky figure in white shorts and white sports shoes seems to beckon. His badminton racquet held high, he hits the shuttlecock across the net towards me. But

I can't see his face. Why can't I remember his face? My tears are blinding me. I can't see him, can't bear to see him. I shut my eyes and rest my head against the railing.

The pale yellow glow of evening was pouring through the windscreen of his car as we drove down Bukit Timah Road, on one those rare evenings when everything had appeared so blessed. I remember The Moon Concerto for Pipa was playing in my head. Uncle Chang was driving and I was seated next to him. He had his sunglasses on, and his white polo tee was open in a V at the neck where the sun had kissed it. His elbow rested on the open car window, and the warm breeze was making the dark hairs of his forearm dance in the setting sun's golden light. I'd said something that made him laugh, and caught a heady whiff of the musk from his sweat-dampened body. Half turned towards him, a violent longing, sudden and sweet, desirable and forbidden, a yearning so strange and strong had seized me just before the evening's golden glow suddenly turned a dark orange.

The sun dipped behind the roofs as our car swung into Juniper Garden. Ah-ku's stern eyes met mine as I stumbled out of the car, holding aloft the bag of goldfish. Shame shot through my frame. Ah-ku knew. Without a word, she turned and walked into the house. Nothing was said. The felt animosity between us had lasted less than a second or two. Yet for a long time I could not forget it. Years later, in the middle of a blustery lonely winter in Boston, not long after my divorce from Jeev, I wondered if Ah-ku had seen me as a Lolita in the car that evening. Would she have felt the same animosity if Uncle Chang had been my real father? But enough! Enough! What's past is past, as Ah-ku used to say. Let this river carry it away.

Resolutely, I step on to the bridge and walk to the spot where John said his father's pair of shoes were found. Lights from the hotel and shuttered shops pepper the dark, restless waters. The tide is coming in. There's no telling what these dark waters hide. Palms together, I face the river and bow three times, whispering his name, aware that my frozen guilt is slowly melting.

"Forgive me, Uncle. Forgive me for not paying my respects sooner."

The moon is trapped in the gap of sky between the towering office blocks. Should I walk farther up the river to look for the spot where the creek used to be? The young taxi driver who brought me here had not heard of the creek where Weng and I used to fish. "Didn't know, leh, madam. Got such a creek, meh?" The young man has smiled into his rear view mirror. Ah well, I heave a sigh, the erasure of place and memory is the hallmark of the city.

The river's tributaries have been hacked off and paved over with concrete. Swanky new hotels and condos with shiny glass and aluminium frontage have replaced the messy boatyards and majestic raintrees. I miss the tongkangs and bumboats with huge black and red eyes painted on their prows.

I had once watched with Weng the ceremony of opening a bumboat's eyes. As drums rolled, the black-robed Taoist priest dipped a large calligraphy brush into a pot of black paint. He walked towards the red and green boat. The drums and the crowd fell silent. The boatmen watched with bated breath. A wrong stroke of the brush would result in failure to dot the centre of the new boat's eye, and misfortune would befall her crew. The priest said a prayer, aimed his brush like an arrow and dotted the centre of each eye on the boat's prow. Huat-ah! The eyes are open! the boatmen yelled. Firecrackers burst above their heads, raining cascades of red papers on to the red and green boat.

All that is gone now. Even the teahouses have disappeared without a trace. The taxi driver was surprised that there had been teahouses behind the river.

"I never heard of them, madam. Last time, this river very dirty. Now, it's very clean. Our gah'ment did good job. And we got win international award." The taxi driver told her proudly.

I think of Weng's father, Uncle Chong Suk, digging in his vegetable plot, his stepmother and sisters in their hut with no running water or electricity. Yes, the taxi driver has every reason to be proud.

"Ping…"

"Oh." I hadn't heard his footsteps.

Weng is standing some distance near the railings, eyes trained on the river. When it looks like he's not going to speak again, I start.

"I looked for you after the prayer service, but twice you left without a word."

"You're the one who left without a word," he says without missing a beat.

His words trigger a sudden warmth that rises to my face, I stammer, "That… that was a long time ago."

"A very long time ago."

The black waters swirl and eddy below us. A brown leaf bobs helplessly in the current.

"I'm… I'm sorry." My voice has dropped to a whisper. My words, I realise, are grossly inadequate.

"I'm sorry too."

His tone is suddenly bitter, but surely that's not what he intends. Not what he wants to say. Why did it come out that way? Why is he saying this now? Tonight of all nights when Ah-ku's wake is not yet over. Why bring up something that happened years ago?

Now my eyes are shut. He must think me a callous brute. Something tensed in his voice, in the way he refused to look at me when he spoke – his silence is making me nervous. I wait for him to speak, thoughts pounding through my head. My mind can't focus.

"I… I wrote to you… many times but… no reply," and hopes he doesn't think I'm accusing him.

"I saw no reason to reply. You had left." His voice is a B flat. A neutral tone. He has not come to the river to accuse me.

"More than forty letters I wrote you that winter."

"I didn't read your letters."

I follow the sound of a car driving out of the car park near the

Asian Civilization Museum. The silence between us congeals; it sits between us as his words sink into the watery depths. A deep weariness fills my heart.

– *Not even one letter?* I want to ask him, but I've neither the strength nor the courage to do it. Instead I ask, "Why have you come then?"

"I phoned. Your brother told me you'd come here."

His use of 'brother' did not escape me.

"So John told you – she was my mother too."

"I've always suspected she was."

"Did he tell you my – my – father was Indian?"

"No," he looks at me, taken aback, and for a while he's silent. It looks as if he's struggling to find words to comfort me, to tell me that it's all right.

"Chinese, Indian or Chindian, your roots are here – in this river, in Pagoda Street, in Chinatown. That's all that matters. All that matters."

I stare into the river, fighting back tears.

"All these years, I thought I was Chinese."

"Identity is an act of will, you know. You can choose to be Chinese or chap jing."

The look I give him must've disconcerted him. His use of chap jing has shocked me. Of all people, he's never called me chap jing before.

"Please. Please don't get me wrong. Listen. Before 1965, we chose to be Malaysian, right? After 1965, we became Singaporean. As a child, you were mocked as a chap jing. Today, people are proud to be mixed. So now, you have a choice."

His smile is enigmatic and beguiling. I struggle to say something equally intelligent, but words fail me. A needle is threading through my heart. Pain and surprise stop me from speaking.

– *He knows me,* I keep thinking.

Despite our years of separation and silence, he knows how to put things to me, and seems more at ease with me than I am with him. How does he do it? Is it his Buddhist faith? Leaning against the railings, his hands resting on the top bar, he's gazing upstream. The sudden desire to put my hand on his seizes me.

Shocked, I hold tightly to the railing, afraid to let go in case desire overwhelms me. I lean hard against the steel. Pockets of grease and light, and eddies of currents swirl and dance in the dark waters below. Neither of us speak until the first drops of rain make him look up at the sky.

"Quick! Run!"

He heads for the car park.

43

A strong wind is blowing at our back. Large drops are falling fast.

"Quick! Under the Old Vic's porch!" he breaks into a run.

We reach the porch just as the storm breaks.

"I hope it won't rain at the funeral tomorrow."

"Rain tonight; clear tomorrow," he smiles, and brushes off the rain from his arms.

Ever the optimist, I think as I watch him shake the drops out of his hair vigorously, a habit that reminds me of our first meeting when he'd run dripping wet up the stairs into Ah-ku's room after he'd fought off the urchin boys to snatch back my little red pail and return it to me. The memory brings a smile I try to suppress. A sudden strong gust whips through the porch sending waste papers and memories flying in our direction. Lightning flashes across the sky. The shower has turned into a sudden thunderstorm. Within minutes, rainwater is flooding into the porch of the city's oldest concert hall. We huddle on its steps as gusts sweep in mists of warm rain, and winds slash the branches of roadside trees, their shadows leaping up like demons in the deserted car park. His face looks wan and drained in the half darkness. The wind has blown a lock of hair across his brow. His hand reaches up and brushes it aside leaving his forehead exposed and vulnerable. I note the fine lines on his forehead, and the tiny crow's feet around his eyes.

Like mine.

"You're feeling all right?" he asks.

I know he is not referring to the storm.

"Ah-ku could've told me."

"I don't think she could. Don't you remember? We were very racist in those days. Non-Chinese were gwai, ghosts or devils. Even in the sixties and seventies when we were growing up, people would spit when they saw a mixed race couple in Chinatown. Waiters in coffee shops wouldn't serve them."

The lively interest is slowly returning to my tired eyes. He looks relieved that we're no longer talking about the letters. He must've regretted burning them, but at other times, he'd felt no regret. I don't blame him. They were useless letters of apologies after all.

"I don't think she could tell you the truth. You were her *ku ai tzi."*

"Her what?" I'm flummoxed by his Mandarin phrase. "What's *ku ai tzi?"*

"*Ku* means bitter; *ai* means love; *tzi* is child. You were her bitter love child."

"Bitter love child, *ku ai tzi*," I repeat after him.

Ku ai tzi. I repeat the Mandarin words slowly, listening to the weight of sorrow in each word. Ku has a bitter taste. It'd never occurred to me to see myself as the fruit of a young and vulnerable girl's embittered hope. He has re-cast the story of Ah-ku with great compassion. And this was the woman who had dismissed him as that noodle boy who would amount to nothing. How wrong Ah-ku was, how wrong.

"How did you meet her?"

"Through the Soka Association."

"Did she know who you were? I mean before you played the dizi professionally."

"I don't think she ever connected me with fishball noodles, if that's what you mean. I didn't tell her that I knew you. If she found out later, she didn't bring it up. But she made a point of attending all my concerts. When she heard that I needed funding, she got her friends to help me find sponsors for the Ming Ensemble. That was how we became friends. By then she was a leader in the women's division of Soka. I heard her tell her life story at various meetings: how she struggled against pride and shame when creditors seized her house in Juniper Garden, how she cried when the family had to move into a tiny Housing Board flat, how she wept for days after she was forced to sell her jewellery. She never spoke about your uncle much at these meetings, or mentioned Old Kim's coffee shop in Pagoda Street or her pipa days. But I don't fault her for leaving them out. If I were to tell my life story, I'd want to tell it my way too."

I remain silent. The sting of memory is smarting in me like a red ant's bite. It had rained like this on the night both of us sat under the porch of the Good Shepherd's Cathedral.

"Why don't you sit down? Looks like this rain will go on for a while," he says, and sits on the topmost step beside me.

His proximity is a little unnerving. He seems so sure of himself tonight, so… so calm and comfortable waiting out the rain while I'm choked with questions and regret. Unable to bear it, I blurt, "I didn't know you were detained by the government till much later." And count the number of beats in the silence that follows. He's staring at the relentless rain blowing through the porch in violent gusts. I listen to the flapping of a canvas sheet on the roof of a closed-up fast food stall near the porch. Loosened by the wind, it is slapping a steady drumbeat in the rain against its wood frame.

"I'm sorry. I shouldn't have brought it up."

"No, don't be. I didn't think you were interested."

Another strong gust sweeps up the road, thrashing the tops of the angsana trees, flinging dead leaves across the deserted car park.

"How long were you in there?"

"Nine months and five days. Three months in solitary because I couldn't give them the right answers."

His voice is flat and off-key. Although he looks calm, his face has lost some of its composure. It pains me that I didn't know at the time what he was going through.

"The worst was the uncertainty; the loss of trust," he says, his voice suddenly soft and low. "And not being able to see my family or play the dizi."

"Nine months is a long time to be detained for a speech."

A shrug of his shoulders.

"Others were inside much longer and had it worse. Much worse," he says.

I don't press him for details. I've read stories like his in books and on websites set up by former detainees living overseas.

"My stint inside was not long compared to the others. Some were imprisoned for ten or more years. "

"But didn't they know that you wrote on behalf of the illiterate hawkers and squatters?"

The impatient look in his eyes tells me not to be naïve.

"That wasn't the central issue. The prosecutor said I was an agitator. A member of the united communist front. My letters and speeches had contributed to the groundswell of anti-government feelings and caused the riot. But it wasn't a riot. It was a protest march by the people evicted from the river."

His jaw line has hardened, and I fear a rupture to our fragile harmony.

"I remember reading on a Singapore website that the eviction orders had to be vigorously enforced. That the squatters and hawkers had resisted change. Failed to appreciate the benefits. It said the government was going to re-house them in new flats and new hawker centres. The area along the river had been gazetted for urban renewal. Some people suffered, the article did admit, but it couldn't be helped. Change was inevitable."

"Excellent slogan – change is inevitable." His finger jabs his knee. "Who decides what to change, when to change? The people who suffered from changes imposed from above happened to number several thousand. Not some. Was that mentioned? I know of such articles. Most are written by civil servants and posted on official websites. ”

His calm has dissipated. He falls silent as the wind dies down.

“You paid a price,” I say as though making an apology.

“A few months in jail; it’s a small price. We lose the freedom to speak if we don’t use it.” He stops abruptly and looks away, clasping and unclasping his fingers as though wishing he hadn’t spoken so much.

“Have you thought of leaving? Emigrating, like some of the others?”

He shakes his head, and when he speaks again, he has regained his earlier composure. “This is my country. To leave is to admit defeat.”

The thought is new to me. I mull over it silently, listening to the drip, drip, drip of rain from the eaves and arches of the porch, dripping with the same languid cadence of our talk, the drops seeping into my dry thoughts and shrivelled-up memories of nights on the riverbank. I used to fear that a catfish might bite off one of my toes when I waded into the creek with him, and he would tease me, using my fears to make me cling to him.

“I was born in a bumboat and grew up on the river. My music comes from these waters. This is where Pa taught me to play the dizi. He never left the river even after we moved.”

His sense of place and roots makes me feel shallow. I’d never asked myself what it means to be Singaporean.

“Besides, I didn’t do anything wrong,” he adds.

“No, you didn’t. What you did was great… admirable.”

“No! Don’t say that! Don’t ever say that.”

His voice is suddenly harsh and hoarse, his face hardening. Have I said something offensive? My guilt returns. But there’s nothing I can do to make up for what I did in the past.

“Look, I want you to understand this. I didn’t do anything admirable. I was a coward.”

His body seems in danger of crumbling into a heap. The urge

to reach out and touch him surges through me. I bring my knees together and grip them hard.

"My one thought was to get out of the detention centre," he says, eyes staring into the distance. "I wanted to get out of there. I couldn't take the daily interrogation any more."

In the end, it was fear and self-preservation that made him sign every bloody sheet of paper they pushed in front of him, he says. They wouldn't let him out unless he signed. He was afraid they would keep him inside forever. Nine long months. They were like nine long years. He felt old and wasted. He was wasting his life and his gift of music. For what? He kept thinking. For what? They were evicted in the end.

"You're not a coward," my voice quavery as an out-of-tune pipa. I want to hug him and hold him close.

He seems not to have heard me. His thoughts are far away, and his eyes are on the heavy drizzle framed by the three arches of the porch. My hand brushes his lightly, but he gives no sign of having noticed when he turns back to me.

"All I wanted was to play my dizi. I thought of nothing but music inside my cell. I kept thinking of Moon On Moon Lake by A Bing, the blind erhu player. I was trying to re-work the piece for the flute before my arrest. When I came out, I returned to my music. I wanted to forget everything. Everything in my past life."

I look away. I can't meet his eye. A deep shame fills me, and I flush under his gaze.

"But I was lucky," his voice is noticeably lighter as he continues, "my lawyer was very good. Very smart. He squeezed the heart of the authorities after I came out. Said I was a young and misguided youth, but very talented. I shouldn't be punished for life. Argued that I should be allowed to leave for further studies. So they let me leave the country and I rushed off to the Shanghai Conservatory of Music."

"I've heard it's very difficult to get into the conservatory."

"I took a chance. Just packed my bags and flew to Shanghai.

Once there, the teachers – they were incredibly kind. They had suffered during the Cultural Revolution. So they understood my problem. They gave me an interview even though my application had arrived late. I played my dizi for them like it was my last performance on earth. Die, die also must play! I know you don't like Singlish. But there's no other way to say it."

"Die, die also must play," I repeat. How apt a phrase it is in his case.

"The conservatory accepted me as a fee-paying student. Even then, life was hard. Students lived in dormitories. Six to a room. We had to be up at five every morning, even in darkest winter. Every day, it was practice, practice, and more practice. I was older than the other students and found it hard going at first. The training regimen was very, very tough, but the professors were top-notch. If it weren't for Professor Mah Shi-fei, I would've quit."

"That would've been terrible."

"It's not us who make music. It's music that makes us, he used to say. He was a wonderful teacher. But during the Cultural Revolution, he was labelled a threat to society, a running dog and other vile names. Banished to the countryside, he spent six long years as a labourer, digging trenches till his hands bled. When he returned to Shanghai, he was a skeleton. He told us his fingers were so stiff; he could hardly hold his flute. He picked up the pieces of his life, and taught himself to play the dizi again, learning everything from scratch."

"I'm surprised you came back."

"I'll never forget what he told me. To hate is to let the enemy win from within. Freedom is in us, and inside the music. Find it."

The rain has stopped. We stand up and walk out of the porch. I'm silent and subdued. Compared to what Weng has gone through, my life in the United States seems self-centred and shallow. The idealistic noodle boy I had loved is still idealistic, but wiser. I look up at the trees; large emeralds are dripping from their leaves. The air smells clean and fresh. Not a word passes between us but our steps are already taking us upriver towards Clarke Quay and Robertson Quay, along the route we had walked countless times when the quays were crowded with boats and coolies. This pleases and troubles me. He has been so frank and open under the porch. Now the onus is on me to do likewise; I owe it to him. And to myself. A light breeze comes up behind us like a nudge from the river gods. We pass the new Parliament House, and cross the deserted road.

"South Bridge Road," he says. "The route you took to go to the convent school. And see, here's the former central fire station." He points to the building with the red, yellow and green windows. "Now it's the Ministry of Information and the Arts."

We walk on in silence. I'm looking for the warehouse and the bend in the river where his house and village used to be. But this river is no longer the river of our youth, and we're no longer lovers. Gone are the inlets and bends, now straightened and neatened into a bland waterway with no unruly creek or meandering ditch. Gone is the lush wild greenery that hid our passionate embraces from view. It's time I tell him about the aborted child and the reasons I left, although I wonder what good would come of it. And yet if I withhold it, it will come between us.

"It's been a long time since we walked like this."

"A lifetime."

"Remember the warehouses?" he asks. "Only one or two are left. One has been converted into a disco. Look across the river. Over there. The hotel and condo. That was where our house and the village used to be. On land owned by the Chang family."

He turns his back to me and gazes at the block of highrises. I try to picture his family's hut and his father's vegetable plot hidden by the grove of trees.

"I might as well tell you. I did a silly thing after our eviction and Pa's death. This place was fenced up. I cut the fence and came back some evenings to tend Pa's vegetable plot. Then one night, I burned your letters at the creek. Your uncle set the police on me and had me arrested for trespassing."

"What? I didn't know. I didn't know about it. I'm shocked that Uncle Chang had done such a thing."

"I held that against you for many years. Now it's water under the bridge. I… I just want you to know that."

I can't see his face; his back is half-turned towards me, a hand on the railing. Gently, I place my hand on his, relieved that he does not move it away.

"Weng, I too have something to confess."

He waits for me to begin, but I'm struggling to find the words to tell him. He turns and holds my hand.

"There… there was a reason why I left Singapore so suddenly…"

Part Eight

Requiem

44

– *Dead. Dead. Dead.*

The incoming tide rushes into my head. *Ah-ku is dead.* The sonorous voices swell and break over my head. *Ah-ku is dead.*

Sweat is pouring down the sides of my face. The electric fans are working at full capacity overhead, but the air in the pavilion is stale and muggy from the warmth of so many bodies tonight. Six hundred members of the Soka Association are chanting, seated in rows of white plastic chairs. A hundred more are standing in the aisles and back of the pavilion. Beside me in the front row are the rest of the family, a group that now includes Dave and Kan Jieh, who looks serene, rubbing her prayer beads between her wrinkled hands. A stab of resentment pierces my heart. She has done her duty by her Madam. This morning, she'd shocked us when she returned our umbilical cords – John's, Kit's and mine. Each piece of shrivelled flesh carefully preserved in talcum powder and dried herbs, wrapped in a red packet, and kept in a red jewellery box. In the old days, mothers would keep their children's umbilical cords to protect them from evil spirits, Kan Jieh explained, looking me straight in the eye. Did Kan Jieh really think these bits of flesh are signs of maternal love?

It troubles me, my umbilical cord. I'm undecided whether to

keep it or burn it. I wish Kan Jieh had not dug it out. That Ah-ku had kept my umbilical cord for so many years, even after I had left home, shocks me. It hints of something in the fifteen-year-old girl who gave birth to me, then rejected me even as she fed and clothed me. Is the cord a material acknowledgement to herself at least that I am her flesh? I want to ask her this. I want to know. My mind is tottering between the child crying to know if her mother had ever loved her, and the adult not wanting the knowledge, for the knowledge is too late. Too late. Mother is dead. Ah-ku is dead. The wind is rattling the hollow in my head. Or is it my heart?

I look at the three of us — John, Kit and I – seated side by side in the front row, facing that horrible photograph with the smiling face next to the altar, bewildered by the outpouring of grief behind us. Did our mother really touch the lives of so many? Mother. The word feels strange on my tongue. Something vital is lost and cannot be recovered; I cannot say the word aloud, and probably never will. I remember when I was five and she was twenty, young and beautiful. I'd yearned to call her 'Mama', and the yearning did not stop even after she left me in Old Kim's coffee shop. This year, I shall be forty-five, and she would be sixty had she lived. I feel almost like her peer now, for the years have narrowed the gap between us. Perhaps… and here I suspect my mind is clutching at a straw… perhaps it's a good thing that I didn't have a child at seventeen.

I hear chimes. Mr Tan, the leader of the funeral service, is sounding the bronze bell, shaped like a beggar's bowl. Its deep, clear tone brings a hush, a silence that slowly gathers the disparate voices into one unifying call to prayer.

"Nam… myoho… renge… kyo… "

"Nam… myoho… renge… kyo… oo," six hundred voices echo.

Adagio, adagio, andante, softly, softly, softly.

I close my eyes. Inside my head, I begin to assign a musical value to each note, and then to each cluster of notes. As the chanting goes on, I focus on its musical and vocal qualities, its rhythm, pitch and tone, a useful exercise that staves off the questions and emotions threatening to invade my mind. I keep it busy, distracting it with the conjugation of sounds, the variations of tenor and pitch, the weaving in and out of possibilities and patterns that will inform a new work-in-progress, perhaps. Perhaps. The chanting picks up speed, the voices rising in unison in the recitation of the Lotus Sutra. I hear the solemn murmurings of pilgrims in temples, the laughter of children running down the backlanes, their wooden clogs clattering over potholes, their shouts scattered like leaves in the breeze.

"Nam… myoho… renge… kyo… "

"Nam… myoho… renge… kyo… "

Faster and faster the chanting. A stormy wind rising, whipping the manes of white seahorses rushing into the river's mouth. The foaming sea serpent is churning up waves and brushing against the bumboats, sending them rocking against each other, their wooden planks creaking and groaning in the wake of the incoming tides, rolling upriver, swelling creeks and ditches, and bringing crabs and shellfish, gifts of the South China Sea.

"Nam… myoho… renge… kyo… "

"Nam… myoho… renge… kyo… "

The wind dies down; the chanting slows to a halt. Has the time gone by so fast? The bronze bowl sounds three times. An expectant silence falls. Kit walks up to the microphone at the side of the altar. Murmurings and whisperings behind me. People are surprised that it is the younger, and not the elder son, who has come forward to deliver the eulogy.

"Dear friends," Kit begins in Cantonese, addressing the men and women in their sixties and seventies, who are more conversant with dialect Chinese than Mandarin or English. "My elder brother, Tai-kor John, and my elder sister, Tai-kah-jieh Ping, have asked me to say a few words on behalf of our family."

Another ripple of whispering goes round the pavilion. My heart lurches forward, a lump in my throat. None in the audience knows that Ah-ku has a daughter. Kit's use of the formal Cantonese term of address, Tai-kah-jieh, has announced to all my true status. It makes me want to cry. My lips are quivering. I feel a joy that no words can describe. Throughout my childhood, I had stood at the margin of Ah-ku's family. With just three words, Tai-kah-jieh, Kit has brought me into the centre. I bow my head, unable to look up for tears are streaming down my face.

"Our family thank all of you, members of Soka, for your prayers and kind attendance at our mother's wake and funeral. Besides her family, the Soka community was our mother's life. It had a profound impact on her. Because of Soka, our mother, a former pipa songstress, became a respected elder and lay leader."

The revelation causes another stir in the crowd behind me. Their whisperings surge and Kit has to pause. I glance at John. He is looking straight ahead, his eyes focussed on a spot behind the casket; his face is expressionless. He had refused to do the eulogy, but he had had a hand in its crafting. Liz reaches over and squeezes his hand. Kit coughs and taps gently at the mike. Quiet returns to the pavilion.

"All of you know our mother as the indomitable Mrs Chang who had prayed with you, who had brought food to the poor, who had sat up all night with the sick and held the hand of the dying. She was devoted to Soka. She'd even threatened to rise from her coffin to put things right if something were wrong with the Soka Association here."

Laughter breaks out. Even John's face cracks a smile.

"Because of Soka, our indomitable mother learnt to listen to others. Because of Soka, she learnt to admit to her faults and weaknesses. But most significantly, Soka taught her to love. Because of Soka, my mother learnt to love me, her youngest child, in the last two years before her death."

The catch in Kit's voice is unmistakeable. Eyes glistening, an air of quiet dignity about him, he faces us. I glance at Dave whose eyes have not left Kit's face throughout.

"From the time I was a child, she had always said she regretted giving birth to me. My father's fortunes changed for the worse after I was born. Then in my teens, my mother found another reason to regret my birth. She found out I am gay. But in the last two years of her life, my mother grew more appreciative of me. I will never forget the day my proud mother apologised to me. She apologised for all the wrong she had done and the hurtful things she'd said to me and my partner, Dave."

Not a sound or movement behind me now; the stillness in the pavilion is so palpable that even Kan Jieh's beads have stopped clicking. Dave's eyes are wet, and my heart is gripped by a terrible ache as fragments of my last conversation on the phone with Ah-ku return. I wish I hadn't lied about the dying battery in my phone.

I catch the quick tender glance Kit exchanges with Dave. It stirs another heartache. I think of Weng. He's due to arrive soon with the Ming Ensemble, but after last night, my feelings are unsure of themselves; I dare not anticipate anything.

"On the night before her death," Kit continues, "my mother had complained of her aching heart. Sum tong, she said, and started to cry. I was shocked. Sum tong could mean she was in physical and emotional pain. She told me her life and personal relationships had caused her a great deal of pain and hardship. The next morning, before I left for work, I told her I would take her to the doctor in the evening. She answered, No need. I'm well. I thought things through last night. I understand now. To get rid of my heartache, I have to let go and forgive. Forgive those who abused me, betrayed me, abandoned me. I had to leave for work. I didn't know…" Kit pauses, eyes gazing into the distance, "I didn't know that my mother would die that same evening."

The weight of silence in the pavilion presses on my shoulders. A woman is sobbing behind me. I hope Kit will end soon.

"Our mother was found sitting on a park bench. She was relaxed with a smile on her face. Whatever had troubled her in life, she had let it go in death. She was calm… and had… had good intentions in her heart in the final moment. Mother, may you rest in peace."

John stands up. All of us in the front row do the same. Kit hands him the mike and joins us. His voice straining, John intones, "Mother, we are gathered here, your three children, your daughter-in-law, your grandsons, together with Dave and Kan Jieh, we pay our last respects to you."

We bow before the photograph of her smiling face. Kan Jieh is keening, a soft mewling as she weeps. One by one, we go up to the altar, take a pinch of incense from the box and sprinkle it into the urn. Ashes to ashes in whiffs of fragrant smoke.

When we return to our seats, I see an image of Ah-ku bending over the folds of pink cloth spread out on the table next to Auntie Molek's sewing machine. Light is streaming into the cubicle from the window, and down in the street below hawkers are yelling their wares for the Chinese New Year festivities. Her long hair tied in a ponytail, Ah-ku holds up the beautiful piece of pink cloth speckled with tiny red and yellow flowers.

– *Molek Ee, what do you think? Will it look nice on Ping?* The question startles me. I've forgotten the occasion till now. I was five, maybe six that year when Ah-ku asked Molek Ee to sew me a new frock for Chinese New Year.

Another memory rises. Ah-ku is lying on her bed, her long dark hair spread out like a fan on the pillow. I see myself, a six-year-old, seated cross-legged on the bed, close to her, next to her head. I'm combing her long, dark strands, and Ah-ku is humming a song.

– *Ouch!* she cries when I pull out a white hair. I show it to her and a smile lights up her face. She reaches for her purse, takes out a coin and drops it into my hand.

– *Save that in your piggy bank for your education.* Tears well up at these words. I'd forgotten those intimate afternoons on her bed. I want to weep.

"Mother." I sink to the floor and kowtow, grateful that, in spite of everything, she hadn't let go of me in all these years.

"Ping, are you all right?" Liz helps me back to my seat.

John places an awkward arm on my shoulders. "Weng is here. His ensemble has arrived. Are you up to playing?"

I turn round to look, fearing cold indifference in his eyes. We had driven back to the pavilion in silence last night. His hands had gripped the steering wheel as he drove, his eyes fixed on the road. When we reached the car park below Kit's apartment block, he stopped the car. I put my hand on the door and was about to get out when he said, "My wife, my ex-wife, she didn't want any children."

I sat in the car unable to move for several minutes. I couldn't speak. His sorrow had pierced me deeply. When I finally opened the car door, he spoke again.

"Will you bring your pipa and join the Ming Ensemble tomorrow?" His question caught me by surprise.

"If you want me to," I replied and got out of the car.

"I wouldn't have asked if I didn't want you to."

The five members of the ensemble walk in, elegant in their black mandarin jackets. They bow before my mother's portrait, and turn to face the audience.

"The Ming Ensemble thanks the family of Mrs Chang," Weng begins in Mandarin. "Thank you for this opportunity to show our gratitude and respect. For more than twenty years, Mrs Chang faithfully attended every one of our performances. Her favourite piece was The Imperial Concubine's Farewell, the pipa's celebrated song of eternal regret. But first," he acknowledges me with a nod, "I'll ask her daughter, Professor Wong Ping-ping, to join us with her pipa."

My heartbeat quickening, I pull out the leather case from under my seat and take out the pipa that Weng's father had bequeathed to me.

"Are you okay?" Liz asks. "You don't have to do it, you know."

I mumble a reply, feeling as though I'm moving in a thick fog. A murmuring of voices surrounds me. Weng seems a long way off. His words are the only sounds guiding me through the fog that has suddenly enveloped my ears.

"Let me tell you the story behind this song," he says. "Zhao Jun, the most beautiful of all the imperial concubines, was banished to the western frontier to be the bride of the barbarian king. Inside her sedan, she wept bitterly over her cruel fate, and called out to her mother. As the emperor watched her sedan being carried away, he realised too late, ahhh, too late, his concubine's kindness and beauty. Let me read you a few lines from the song before we play."

There is an expectant hush. This is a novelty – poetry and Chinese classical music at a funeral service; it has never happened before. Weng begins in his elegant Mandarin:

"At Chang-an's Gate, she turns back her tear-stained face
With eyes that gaze back at him full of love.
Few has he seen so beautiful to his anguished eye.
Too late… ah… too late."

At his nod, I strike a lun on the pipa's strings. Sharp as glass, the lun slices the pavilion's silence in a cry of pain. A bus roars down the road. I hit the pipa's soundboard. Once. Twice. Thrice. Like three kowtows to the dead. And launch into the first movement.

Tu. Shui. Mu. Qin. Huo.

Earth. Water. Wood. Metal. Fire.

Five notes to desolation. Ma! The pipa lets out an anguished groan. The Ming Ensemble joins in with a sobbing of erhu strings. The guqin gives a rippled cry. In a lilting undertone, the dizi sings a sorrowful accompaniment, underscoring the pipa's grief. When the pipa rages in the desert storm in a fury of plucked strings, his dizi soothes in calm counterpoint. When the pipa weeps among the bleak sand dunes, his dizi comforts with brief snatches of melody. The rapt assembly has never heard the likes of this before. As bamboo, wind and strings sweep across the desolate plains beyond the Great Wall, weaving an intricate song of bleak beauty and sorrow, some people in the audience weep. When the pipa grieves her loss, the dizi consoles. When the dizi queries, the pipa replies. You left, he rues. I left, the pipa sighs. Like a pair of weaverbirds, our musical replies intertwine the threads of tangled lives. But does it matter who left and who stayed when the leaving was never in the heart? the guqin asks in a rippling of strings.

In a burst of joyous trills, the dizi leads the pipa out of the desert plains. Their duet in Spring Comes to the Valley brings smiles all round, for the song celebrates the return of a pair of mandarin ducks, symbols of love, to the river's creek. As his dizi trills masterfully in his signature long notes like the cry of the mandarin drake to his mate, I pluck my strings lightly in reply. The duck and drake are paddling in dappled sunlight on the rippling waters now, and I feel Mother is watching us, looking down and smiling. Smiling on her American daughter – who finally feels she has come home.

A Grace Note

"Jeev, stop shouting. I can hear you. Listen. Text me daily if you wish, but my mind is made up. I'm not coming back so soon. My work-in-progress is here and now. My head is brimming with so many ideas and sounds. Yes, yes, I'll complete it in time for rehearsals. Listen. I'm adding a new sound. A new instrument. The dizi. You've never heard of it? The dizi is a Chinese flute made of bamboo. Please don't fret, darling. I'm fine.

What d'you mean the mourning period is so long? I'm already rushing it. Traditionally, it used to be a hundred days of mourning. I'm doing it in forty-nine days, reducing it by half. No, I'm not pulling your leg. It's true. That's the tradition. Oh, you've already checked out the Soka website? They don't have this tradition? But I'm following the Taoists… Hey, you forget I grew up in Singapore. This is the great city of multi-cultural mix. We mix and match our traditions. Who is going to excommunicate me? The pope or the Dalai Lama?"

I hear Jeev laughing at the other end of the line just as I know he would.

"I will finish it," I assure him again and switch off my phone.

I look out of the window.

The glint of glass from the apartments opposite no longer

hurts my eyes. The sunlight no longer appears as harsh as when I first arrived. It's more than two weeks since the funeral, and I am still staying in Kit's flat, working on a new symphonic poem for orchestra with pipa and dizi in collaboration with Weng. It has not been an easy two weeks, I admit, this period of intense feelings and heightened sensitivities. What the future holds, I do not know, but I know I will not be returning to Berkeley this summer till the symphonic poem is complete. I keep thinking of two solitary crabs Weng and I once saw. The crabs had climbed out of their mud holes at the river's low tide and touched claws. A rare and wonderful sight.